Leading to Texas-2

Aled Smith

Parthian, Cardigan SA43 1ED
www.parthianbooks.com
First published in 2019
© Aled Smith 2019
All Rights Reserved
ISBN 978-1-912109-11-1
Editor: Carly Holmes
Cover design by Syncopated Pandemonium
Cover image: Charlie Kinross/Millennium Images, UK
Typeset by Elaine Sharples
Printed by 4edge Limited
Published with the financial support of the Welsh Books Council
British Library Cataloguing in Publication Data
A cataloguing record for this book is available from the British Library.

Contents

DAY TWO

DAY ONE

A Long Journey

It was dark under rumbling wet mackerel skies and passengers on the warm, dry bus seemed electrified. The non-stop chatter and constant beat had a distressing roar to it inside Hank Evan's skull. New medication. He had been stuck in the hospital for over a week, undergoing his regular epileptic medical tests, and had only just managed to catch the 97B circular. It would take the long route back.

Hank felt like shit. He had had a nasty fit that morning in the hospital. He'd damaged his left foot, and a scrawny nurse coated it in plaster and plastic sheeting whilst warning him about the weather conditions outside. She had given him the stiff metallic crutches and said goodbye. He'd stood on aching limbs at the hospital bus stop and clambered onto the first one that pulled in.

Their county hospital was perched at the top of the valley and shared by all of the ex-mining towns below. The bus Hank was travelling on would drive right down the valley, around the base of Blackmill mountain, through Cooperstown, Stanleyville, Evanstown, Aberpant, Morristown, Ynys-y-Pwll, Brownsville, Pentrecoch, and loop back up past the rear of the hospital into his small town of Cwmgarw, eventually coming onto the Bevan Estate, or Texas-2 as the locals liked to call it. He didn't want to look out at the litter of settlements named for mine owners and the ransacked landscape.

The bus slowed and strained to another juddering stop. Hank found himself staring straight ahead at the two pensioners sat opposite. The man hesitantly touched his plain tie and nodded towards him. Hank was aware he must be looking pretty vile that afternoon with a pair of broken, ill-balanced glasses on his nose, oily uncombed hair, and a carrier bag full of dirty clothes resting between his sore feet. The man looked away. Hank looked to the side and they drove on. He was chewing at skin on the side of his thumb and trying to keep Cheyenne out of his head. He had been annoyed with his girlfriend for days. She'd barely spoken to him since he went into the epileptic unit, and he'd had no text or call from his mate Masaki either. They both seemed to have vanished. Hank felt as forgotten as the ragged communities that greeted his tired eyes.

Each blink turned him black inside. He opened his eyes and sighed. His epilepsy had leapt at him from nowhere, and caught him standing still. It was at the end of his second year in college; he'd gone home for the summer break and never went back. Home was no longer the same either. Mam died, and dad drank. Hank knew it would never be the same for him again. He saw everything differently. Each time he plunged out of the world, another one waited for him.

The growling noise of the bus's engine became mixed with the cold, tight noise inside his head. He was shaking. He noticed it had gently started to rain again. He felt he was about to take the plunge. Hank swallowed. Shut his eyes. And waited.

Croeso i Gymru: Welcome to Wales

The American couple yawned in unison. It had been a long journey and they weren't there yet. Their large bodies made the small car feel cramped as Ed Evans drove carefully up the mountain road against a barrage of wind and rain. He was hunched over the wheel, trying to see the battered concrete in front of him as it transformed itself into a mini brook. The fields that ran alongside the car had flooded, and brown water flowed through the rooted hedge onto the road. In the dark morning light, Ed stared silently in concentration.

He hadn't spoken to Betty for fifty-six minutes and was aiming for the sixty minute mark. Ed had not wanted to go on this off-beat road trip. A retired police officer, he felt it was a mistake to travel this far from his home. She had told him it was to be the "holiday of their lifetimes". To visit Wales. The country of their origin. The woman had spent weeks pestering and nagging him to make those small steps to board the transatlantic jet, and from what he'd seen of this gnarled country so far it wasn't hard for him to guess why people had left.

A heavy yellow truck trundled toward them and beeped. Betty couldn't help follow the crawling beam of its headlight as her husband's miserable, wrinkled face was abruptly illuminated. His eyes held firm under a fixed scowl. His heavily veined, alcohol-brushed nose. His enormous drooping moustache. A moustache which had been hanging there with those grey sideburns since the Sixties. Betty had known that face for most of her life. Feared it. Loved it.

Loathed it. She'd recently wondered how big a distance there was between them now. She wondered what had caused the gap. And she thought she knew. It was her. Betty painfully felt she'd failed her husband years ago. They didn't have any real family, and she had fooled herself into thinking this wild trip to Wales was somehow going to fix it for them both.

Ed slowed the car and let the psycho trucker roll on by.

Betty knew she needed sugar. She felt faint and figured she was having some kind of elderly body sensation that needed the sweet crystalline substance of sugar to boost her. It could happen. They'd been stuck in the airport half a night, waiting to get through the darn doors. She had eaten only one flimsy peanut butter sandwich and drank what felt like thirty-six cups of nuclear-hot coffee in four hours. She felt jittery. When they finally got out of Heathrow, Ed insisted they just find themselves the cheapest car and drive on. If they were going into Wales he didn't want to waste any money on jetlag in any English motel. They could get their sleep in the next country.

Beneath the tumbling rain outside, Betty was sure she could hear something. A rattle. Some sort of metallic clank. A thin clatter inside their tinny hire-car. Every few metres she waited, and listened for a rattle. It was coming from her door. She was sure she had shut the door firmly back at the airport, yet she could hear this noise and it had begun to unsettle her. A rattle.

Ed yawned again, and pushed his saucer-shaped driving glasses back up the bridge of his nose. The empty can of diet soda on Betty's lap was teasing her, and she was beginning to get bored with this cold chunk of Mormon-car-silence. She hated this game. She'd thought she could bear the chastisement but she couldn't. She needed to use the bathroom. She raised her voice above the downpour.

– You going to speak to me, honey?

– I'm driving, Betty.

– I know you're driving, Ed. You've been driving for quite a while now. And you haven't said a damned word!

– I'm concentrating, Betty. What you want me to say?

– I don't know. Sorry?

– Hell, I'm not the one that needs to apolog…

Ed's mouth stayed open. Shit. He'd spoken. He peeked at his wife. There was a glint of malice in her eye. A trace of a smile on her worn face. The bitch'd beaten him. His wife had won. She'd slipped one in. Broken the car silence and caught him out. He trembled. Then exploded.

– BETTY, CAN YOU SEE THAT STINKIN' RAIN OUT THERE? Can you see that rain? I CAN. I see more of that rain than the goddamned road in this place. And it ain't easy driving on this petty little mountain road, in this shabby little country you brought us to, Betty! I'm trying to focus here! I *need* the car silence! It ain't no easy punishment I'm giving you here, neither! It ain't a game, girl! IT IS NECESSARY.

– Yeah? Well you just passed us another one, back there, didn't you, Ed!

– Another what?

– You just passed another service station! Don't tell me you didn't see it, Ed.

– I didn't see it.

– Bullshit. That's seven you've passed! I'm gonna piss myself 'lest you stop at the next one. Hell, it took you awhile to get this thing started up, but you *can* stop it, right?

– Why don't you wait till we get to the motel?

She watched as the rain whacked brutally against the car windscreen and they drove on slowly up the never-ending mountain road. She'd wondered earlier whether they'd actually taken the right turning. At least she'd gotten the old dog talking.

7

Ed let his head nod calmly at the passing sight of a half bent, iron road sign: *Cwmgarw 3 3/4*. He took his hand from the steering wheel and pointed. Planted high on a ridge in a rain-soaked field behind the first sign there was another. A sign made from garden fencing. It was over five metres tall and stood on thin wooden legs that wobbled against the wind. Ed squinted and read the words roughly written in a bright orange paint: **Leading to Texas-2**. The words were underlined with a curling black arrow which pointed directly downward into the field. Ed saw a dead sheep as it bobbed, floating in the muddy water beneath the sign. He turned to see whether his wife had noticed. She hadn't. Ed fumbled with his glasses, pushed them back onto the bridge of his nose and briefly glared at his cherry-faced, gasping wife. Her seat belt had locked around her body when Ed's hand left the wheel and he quickly steadied the car. She yanked the tight belt loose and squeezed at the tip of her bumped elbow.

– I'm sorry, he said.

– So am I, she said.

Family Love

– I'M SORRY! Alright? There, I've said it. I. Am. Sorry. Fuck's sake, Leanne, how many times should I...

– Don't matter how many times you says it, does it? said Leanne.

– Awww, come on mun...

– Don't CHANGE nothing, does it? said Leanne.

– I forgot. Fuck's sake. I forgot.

– Yeah? Well you never forgot to go and order us a sword from the Dogman, did you, eh? Naw. Big giant sword? Got that lined up. Easy. Easy peasy, like. And you never forgot to dress all neat and tidy yourself, did you, eh? said Leanne.

– We needs that sword, said Donna.

– Hhhmmm.

– Aaaaw, come on Leanne, you look fine.

– I looks like a battered old fucking waitress. Someone who dun have the frigging brains to change outta her greasy uniform, on her day off. On her fucking birthday, Donna! And all cause my sister here tells me that she's got my clothes all neatly tucked away, in the boot of her frigging car. And me? Yeah, me? I'm stupid enough to go an believe the manky tart.

– I'M SORRY, said Donna.

Leanne Evans stopped nibbling on the corner of her tissue and wiped at her nose. They'd been driving in the car for forty minutes and it was only when they'd reached the long road crossing the top of the valleys that Donna bothered to mention she hadn't brought her a change of clothes. Today. It was her twenty-third birthday, and Leanne sat in the car wearing a pink dress that was baggy on her skinny hips and covered in cooking oil.

Leanne licked her fingers and picked at a dried patch of sauce smeared across the chest of her uniform. She was feeling older already. She knew her bruised face made her look rough, and the dress wasn't going to help. Donna had collected her earlier that morning when her shift at the 24-hr McDonalds finished. They had just begun a theme month doing Classic American Diner; the waitresses had to wear a 1950s pink outfit with the men wearing a white shirt and slinky black tie combo. If Leanne were a bigger woman maybe the uniform they'd given her wouldn't have looked so bad, but she didn't have 1950s curves.

– I'm sorry, said Donna.

– Piss off.

In the wet morning light, the charred roadside trees were standing dead. The wet fields were black and burnt. Small wild ponies stood together. They shivered against the wind and watched Donna's car drive past over their ravaged mountaintop. The sisters had come too far to turn back now, and Donna drove on. She tapped her gold-ringed fingers on the brittle steering wheel to a tune Leanne didn't recognise. It was cold in that car. Leanne leaned forward and started to fiddle with the heater again and Donna hit her hand away.

– Leave 'em, Leanne.

– It feels fucking freezing in here.

– Leave 'em, said Donna.

– IT'S FUCKING FREEZING IN HERE.

– Leave. My. Fucking. Heater. Alone. Leanne.

– MY TITS ARE 'BOUT TO DROP OFF!

– Leave 'em, said Donna.

Leanne folded her arms across her chest and stared out of the passenger window.

– Well, happy fucking birthday, she mumbled.

– Yeah, happy fucking birthday, said Donna.

Donna could *be* the boss. Growing up, Donna had thought Leanne was always dumb enough to simply nod her head and agree. And Leanne often did. It was her act. In her own head, she knew being the younger sister never really made her the second in command. But waiting for her sister to pick her up that morning, she had started to think she shouldn't have agreed to what they were doing right now. It was all more Donna than Leanne, and she was beginning to think she was daft for nodding her head this time.

Leanne had waited twenty minutes for her sister to fetch her. She knew it would happen. Leanne had sat, freezing, in front of an empty store, trying to get her mobile to work, and watched three boys turn the road on the edge of town into some sort of racetrack. Leanne stared in stupor, smoking her Regals, as they zoomed round the abandoned shops and Carphone Warehouse.

– So, what's the matter, Leanne. You gonna tell me?

– I dunno, do I?

– Dunno what?

– If this seems right. Is this right? said Leanne.

Leanne could see her own breath and glared at her sister. Donna pointed at her. Leanne was worried she was looking at herself in a few years time. She shook her head as a car raced past. Donna lowered her bony finger and clenched hold of Leanne's arm. Her sister raised her head.

– This? This is fucking right. This is your day, innit? Your birthday. Right? And I is gonna get you the best present we could ever hope for. Right? We gonna do what needs to be done here, Leanne. Right? We been planning this all week.

– I dunno, Donna. It's you, really. You been talking about this… going on about doing it. Not…

– Right!? said Donna.

– Yeah, said Leanne. Okay, right.

– Good.

Leanne let out a small groan. She touched her bruised cheeks and wiped a tear away from her face. Donna always had the upper hand in their decision making. It didn't seem fair she was that weak.

– It's a strange thing, love, innit? said Leanne.

– NAW. NAW. DON'T FOOL YOURSELF. It ain't strange, Leanne. Love? Love is a simple thing. You never loved tha' man. And he definitely never did love you, did he?

– We was never proper lovers, Donna. We was friends.

– You wasn't friends, Leanne.

– Yes we was. We were house friends.

– Yeah? Well friends can love each other too, innit? But you don't go sharing a house with a friend, waiting for the day the fucker tries to kill you, does you?

– Spose not, said Leanne.

– Cause, love? It certainly don't involve beating the shite out of you, does it? Love? It don't involve dragging you screaming across the floor by the hair. Shite, it don't involve holding a knife to your throat, and threatening to kill you. Love? Naw, love ain't that, Leanne. No. Peculiar fucker always loved his dog more than he could ever love a human. Now, that's strange.

– Spose.

– And yeah, I wants to do this. It's true. Cause tha' fucker is gonna find out what love can feel like. Family love. And you know what family love can mean? Means we are gonna make tha' cunt weep, Leanne. And you know what it's called?

Donna was smiling.

– Love? said Leanne.

Donna shook her head.

– REVENGE.

The Oxytocin Stare

When the seven-tonne industrial snow-gritter went past, it was barely light at the top of the valley and Boyd Evans had been stretched out in the back of his 1989 Ford Mondeo. He woke so fast his forehead hurt from frowning as he leant toward the noise of the vehicle choking its way past the lay-by. Boyd peered at the back of the yellow snow-gritter and caught sight of the pissed town councillor, Mister Merlin Gunter. The man was testing his newly bought vehicle for speed, and spread the grit with a damaging force onto an ice-free mountain road. Every three seconds rock salt bullets were spat out of the electric pipes and Boyd watched the driver joyously yell, enrapt with the bellow of the engine.

Boyd had worked for a different town council division in Pentrecoch, only a few miles away. It had been a real shock when his own borough announced they could not afford, nor did they need, a new snow-gritter, unlike Mister Gunter's happy bunch. After the Christmas disaster last year, the Cooperstown council were determined not to be mocked by the national press ever again. They had put themselves on a high alert, prepared for any sudden change in climate, and were calling it *Operation Snowflake*. They had bragged in the local press non-stop for five months about the one hundred thousand pound snow-gritter they'd found on the web. And there was a general agreement that everyone in their constituency seemed proud of the mammoth vehicle. It was worth the costs.

The yellow snow-gritter had been placed on display in the neighbouring town centre for days. They had sealed off the roads and parked it next to the statue of a local worthy. They covered it with purple baubles, fairy lights and tinsel. Children were invited to sit on the huge wheels, and pay for their Christmas photos to be taken by one of the several dancing elves, and Boyd knew there was a growing sense of jealousy between the two towns.

Boyd turned his wipers on and watched the thin rubber sticks scratch brown rock salt and rain across his windscreen. He yawned and leant back, trying not to think about what had happened to the outside paint job of his car. He had to rub at his face again to calm himself. Across the road from the lay-by he looked at the knackered service station. Shite, he knew he had to get over there. He couldn't concentrate. He slipped out a cigarette.

Pinkie, his dog, noticed he was awake and started to pay him some attention again. And for a moment, when he realised little Perky would not stand up, Boyd felt he was letting Pinkie down. He tilted his face back towards the scarred dirty vinyl, hanging from the ceiling of his car, and groaned.

No. Boyd didn't have time for this. The frantic slurping and panting around his cock was making him more nervous. And he could not get hard. He didn't want to.

– Aaaww naw, mun, Pinkieee, no. No. Stop it. We gotta stop, stop mun…. sssSSStoooaaaaaop.

They hadn't come up here for this. And Pinkie bloody knew it. Perky does not come out to play before a job. It was an agreed fucking rule. He was the one being let down here, not his partner. Stick to the guidelines. The routine.

Boyd looked at the top of the gorgeous hairy head, rolling between his thighs. It had to be done. He took a breath and punched Pinkie away from his cock. The frightened dog barked loudly in displeasure. Stunned. Aggrieved. Boyd knew it would be tricky.

– I'm sorry, love.

Pinkie was a big hound. The size and shape of a fat pony, covered in masses of fluffy black fur that Boyd spent hours combing and perfuming to give his dog an elegant touch. He stood seven feet long and thirty inches high. Weighed thirteen stone and four pounds. And this massive Newfoundland did not easily accept defeat. He was barking at Boyd. Wailing. Boyd pushed him back and Pinkie glared at him. The dog was breathing heavily. Warm threads of spittle and pubic hair hanging off the tip of his muscular tongue.

No. Pinkie pounced back down there and continued to repeatedly lick at his crotch. He didn't want to treat the dog like this. But things had to be done. They'd come up the mountain for a reason and he realised he was lucky the snow-gritter had woke him. He spat out his cigarette. With two hands Boyd grabbed hold of the dog's firm leather collar and pulled it with all his might. He wrenched Pinkie a foot into the air, and the dog leapt forwards onto his chest.

– Aaaaaaaaaaahhhhh.

Boyd screamed as he found himself crushed by the enormous weight of this fighting beast and lost his grip. He struggled to regain control and tried to slip his arms back through the mass of black fur, wriggling his fingers to connect. Pinkie was ecstatic. He thought it was part of a new game. There was delight in the dog's bark and Boyd felt its heart pump as litres of blood smashed through an eager body and up to a wagging tail tip. The dog writhed in excitement as Boyd winced in pain. It wasn't until his hands found each other and locked around the dog's neck did Pinkie understand they weren't playing. Boyd squeezed, and listened to his dog choke.

He pulled the flailing animal tight and got a face full of fur. Boyd spat and Pinkie made spluttering sounds. Kicked hind legs against the radio. Boyd pulled harder. He had his dog on top of him. He knew this was the only way. He used his arms and chest to crush the windpipe and strangle away at the dog's aortic arteries. He could feel Pinkie going. And he continued to squeeze. The dog stopped kicking. Pinkie had lost. The dog was still. He rested on top of Boyd, and the dead weight pushed him further down onto the seat. Boyd shoved the animal to the side and grinned.

– Sorry.

Pinkie was slouched against the car door, his head against the cold window, and he made that whimpering noise. One big, drooling dog. Barely breathing. Beautiful. Boyd loved that dog more than he could ever love anyone. He wiped cold sweat off his forehead and let the fish-grin spread. Shite, dogs like that should come with an addiction warning. He shook out another cigarette and lit it, staring at Pinkie. Boyd swallowed a heavy lungful of smoke. He could sense Perky coming to life.

He sat and watched Pinkie slowly but steadily regain its senses. The dog had become his life. Boyd puffed his chest out and laughed, coughing a mouthful of smoke into the cold car. Pinkie opened his eyes and instinctively growled at him. Boyd gently stroked his neck and let the dog lick his hand. Pinkie let out a whining bark and growled at him through the smoke.

– Aaawww come on, love. Listen, Daddy made a mistake, didn't he? Daddy was naughty. We was bored in the rain. A silly Daddy, yes. Silly. Should never have taken Perky out. Silly.

Pinkie let out a muffled bark and moved his head away from Boyd.

– Aww come on Pinkie, mun, don't do this to me. Not now. Not today, mun. I got other things to worry about, right?

The dog turned back toward Boyd, stared at him with tawny yellow eyes, and licked its wet snout. He wasn't pleased. Boyd sighed. This didn't feel right. He reached into his pocket and slipped out a Winalot bone shape and offered it to Pinkie, but he wasn't interested. Boyd chewed on the biscuit himself.

– Jus wait here, sweetheart. Daddy'll bring you a little present, yeah? What you want? Eh? A Twix? A Twixy? Nooo? What about a Mars bar? Eh? Likes 'em, dun you? Eh? Mars bars? All chewy like?

The dog barked in intense response. Boyd knew he liked the Mars bar.

– Alright 'en, sugar, Mars it is.

– Woof. Woof. Woof.

Boyd leant forward and opened the glove compartment; he put his hand inside and brought out a plastic bag with a quarter gramme of grainy white powder he'd bought. He believed it would give him a bit more power, a bit more energy for the jobs, and Boyd had got into the habit of using this cheap stuff. He eked a speck of it onto the top of his hand, and snorted it all up his left nostril.

He reached under the car seat and carefully pulled out his heavy gun. It was a copy of the old-fashioned Smith and Wesson six shooter. His dad had it made years ago. Silver-plated iron, with a star clipped onto each side of the wooden handle. Boyd's mam never understood his dad's cowboy passions, and wouldn't allow the gun to be placed alongside him in his box when he passed away. Boyd knew he'd never really use it. Felt weird in his hand. Excited, Boyd kissed Pinkie on his drooling snout. A tender look of quiet love passed between them both and he stroked the dog. He felt his cock rise.

17

– Won't be long, love.

Pinkie placed his elegant head back down into Boyd's lap, and compassionately rubbed at Mister Perky. Boyd shook his head. He was hard. Perky was standing tall. And Pinkie knew it. *Shite.* He couldn't help himself.

– Fuck, you're good, Pinkie.

Cheyenne's Lucky Day

A fleck of shiny red blood popped from the needle nick on the side of her forefinger and Cheyenne Evans moaned in anger. She spotted the dropped name-tag resting on the countertop and threw it with some force at the bin. The badge bounced off the wall, slid across the linoleum floor and over towards the Bargain Snacks.

– Yeah, sod off Nelson.

She plumped back down behind the till. Cheyenne had been tired, sitting there throughout the night with old Nelson's plastic name-tag on her chest, and had only just noticed. She was sure she'd been having a thought at the time. A good one. She let her head drift off the badge and up to the electric doors. She sucked her breath in tight, and thought. Hard. If she was superstitious, she'd probably think it all meant something. She wasn't though.

Work at the petrol station was dull. Cheyenne would sit and read a magazine, eating the nearest chocolate bar, drinking her Tango and admiring the latest hairstyle in a copy of *Hello*. And the night-shift slot was even worse. It took her a while to get used to it. To stop falling asleep and dreaming. There were plenty of savoury pot noodles to guzzle through, but Cristiano Ronaldo, semi-naked in a pair of tight fitting Armani pants, never did wander by. It was mainly lorry drivers. Beer-bellied men in their fifties, grunting and groaning toward her. Asking her why they'd shut the Little Chief restaurant over there, and watching her delicately finish off a packet of crisps before she even noticed them. When she got the call a day ago, she'd been surprised. Mister Hardy sounded as if he'd been sobbing when he asked her whether she could fill in for his nightshift duty.

– Yeah, course, said Cheyenne. Wouldn't Nelson normally do it, though?

– Ha, yes, yes, only I can't seem to get hold of him and I've had a little problem. Something serious happened to me, love.

Cheyenne had phoned her part-time boyfriend, Tetchy, to tell him his date was cancelled.

– Some nutter's gone and assaulted Mister H right outside his house. He was stepping out the front door when some disguised psycho-midget charged him with a sword.

– A psycho-midget?

– It's what I heard. Nutter was four foot something, wearing this lacy black cape outfit waving a…

– Ha, sounds like your Nan, don't it?

– Don't dare say that!

– Well, we both knowse it, Cheyenne, she don't like…

Cheyenne was disturbed. He may have been right. She remembered when the mouthy local hairdresser had first told her gung-ho Nan that she'd got the job up at the station. Nan'd come bolting round their house with her hair half fixed. Not the right frigging work for her young grand-daughter.

– Stop it, Tetchy! This is *serious*. This nutter had some massive steel broadsword. Mister H legged it back in, and called the police. Psycho-midget never got him. Disappeared when it heard the sirens go. He's shitting himself. Decided to step back from the counter. Probably means I'll be getting asked to do a load more work here.

Tetchy had reckoned it could be her lucky day, and he'd be able to come around to celebrate with her. Cheyenne had said no. She was young, but she wasn't dumb. When your boss gets attacked you don't go out celebrating. It wouldn't look right. It was creepy. And she told him so. The truth was, her second part-time boyfriend would soon be leaving the hospital. They'd almost completed his eppy tests, and she knew he'd be calling in to see her and check on his own work schedule.

She'd met Hank at the petrol station on her first day. He'd been lounging about, trying to impress her and lying about things. Hank had told her it was he who'd installed the CCTV cameras. All six of them. She loved the CCTV cameras. They were everywhere. She'd learned it was his dad, Nelson who used to be the electrician, so she wasn't sure. The cheap petrol scam Mister Hardy was running relied on Bio-Fuel. Hank, his dad and Mister H, had warned her never to talk openly about the Bio-Fuel in front of one of the cameras. You took the driver's money, smiled, but you didn't mention the deal.

When there was nobody else in the station, Cheyenne couldn't help practise in front of one of the cameras. Showbusiness was where Cheyenne was really heading. She knew it. She'd make the perfect celebrity. Dead right for a part in any Soap. Hank always bragged he'd soon be selling his own work over in Hollywood. His brief stint on some college course a few years back had boosted his hope of success. Cheyenne knew the dork was living in fantasyland. X-Factor was coming to Cardiff in January, and she was going to be there. It was why she'd started to dye her thick black hair blue and use the silicone tit-lifters. She was the one who was going to be leaving this stinking shithole, not Hank.

The dirty fuel sold at the station was 80% veggie oil, the rest being cheap vodka brought back from the Ukraine. They had hundreds of soaked cardboard boxes stacked in the corner of the shed. The dump was bursting with vodka. Hank saw her once standing near the boxes, thinking of nicking a couple. He'd told Cheyenne not to be tempted by it.

– If you've a mind to steal, then you steal the vodka on display. Do not touch this one. Not even my dad would touch it.

Hank explained to her this lethal vodka was to light it all up. Make the engine go, like. Any leftovers of that dangerous liquid, they'd pour down the drain in the Chip shop. It killed the rats. They had these special pumps at the back of the station, and every week or so it was Hank's stinking job to fill them to the brim with the tons of cold grease and mangled chip fat that got passed out of Adumchuk Gogol's eighteen chippies down the valley. Adumchuk Gogol and his ever growing family had always upheld the local passion for the deep fried chip. To fry the food item only in fresh oil. Dirty oil had to be buried. But the Gogol family had buried so much of it over the decades it was beginning to get noticed. And it was the petrol station who knew how to help.

Hank brought the hot fat from the chippie in the sealed trunk of his dad's car and stored it in the shed, and when the temperature dropped he'd work over the top of the fifteen barrels, taking out all the bits of food with the clever plastic filters Hank bragged he'd made. It reeked. Hank always had a smell on him. Cheyenne'd grown used to it. You knew when he was coming, alright. He was embarrassed by it.

On the day they'd first met, Hank told Cheyenne he'd usually spray half a can of Lynx Leopard deodorant onto the inside of his work tracksuit before he ever went into town. Reckoned it didn't stain or nothing, long as you used Lynx Leopard. She'd been well impressed. Lynx isn't low-priced. After ironing his tracksuit, his mam had once used a cheaper deodorant, Physio Sports Endurance. He went mental.

– No, Cheyenne. No. If you do it, you do it properly. Right?

She knew that. I know that. And I didn't need to tell her that. It's Lynx Leopard. Simple. She was just messing around and eager to use one of the cheaper ones. I don't even know where she got the Physio from, Cheyenne, because believe me, I don't use the Physio deodorant, Cheyenne. Ever.

– Does you use Lynx for the pits as well?

– Don't be frigging silly, girl.

– Wha' does you use 'en?

– Come here.

Cheyenne looked at the long-haired, bespectacled young man standing a foot in front of her and laughed. He was a right geek.

– Get lost, she said.

– Come on, mun.

– Why?

– Just come here, I'm not going to hurt you, Cheyenne, am I?

– Hank, she said.

– Come on.

Hank had taken his shirt off and lifted his arm. He was pointing at his arm-pit. He rubbed a batch of stringy hairs between two fingers and smelled at the delicious scent with delight. Cheyenne stopped giggling and moved toward him. Hank nodded his head and Cheyenne smelled under his arm.

– Now tell me, Cheyenne, what is that? Hank said.

– I don't frigging know, do I?

She pulled back. Hank stood there, both arms raised and doing his snaky wriggle dance.

– Bet you've never ever smelled a scent like that before have you, Cheyenne? A real beauty, right? A real swooner, eh girl?

Cheyenne shook her head and had another sniff.

– Old Spice.

– Fuck off. You couldn't afford Old Spice, she said.

– It's Old Spice Classic, Cheyenne. Five quid a stick. Quality stuff.

He was dancing again. The nerd was trying to chat her up. Cheyenne had never really understood why she liked Hank. She didn't, she supposed. But he was certainly different to everybody else she knew around there. And he was available. And hell, she knew he always would be.

*

Cheyenne stretched over the magazines on the counter top, and leaned forward on her elbows. She sucked her breath in again. Held it, and counted. In that week's edition of *Hello*, Mystic Maggie had described this new type of Yoga art. All to do with holding your breath. Good for a tired brain. If you could hold on to it for long enough, any previous ideas would flow back in. Cheyenne had another go. Her breath shot out of her mouth when she heard the crash at the back of the shop.

– Sorry, honey.

– Leave it, said Cheyenne. I'll clean it later.

She'd forgotten they were even in there. It'd been dead all night. Just Hank and Tetchy texting. No customers all morning until them two. Seven-fifteen and the lost-looking American lovebirds had hurried through the doors. In their eighties, Cheyenne reckoned. They went straight to the back of the service-station to use the toilet, then started searching through all the out-of-date crap lying damp on the shelves. Cheyenne had ignored them.

She looked up at the CCTV camera on the wall and nodded at herself. This was her lucky day. She looked at the electric doors. She could hope.

The Cost of Living with a Canine

HowdeeeeeDooDeeeee!
How'd you like your eggs treated?
Fried? Scrambled? Fluffed?
It's Your Choice on our New Breakfast Menu
for the Early Morning Starter

Before it shut down, the Little Chief Restaurant had been awarded a Good Egg Certificate. Boyd found himself reading the plastic menu hanging inside the large shattered plate glass window. He never did understand why the company had closed all its restaurants in the area. Whenever he went into one, there had always seemed to be people sitting at their tables. Since Little Chief won the award, Boyd and other customers always felt obliged to buy an egg dish. Mind, he knew his passion had really been their bacon special.

He turned away from the menu and pulled the light stocking down over his head, then took the gun out of his jacket and rolled it in his hand. Boyd looked across the restaurant's ramshackle car park towards the petrol station and drew a breath. When the restaurant had closed most people assumed the petrol station would follow but the Cwmgarw mountain road didn't shut, and the station was always in use. It linked the two valleys and the petrol station's owner had been canny enough not to sell the place.

Boyd kicked an empty beer can through a puddle and pushed his chest out. He started to walk across the rain-soaked car park towards the petrol station, the gravel beneath his feet a mix of broken glass and burnt black plastic. The car park was mainly used as a meeting place for swingers or drunken teenagers. Boyd had visited the location a few times in the past week. In the morning there had never been anyone around other than Nelson or the owner.

The electric doors opened and Boyd entered the station like John Wayne.

He held his gun out, clicked the hammer back, and stood there. The spot behind the till where Nelson should be resting was filled with the sight of a terrified teenage girl. And the countertop was covered with a collection of celebrity magazines. Boyd got a nervous tinkle in his bladder. He didn't like this. This wasn't the routine.

The open-mouthed girl nodded slowly at Boyd as if she was expecting the event. They were both silent. Boyd felt wasted. The minute rush of adrenalin had abandoned his veins as soon as he saw this blue-haired muffin. He delicately waved the gun at the girl.

– Money. I want the money.

She tidily shuffled the magazines on the countertop into a neat pile and quickly fixed her hair back with a clip. Her eyes flitted away from Boyd and focused on the security camera behind him. She raised her arms straight above her head and screamed hard at a loud peak. Boyd trotted a few feet towards her, his gun levelled at her mouth. The girl swallowed her scream and waited.

– I said, get me the money out. NOW!

She took a step towards Boyd and whispered,

– This gonna be national, innit?

– What is?

– This! This! It's gonna get on telly, innit? I'm gonna be famous here, innae?

– JUST FUCKING DO IT. Get your frigging arms down, and shove the money in the bag. Come on. DO IT.

– NO, please… no… DON'T shoot me, sir… PLEASE…

The girl was talking to the camera. She pulled her arms down, looked at Boyd and, quite magically, she started to produce enormous tears. Boyd burped and swallowed the bile as he watched heavily applied mascara jolt in a stream down this freaky kid's face. Boyd lowered the gun and stepped up to the counter. He got a glimpse of her name-tag.

– Cheyenne? I'll need a bag. A carrier bag, please, Cheyenne.

– They're under the counter, sir.

– Okay, well get us the bag, go on Cheyenne, get us the bag.

Cheyenne ducked under the counter and re-appeared with a carrier bag. She opened the till. She was sobbing. Sobbing in what Boyd thought wasn't a very convincing fashion. Melodramatic. She shoved the used tenners and fivers into the bag. Boyd scanned the dough. Not much. He kept turning towards the doors and back to this idiot. He raised the gun and talked to Cheyenne.

– Fuck's sake mun. I ain't gonna shoot you is I, Cheyenne? If I'd have wanted to fucking shoot you 'en I'd have fucking shot you already. C'mon, HURRY IT UP, MUN. Not the fucking coins. NOT THE FUCKING COINS, MUN.

– Sorry sir, I'm boiling hot though, innae?

– What?

– Does you mind if I undoes my… I think I'd work better, at a faster speed like, I think, if I took off…

– Wha'? No. You ain't taking nothin off. Get on with it.

Boyd spun around and waved the gun over to the back of the station. He'd heard something. He was sure he'd heard someone's voice. A whispering voice.

– What was that?

Cheyenne shook her head and continued to fill the bag. Boyd thought he'd heard a voice. He had. He'd heard someone whisper at the back of the place. He was sure of it. It was the voice of a woman. He ordered Cheyenne to stop.

– Who's there?

– Hello? said the voice.

– Hello? said Boyd.

– Dang it, Ed. There's no signal up here.

Boyd took the gun away from the side of Cheyenne's head and jumped onto the counter. He scanned the place but he couldn't see anyone.

– Right, whoever you are, appear now. I'm giving you five seconds to appear. If you don't appear within five seconds, I'm coming to get you.

After twenty seconds Boyd got down and walked away from the countertop. Gun raised. Searching. He got to the electric doors. Moved to his left. Waited. A blast of air rushed past his ear and a bottle of HP sauce smashed against the wall beside him. Cans of baked beans fell off the shelf and scattered. Boyd launched himself into the aisle. His trigger finger slipped. His arm was wrenched into the air. The bullet tore its way through a fridge with a heavy whump and several plastic bottles of orange juice were blasted apart all over an odd looking couple, drenching them.

– WHO THE FUCK'RE YOU?

– Uhh, we… we're… Americans, son.

– I cun fucking see tha', can't I? Get the fuck over here. NOW.

The soaked American couple waddled over to an angry Boyd. He snatched the mobile phone from the woman's hand and pushed her past him. He stood back to let the man pass, he must've been at least six-foot-three, wearing a black suit and tie, with a moustache that Burt Reynolds wouldn't wear. The enormous woman had started to pray.

– God no. Jesus help us...

– Who was she trying to phone? said Boyd.

– Uhh, who'd you think? Our best friend? said the man.

– ...please save us from this beast...

– You're relaxed, said Boyd.

– Someone has to be, son, said the man.

Boyd spun the gun from the couple to the girl. Cheyenne was staring out of the side window. He edged around the customers to the countertop. He couldn't understand what the kid was interested in.

– Oi, Cheyenne? OI, CHEYENNE. What the fuck're you doing? Who're you looking at?

– Nothing.

Boyd couldn't see anything. The lollipop stand was blocking his view outside. He shook his head at Cheyenne.

– Stop it, 'en.

Cheyenne stopped hopping and Boyd pointed his gun at the American pair.

– What the fuck're you two doing in here?

– Uhhh... we've come to fish around... said the man.

– We pray for our saviour... said the woman.

– SHUT UP. Fishing? For wha'?

– Our ancestors.

– We pray for our rights...

– Cun you SHUT HER UP?

The large lady had gone into some sort of religious rant.

– Uhh... Betty, you'd better do as the *gentleman*...

– SHUT THE FUCK UP. Both of you. Lie down on the floor. C'mon. Lie down. ON THE FLOOR. NOW. DO IT. BOTH OF YOU.

They struggled to lower themselves. Boyd had to watch and wait as they puffed and wheezed their limbs down, inch by inch, onto the worn linoleum. As soon as they were flat, Boyd

29

knew he had made a miscalculation. The American couple were the size and shape of two beached whales lying there in the aisle, and he was standing behind them squeezed up against the countertop. They were blocking his way to the exit.

– Please Lord…

– Shite.

– …if you decide to take us, in this foreign land…

The woman continued to pray. Boyd scratched his head in disbelief. He turned to Cheyenne, who had vanished.

– CHEYENNE?

– Yes, sir?

Her voice trickled up. He poked his head over the countertop.

– What you doing?

– You told us to lie down a second ago?

– No, mun, not you. Get up.

She was up in a jiffy. She'd taken off the company shirt and was stripped down to the bright T-shirt she wore underneath. Boyd nodded towards her bleeding finger.

– Oh, I had to move my name-tag badge. Needles, eh? Second time it's happened. Clumsy fingers.

She looked up at the CCTV and stopped chewing gum. She started the tears again, threw her hands out towards the carrier bag and stepped back.

– That's it, dude. Leave me be, please. Go now.

Boyd put his hand on the bag, and Cheyenne stepped forward to take it back.

– No, no, hang on. That sounded funny, didn't it? Hang on. Let me do that one again. *THAT IS it, sir.* Please, don't take me with you.

She lowered her hands and allowed Boyd to take the bag. He looked at her in astonishment.

– Was tha' better? she asked.

– Yeah, yeah. Listen, I'm not stupid, Cheyenne. I know what you lot does up here. I WANTS IT ALL.

The juice-stained American lady was still praying. Boyd kicked her in the side with the toe of his trainer, and he waited for Cheyenne to swiftly return from the back office with the box. Cheyenne handed it over.

– That's all of it, sir.

– Right, thank you, Cheyenne, didn't hurt did it?

– Nuh.

– Right 'en. I'm gonna go. Nobody fucking moves. And we're all done and dusted. Understand?

The Americans looked up.

– Yes.

– Yes.

– Good.

Boyd turned and waved his gun at Cheyenne.

– You gonna take me as well? she said.

– Uhh, now why the fuck would I want to do tha'?

– Kidnap, maybe?

– No. I wants you, Cheyenne, to get back down on the floor like 'em two and when I leaves here…

Boyd's sweaty finger slipped on the cold metallic curve of the trigger. He stared at the silver pistol in his hand and realised it was pointed at the kid. It fired. Cheyenne, with a look of disbelief on her baffled face, was glaring at the security camera. Her bleeding finger was raised at the lifeless object on the wall. It hadn't been turned on. She had missed her chance. The bullet went through her. Boyd watched blood bloom from her chest. Cheyenne slid down the wall.

– SHIT.

He turned, jumped on top of the American woman, and bounced right down her back to the exit door, running out of the petrol station and over to his car.

31

– SSHHHIIIITTTTTTTTTTTTTTTTTT.

He got in the car and slammed the door. Covered in sticky blood, he chucked the money and the gun onto the back seat. Took off his wet nylon stocking and looked down the road in shock.

– Shit.

He started the engine and wondered why he could feel a breeze caress his face. The passenger door was wide open. His dog wasn't sitting where he'd left him.

– Pinkie?

The car was empty.

– PINKKKIIEEEEEEE?

Friendless, Electric, Hospitals

A noise shot into his ears, echoing from someplace in the valley outside, and he felt his skin prickle as the dead-bang explosion brought the image of Cheyenne popping back into his otherwise barren mind. Hank had been feeling sicker than usual in the hospital earlier that morning, and was looking forward to his trip home.

Like most NHS relaxation-rooms it stank of feet, Dettol and human shit. Friendless, electric, hospitals. What made this one worse was the fact that it featured four rooted epileptics, listening to the sound of the Specialist Nurse's radio, drifting down the narrow corridor. Each one of them trying not to twitch. Each one of them knowing it was there, somewhere. Waiting. Each one of them secretly desperate not to take *the plunge*.

Hank let out an embarrassing fart. He'd been staring at the stained wall for hours now and felt knackered. Some individual parts of his gangly body were beginning to rebel. A violent shuddering in his left arm had started to snap him back into a numb reality. He slipped his glasses back up his nose and rubbed at a muscle tic in his jaw. He had a portable EEG Unit attached to his head and his tingling legs hung beneath him, entangled in five feet of electric wire plugged into the wall socket. It didn't matter how much medication they fed him, staring at a wall can become *difficult*. Dangerous even. One lonely jerk and he'd be on the floor wrapped up in these electrical cords for quite a while. He knew it could happen. It had.

One hundred and fifteen hours. Forty-five minutes. Eleven seconds. They'd been scanning his brain for its problematic pulse. The energetic timer that rested on top of the enormous battery shackled to his left thigh had given him the silent numbers to count. Green numbers. They blinked past his eyes at a speed as identical and boring as life itself. It was aggravating. Burning. Making his eyes tire. Tremble. He yawned. No, he couldn't. He shouldn't. He didn't want to take the chance.

They were in a room painted tangerine, and sat on lime green foam chairs. Christmas was only a week away and faded tinsel hung from the walls like a thin dead smile, metres long. Outside, the rain hadn't stopped all morning, hurling itself against a colossal wire-laced glass window, desperate to get in. A mute TV was on the small table, showing a special edition of *Sesame Street*. By the open door, to the right of Hank, sat Custer, a teenager proud of his first moustache. Custer was quivering the most and looking as if he needed a teddy bear. A few feet away sat Carlton; a big bloke, constantly fiddling inside his tracksuit bottoms. Ivan was a man in his seventies who was flopped there in the corner wearing Hank's Transformer T-shirt and spare pants. A constant grin on his face. Maybe the fixed grin was helping him forget he'd shat himself three hours earlier. One of the professional thugs had pretended to clean him, but claimed she couldn't track down any spare gown for the sodden git. Ivan was handed back a sopping pair. Carlton? Sure, he had spare clothes. The tight twat had come in with a suitcase full. Hank had been daft enough to think Carlton would hand over his extras. Ivan didn't even ask the man. He had asked Hank.

Hank had first met these two five years ago in the hospital, and knew all the details. Their seeping hatred for each other had hardened over the years. It was solid. They were fixed.

Neither had ever left the valley. The nonsensical chit-chat between them sounded marital. It was bitter and Hank had to swallow it steadily.

– …what the hell'd you mean, like a sodding snake? asked Carlton.

– You know. A snake. Innit? said Ivan.

– A snake?

– Yeah, mun. Like a snake. You know snakes, dun you? The Black Cobra? The Asian Copperhead? The Mamba? The Viper?

The couple were having one of their baffling disagreements and Hank was finding it difficult to ignore. They both wanted him to step in and take control of their problem. They knew he was awake. They wanted him to act as some kind of intelligent referee.

– You awake, Hank, love? said Ivan.

– No, Hank lied.

– Custer, you awake boy? said Ivan.

– Naw, lied Custer.

Hank was beginning to like Custer. Good kid. Following his example, like. Scared shitless when he first walked in a few days ago. Hank had told him he'd soon get bored. Custer was out of it now. Zombified. Getting ready for *the plunge*. He was still clinging on with the copying lark though. They'd made an agreement to do it when they met. No point faffing about. The youngest in here become mates, Hank had told him. If you went into one, you knew you could rely on the other to keep watch. If you went into one, you'd be safe. And Custer was about to go into one.

– Quick question, Hank, said Carlton.

– I'm asleep.

– …like a snake, innit? The carnivorous reptile, the legless lizard…

– Yeah, and fuck you too, said Carlton.

Ivan had opened his eyes. A dark dried tongue darted out between the crisp parted lips on a grinning face. Again and again. Ivan was waving it at Carlton. He was trying to upset him. Hank moved his dizzy head to the side with a slow purpose. His movement caught the attention of the Pantomime Act.

A humming tranquillity crept into their room as the patter of rain outside stopped its assault. The place began to seem different. Their yellow light bulb wasn't strong enough to hold back a dark pressure from outside and their room felt crushed by heavy storm clouds in an intense morning sky. Hank could hear water gurgle in the ancient iron radiator beneath the window. He looked at his arm. It was frozen, inches away from his face. Stiffened at an angle under his chin. Jesus. Was he trying to pray? Hank wondered whether you had to put both hands together in a more formal, pious manner. Pointless, he knew. He pulled his arm down and sat there motionless. He inhaled the dark light, waiting for the rain to return, wary his mind was set to concoct those rusty roller-coaster thoughts which would help send him into the familiar spasms.

Hank was listening to the small noise of walking feet down the empty corridor. Custer was twitching at a more frenetic pace. And Hank couldn't help it, he started to join him. A gloating Carlton and Ivan watched Custer and Hank. Ivan shoved his tongue out and wiggled it.

– Here it comes 'en, said Carlton.

– And here comes *The Eyebrow*, said Ivan.

– Ow'd you know it's her? said Carlton.

– Smells her. Like a snake, innit? Cun smell her hairspray, said Ivan.

– Piss off. How'd you know so much about snakes?

36

– Keeps 'em, dunnae? said Ivan.

– Tha' legal? said Carlton.

– Could be.

– So how does you smell like a snake 'en?

– 'ey got special powers innit? Can't see fuck all, cannae the snakes? So 'ey uses their tongues to sniff out the air, and it shoots up to their brains. And Bingo.

– One of 'em two's gonna go in a minute, said Carlton.

– Yep.

– Fancy ah bet, Snake-oil? Tenner, on who goes first?

– Oooooohh tricksy, said Ivan.

– Yep. New boy's been wobbling all morning, 'an he? said Carlton.

– Hhmmm. Go on 'en, I'll take Hank, said Ivan. Lad's always on the edge.

The sound of feet on the plastic flooring grew louder. They watched the open doorway as the female nurse appeared. She had the decency to pause at the doorway and examine them. Hank couldn't control the faltering surge. His jaw was clamped tight. He couldn't speak. He caught her eye and motioned toward Custer. She raised an eyebrow and walked on past.

Hank spat out in front of him, his body as stiff as a tree. His jaw driving down into his chest, eyes clamped shut. A Dolly Parton song came on the Specialist Nurse's radio, 'Islands in the Stream'. And a shaking Custer simply stopped. He came out of it. Wiped the phlegm and blood from his gob and looked over at Hank with a triumphant smile, shook his head and looked at the old men.

– Hehhe, you alright sweetheart? said Ivan. Never seen tha' before.

– Yeah. Fine.

– Lucky bastard, said Carlton.

– Tenner 'en, said Ivan.

For a moment they sat in quietude. Listening. Bored. Drugged. In a soulless state. They watched Hank, waiting for him to drop. Hank rattled along in a series of nasty spasms and was having trouble with his breathing. His jaw jumped further downwards onto his chest. And then one by one, Ivan, Carlton and Custer started to sing along to the song.

– Islands in the stream, that is what we is…

Hank sat grinding his teeth. He couldn't break out of it. He couldn't sing. He didn't realise, but he couldn't stop thinking of Cheyenne. He had heard ambulance sirens wailing outside, shouting voices, and trundling trolleys as hospital staff and policemen filled the corridors. He started to chew on his tongue. Blood dribbled down his neck. It was going to happen. It had happened. He'd lost it. He'd taken *the plunge*, and for a minute in his life he was somewhere else. Somewhere. Every muscle in his body would ache for the rest of the week as if he'd run the London marathon whilst fighting Rocky Balboa.

He sprang forward, and fell to the floor. *Thump.* His nose exploded. The arm of his glasses snapped. His body froze. And he started to convulse at a faster pace, tangled in the pulsating EEG wires. His legs kicked hard at the floor as he sucked for air. Convulsing in uncontrollable spasms, Hank pissed himself. He lay there briefly unconscious, slightly blue, then felt his head twist to the side and looked up. Three men were watching him. Singing. Giggling.

– Second time for Hank this week 'en, said Carlton.

– Yep, said Ivan.

Caught

Pinkie had stopped barking. He'd been disturbed by what had happened and Donna had fed him a sleeping pill. Leanne looked at the huge, sad thing, sitting on the back seat of her sister's little car. She looked as worried as the dog. Pinkie pushed his massive, drooling snout through the gap between the front seats. Leanne stroked him. He lowered his head. Doped. Defeated.

– Happy birthday, said Donna.

– Yeah, thanks, said Leanne.

Donna looked down the road at the undulating streams of terraced houses in the valley beneath them. Tiled roofs black with the constant rain. The cheap speed she'd taken earlier for the trip had trickled out of her body and she was wishing she'd bought more. It felt a long drive. Sitting in her car with Leanne, arguing. Arguing over a little error she'd made. It was her birthday, and Leanne should be treating herself, not fighting like a child.

Donna was feeling rejected. She was getting the sense her sister did not want to do all this as much as she did. Donna could admit it was her idea like, but fuck, she was only doing it for her sister. When Donna saw the battered state of Leanne when she came to stay, it got her thinking. And when Donna heard about the man's love for his dog, she had told Leanne she had a plan. The plan was, they were going to make a little film. A little snuff movie. All they needed was a sword, and of course the star. And the star of the film was to be the man's doped dog. It was easy.

Leanne was feeling dejected. She and her sister had been kicking and quarrelling since they'd first appeared. They'd argue over a blade of grass. It was natural. It was what they did. They were brought up by their oldest aunt and never met their real mam. For years, an innocent little duo would often repeat the same tiresome question to an annoyed aunt.

– Where's mam?

And the question was greeted with the same answer, always.

– She's run away with a black man.

The young girls always guessed this was just a saying, but they were never sure. They loved aunt Aggie. But secretly, they knew she was only second best. The sisters figured their real mam was the better looking one, the one who lived up in a nicer home, somewhere. The truth was that their mam, Elsie, had run away with a black man. Devon Raymonde Jr was a handsome man she'd met when she was working at a pub in the next valley over. The young couple had bungled their first bank robbery in Birmingham by killing a security guard and two customers. They ran away to escape the police manhunt and left the country.

They managed to get as far as the state of Utah and were peacefully travelling down an empty Highway on their way to California when a buck-toothed state trooper, Wayne Spurlitz, caught sight of them and made his famous claim of mistaken identity.

Wayne Spurlitz was a nineteen-year-old officer who would spend every morning studying police photos and fax details that held information about state criminals on the run. One day, he believed, he'd get lucky. He left his breakfast uneaten on the morning he spotted Devon Raymonde Jr and Elsie Evans drive past Big Burt's roadside diner.

Jessica Sharpe and Leroy Love claimed they were leaders

of an anti-capitalist, military organisation. It was the reason they had murdered thirteen corporate people in the finance district of Dallas, Texas. And when Wayne saw the couple go past the Diner in a light blue Sedan he had almost shat himself with excitement.

Ed Evans was the Senior Officer in charge of the trainee kid. The old dog had been chatting to his buddies at the counter top and only turned around when he heard the skidding wheels of his car in the parking lot. He was surprised to notice the table where the two of them had sat was now empty, and an awkward sense of fear and guilt spread quickly through his body as soon as the waitress pointed him in the direction where the young officer had taken his patrol car.

In court, Ed dutifully claimed that Wayne had shot the couple purely in self-defence when they didn't heed his warning. And Officer Spurlitz was hailed as a hero in his hometown of Kanarraville. He received police military honours which promoted him to the rank of Deputy Marshall, and Ed never spoke to him again. The correctly identified bodies were sent back to South Wales. Nobody knew where Jessica Sharpe and Leroy Love had gone.

Aunt Aggie didn't tell her nieces all the facts about their mother, and made sure nobody surrounding the small family ever mentioned the truth. She was a strong woman who held strictly to her own individual beliefs. The girl's problem was that Aunt Aggie had never really moved beyond 1976. She disliked modern day trivialities such as the mobile phone or the internet and the idea of Sky TV being beamed digitally into her home was meaningless to her. She had a large VHS recorder, bought in the early eighties, and hundreds of big, dusty video cassettes containing her favourite shows.

Leanne looked out of the car window and pulled her arms tighter to her chest, hugging tight to her bitter memories.

They had travelled past the Cwmgarw hospital, and Leanne sighed. Donna was driving at a faster pace now, in an attempt to get the heater working. Leanne was remembering how each week they would watch an episode of a cop show, *Cagney and Lacey*. The sisters would play *Cagney and Lacey* out the back. You had the cool cop. The blonde one. And then there was her partner, Lacey. Leanne always had to be Lacey. She wanted to be the cool one. But no. No. Her sister was always Cagney. Cagney was blonde. Donna is blonde. They were match-fit lookalikes. So she claimed.

Leanne was always Lacey. The fat dumb one. Leanne used to hope Lacey would dye her hair, or lose some weight, or get shot. But no. Her sister played the tough blonde cop, Leanne played the other one. Cagney and Lacey went on for six years and Aunt Aggie had recorded every single episode. For six years in Llanbradach Street, every Tuesday night, the young girls would sit in their living room in front of the TV and watch. Afterwards they would act it out. Leanne knew it was what they were doing right now. Being Cagney and Lacey.

Donna turned the heater up and put the radio on. The local station was playing 'Islands in the Stream' by Dolly Parton. It was a special celebration in anniversary of Dolly Parton's pleasure park, Dollywood, and the radio presenter was offering any listener a pair of tickets to a Country and Western theme night over in Brownsville, if they could answer who Dolly was singing along with. Leanne shut her eyes.

– Tha's easy, she said.

– Tha's the bearded bloke Aunt Aggie used to like, said Donna.

– Kenny Rogers.

– Yep, that's him.

– I'd love to go to Dollywood.

– Yeah? said Donna.

42

– Yeah. Reckon it'd be a right laugh.
– Naw, it'd be shite, said Donna.
– Yeah?
– Yeah.

Lost

Boyd drove away from the oncoming flashing blue lights. He was in shock and his thoughts were spinning faster than the wheels of his car. He had to scratch at his forehead when he heard the double-act sound of Kenny Rogers and Dolly Parton leap onto his radio. He lit a cigarette. Hell, he knew he should turn the radio off. Pinkie would've snapped at the radio by now. Boyd agreed and followed his missing dog's advice. He turned it off.

He smiled, and stroked the empty passenger seat. Had his dog dumped him? He coughed and shook his head. Pinkie was only a year and a half now, and still had the learning to do. Boyd knew they were a dog to be taught. He had driven away from the petrol station and scanned each of the empty fields besides the road, the noise from the emergency sirens diminishing behind him. He wanted to pull over but knew he had to return home.

Boyd was in a daze. He was a man who had always loved dogs. And Pinkie was his special one. The first time he was introduced to the Newfoundland breed Boyd knew he'd have to own one. He would be honoured to own one, despite the cost. He knew that in the present day only a select few shared the secret of the Newfie. He was one of them. And he knew the problems ownership could create. Boyd was not a rich man. He was an undernourished thirty-eight-year-old, who'd never stepped much outside the valley. Acne scars covered his closely shaved taut cheeks which would turn pink in the cold weather, and drooping skin under his deep black eyes always gave his clean-shaven face an untidy, hang-dog expression. He had known, if he dared buy a Newfie, he would be a man in debt for most of his small life. It was the reason he had left his council job and become the criminal he now was.

The dog had sheer passion and strangely small teeth, a purpose-built dog, one whose nature was to adore its master. And Boyd Evans was pleased to be part of the long list of honoured men who had once adored a Newfie. He understood he was part of that select elite which had been seized by the spirit of the dog. The Dogman had given him gazillions of names, well into the nineteenth century and beyond who he claimed were linked to the Newfoundland: Schopenhauer, the Grimm Brothers, William Tweed, Tokugawa Yoshinobu, even Lewis Carroll had such a curiosity. Shite, the dog was a wonder and Boyd felt a noble man. It was part of his life.

Lewis and Clarke loved a Newfie. They had named him Seaman. They shared him the seven thousand miles all the way across North America to the Oregon Country. Boyd knew that his own hero, the great Civil War champion, George Armstrong Custer, had captured one in the state of South Dakota, back in 1862. Called him The Bull. He never figured out why, assumed it was probably something to do with the size of the dog. Boyd learnt the breed was also popular in Europe. Bismarck secretly purchased his first one in Paris. And tragedy had struck Lord Byron's Newfoundland dog, Botswain, when it died of Hepatitis B.

The popularity of the breed grew well into the twentieth century. Boyd learnt that in the nineteen-fifties both in America and Great Britain the Newfoundland had become the classic suburban dog. Mass produced. It was the large dog you always saw sitting outside the calm pebble-dash bungalow in Sheffield, or a lime green caravan somewhere up on the coast near Aberystwyth. Unfortunately it was because of all this that the dog went out of fashion. The Newfie had somehow become the user-friendly, plastic dog. Americanised, like the encroaching phenomena of supermarket chains that could sell you a Chicken Kiev TV Dinner for two, or pre-cut vegetables, and frozen peas.

It became the latest fashion treat. It was cheap. It was too well-known. And, as fashion changed, it almost disappeared in the early seventies. Boyd shut his eyes. He licked his lips and shook his head. Those flids had almost destroyed the true value of the Newfie. If it wasn't for the remaining, tenacious supporters of the breed, those that worked in remote kennels in deepest Sweden during the late seventies; if it wasn't for the honourable members of the secret Newfoundland societies; if it wasn't for the desire for the dog which was still held in the hearts of men in privately owned council houses throughout Essex during the mid-eighties; then Boyd knew he would never have had the opportunity to own the big dog. The passion for the Newfie was kept under wraps. Hidden. They had become an exclusive, secret brand once again.

– Expensive, the Dogman had told him when he had introduced him to Pinkie. And now Pinkie was gone.

Boyd came onto his street and parked in front of his house. The car felt empty. He rubbed at his face and turned the engine off. He pretended the flutter he sensed in his hand was due to the cold air. He sat there, lit a cigarette and allowed his eyes to focus on a yellow spot miles away. It was the council snow-gritter somewhere in the distance, travelling down the mountain road. Boyd was trying to turn his thoughts away from what had happened at the petrol station. He'd become confused. He angrily flicked his cigarette out of the window. It wasn't working. Why should he care about their gritter? What had happened to Pinkie? It was all he could think about.

Mountain Men

A crow came down from a gap in the trees to land on the decaying corpse of a rat. In a microsecond Morgan had reacted. He missed. The pellet had disappeared into a slab of melting mud five feet from the pecking crow. It didn't have the distance. The bird looked up from the corpse and jeered at Morgan in a way only a bird could laugh at a boy. A hunter. It tore at the remains of the rat and then shot upwards through the falling rain. Morgan Evans stood there staring. He was thinking about the Dogman. For the last few days he'd noticed that whenever he missed his target, he was thinking about the Dogman.

Wearing pyjamas and his damp blue Parka, Morgan crept through the sparse black trees on the cold Cwmgarw mountaintop. In his right hand he carried the Shooter. The new K9 Scorpion Shooter. Detachable telescopic lens. Zoom-scape focus-pull. Total sporting style. It was the air-rifle Dogman gave him for his eleventh birthday and it was perfect. Or, almost perfect. Morgan wanted the *BANG*. The explosion. He wanted to frighten, to terrify, all the tiny animals. The Shooter didn't have the same strong noise as the Dogman's Longthorne shotgun. Instead, all he got was the *Pop*.

Morgan had the rifle pointed at the Cwmgarw hospital. It was out of his range. He heard a buzzing noise trickle up the mountain from the estate below. He spotted an electric milk van and instinctively raised the Shooter. He stared at rocking bottles through the cross-hair. They became so large he felt he could touch them. Mega-magnification. He hadn't killed anything all morning and was dying to watch the bottles shatter. But he couldn't. The hunter wasn't up the mountain to shoot at milk bottles. He crouched. He watched the rain travel downwards through the rotting leaves at his feet. He waited. He spat on his fingers and worked it through the rip in his pyjamas to rub at a bramble-scratch on his thigh. Morgan knew he had the patience. The true mountain man.

He'd been getting up early now for five days in a row, searching the Cwmgarw mountainside for his kill. He'd not been to school since his party and had managed to shoot his way through one hundred and three Red-Beck pellets. He'd taken charge of the straggly woods that sat alongside the Dogman's farm, and assured himself that he was now enough of a man to take on any beast lurking in them. Any target. He shot with a purpose, and a style. He waded into the wet. Strutted through the mud. He hunted. He collected. And he killed. It was the purpose of the small hunter. It was what the Dogman had taught him. It was cats mainly. He could kill a bird, but a cat was the easier target. There seemed to be so many of them drifting up from the Texas-2 estate. The Dogman wasn't interested in his success, in his growing collection. The Dogman had ignored him all week. Since the birthday party, the only thing Dogman was interested in was drinking. Morgan heard a rustle. A twig cracked behind him. He raised the Shooter and spun around, yanking his little finger firmly down on the trigger. *Pop*.

*

When Morgan first met Dogman-Dean Evans, he could see there was a quality in the man he thought he'd never get in a dad. A dad who could hand over a K9 Scorpion Shooter as a

48

birthday present? Now, that was quality. And for three months, the three of them had been living together on the Dogman's smallholding. For Morgan, it was paradise. His mam was fussier. Morgan's mam, Dolly, had a regular tendency to change his dad. His mam had had seven and a half so far. It used to bug him but he learnt he had to make do. To choose from the best on offer. It was what his mam did. It was why he'd been feeling funny all week. Dogman seemed a good one. A decent dad. He could see that Dogman wasn't as handsome as some of the others: his small ears didn't match the size of his shaved head, his staring pebble blue eyes never seemed to flicker. But once you got to know him, you'd know there was always a hint of cleverness, at least in some of his thoughts.

Morgan remembered the day they arrived at the farm. His mam was lucky to have met the Dogman. It had been early one morning and they were the only two people left in the bar. Dogman and his mam were drunk, with Morgan asleep under the snooker table. His mam had claimed Dogman could do with a little family. He agreed, he could use a wife. And with their bags packed, Dogman took them up to his place. His mam didn't like it from day one.

– Now, I know wha' you're thinking, said Dogman. It is out of the way a bit.

– A bit? said his mam.

– Well, I did say it was…

– Uhh, no, Deano love. You told us tha' you had a glorious fucking house in the country. Not this shithole above Texas-2. I ain't come to live in the jungle. My name ain't Jane, love.

– It's peaceful, up here.

– No.

– Aaaah, come on mam. It don't look too bad, does it? said Morgan.

– Thank you, boy, said Dogman.

– No.

His mam was a townie. She didn't like the farm flies. She hadn't liked the mud. And she hated the non-stop barking noises. She'd made a drunken blunder with Dogman. Morgan had been embarrassed by his mam's behaviour. She had sat in the Dogman's parked car for an hour with a bottle of vodka and worked through every number she could find on her mobile to get them a different place to stay. She failed and Morgan was shown around the farm. The place was special. The Dogman farmed dogs. He made them. And he flogged them. It was a canine wonderland.

On the farm he had dogs in all shapes and sizes. Brown dogs, white dogs, dogs with stumpy legs, dogs with pointy ears. Small dogs, large dogs, guard dogs, pampered dogs. A digger, a racer, a hairless dog, a dog with a thick coat, a dog with a large dick, a lap-dog, a long dog, a fat dog, and a mad dog. A dog for the grieving widow, a dog for the playful child. Poodle-types in different colours and any size or form you wanted. Doe-eyed beings that would thrill Disney.

You could order by post or on the net. People came to pick and choose the puppy they wanted. Families from as far as England. Dogman Evans had a good reputation. He could make the dog. And he made the money. Morgan was wonder-struck. The Dogman sold the man-made-dog.

He kept the dogs round the back of the farm in steel cages, packed in tight. Side by side. These were the pretty dogs on display. Dogman called them the Plastic Dogs. The place was bursting with the whimpering beasts. Morgan saw animals he couldn't name. Dogs with perfectly shaped ears that belonged to Mickey Mouse. Dogs with long snouts and pink tongues, too large for their mouths. Dogs with bodies the size of a kitten and heads stolen from a Rottweiler. Dogs designed for a Surrey housewife or a resident guest at the Ritz, all cramped into their dirty cages and taken out for the eyes of the drooling, potential buyer.

Morgan learnt the Dogman sold other things as well. He had asked Dogman what type of dogs were kept behind the padlocked door, and was shown inside the concrete bunker. It was a square room brimming with weapons. Swords mainly. On each of the four walls were seven metal shelves, on which he stored long boxes containing swords. A Don Quixote, a Crusader, the Highlander blade, the Braveheart, Gladiatorus, the Conan, Paul Chen Ninja grooves, the Sword of Isildur, and tons of stuff from the Lord of the Rings. South Wales people liked their sword. It was a fact. And what you did with the sword, like what you did to the dog, was none of the Dogman's business. He simply sold them.

For the first couple of months Morgan was floating on a cloud. He read with fascination the weaponry booklets Dogman gave him, and he helped out in farmyard duties. His mam was stuck and Morgan was bubbling. He worked alongside the Dogman, feeding and washing the dogs. Helping to find right ones for mixing. Taking care of the phone calls and sorting through the mail. His mam found casual bar work in Pentrecoch and was rarely on the farm. Morgan quickly became best friends with the Dogman. The Dogman was a real dad.

Morgan was about to become eleven and when he woke on the day of his birthday he thought it was going to be the best party ever. The Dogman had the living room full of colourful balloons and his mam had made a hand-painted sign, which they'd hung over the door: *Happy Birthday Morgan!!!*

When she winked at him and told him that he had a great surprise coming, Morgan got excited. He guessed they'd hired the Pentrecoch Panda to come up and do his tricks. But when the Dogman walked in with the Scorpion Shooter in his hands, Morgan was jumping up and down. He'd never owned an air-rifle before, and as soon as the Dogman gave it to him Morgan couldn't put it away. All day he snooped around the farm with the rifle glued to his small hands. Chairs; trees; tables; rocks; fruit; cans. He was shooting at everything he could find. The Dogman had to tell him he should only do his killing up on the mountain.

– I seen you now, boy, skipping round with tha' Scorpion Shooter stuck in your hand. Shooting at anything and everything today. Naw, mun. It's wrong, Morgan. Just showing off, innit? See, a mountain boy's gotta learn his Shooter is special, like. Gotta be using his pellets with real purpose. Every time. It's the challenge. No playing round, like. Naw, mun. Every pellet used, is used to kill. Pellets shot with a purpose. A true hunter.

Morgan had gone mute.

– Cun I do dogs?

– We do not kill the farmed dog, son. We makes 'em, and we sells 'em for profit.

– Sorry.

– S'alright, should've explained, shouldn't I? I should of said. See, once the first pellet jolts from the barrel of the gun the challenge is set. The mountain boy shoots with a reason. You becomes the hunter. You don't go round shooting the beer cans or stinking bin-bags. You shoots with a purpose. You shoot to kill.

It kind of spoiled the party when some bloke from the Cynon Valley turned up in his Vauxhall Astra. His mam started waving her arms about in merriment and kissed the man. This was her great surprise. Her present. Morgan and the Dogman found out when it was announced, this sleek runt was to be his new dad, Martin. His mam proclaimed a big, *Ta-Ra-Ta-is-No-More*. Martin had come by to collect Morgan and her.

Morgan tried to tell her she was making a mistake to leave the Dogman for Martin. His mam was a pig-headed person, and she often refused to accept the advice of a boy. She took her pleading son to one side and informed him of the reasons why they had to leave. She claimed it was personal. She whispered in his ear:

– What you don't know about the Dogman, Morgan, is tha' he's a real violent person, love. He don't like the way I spends the night in town with all the girls, does he? He don't like the idea that he has to spend every night here, at the farm, looking after you, does he? An when I come back up, the next day? When you're in school, love? Tha's when he does his wobbly, innit?

Morgan pulled his head back from her whispering gob, and left her bad breath hang beside him. He looked at his two dads. They'd been fighting. Dogman and Martin had been going steady at each other in the living room for five minutes, and Martin looked like the winner. Morgan wiped a tear from his red face. The drunken Dogman was sitting on his chair, drinking from a can of Red Stripe and trying to stem his nosebleed, whilst Martin, standing next to him, danced gaily with two red balloons. Laughing.

His mam started to shove bags full of their stuff into the back of Martin's car and Morgan sat in the kitchen with the Dogman. Dogman had managed to stop his nosebleed and wiped at the bottom of his face with a ragged tea towel. He brought his coarse hands up and winced in pain as he touched the tip of his broken nose. Morgan stood and went to the window, from where he saw his new dad and his mam out by the car. They were kissing. Heavily, and noisily. Morgan turned. The Dogman was behind him. He looked down at Morgan who was crying.

– A lot of people fail, boy.

– I'm sorry, said Morgan.

– I just thought your mam was a different one.

Morgan and the Dogman watched his mam and Martin. The Dogman put his hand on Morgan's head and tenderly stroked at his hair. He couldn't bear it. He whirled around, took his Longthorne double barrel shotgun from the mantelpiece, and strode out.

Dogman walked up to Morgan's mam, rammed the Longthorne shotgun into the back of her neck and pulled the trigger. *BANG*. His mam fell to her knees with her head torn in two, the blood covering Dogman's clothes. Martin fell to the ground and was screaming in fright. Morgan ran outside and watched Dogman turn Martin over with his boot, and poke the Longthorne into his eye. Morgan felt a bit funny.

*

On the Blackmill mountaintop, Morgan had made his way over the bridge to Dead Man's pond. The stones were covered in a frosty, light slime. Glistening. Green. It was where they'd put mam. They'd put his new dad, Martin, in with the dogs.

Morgan cracked the Shooter open, and touched the dark blue steel with his hand. He slipped in another pellet. He only had three pellets left. He shut the Shooter and put the safety on. Firm. He'd been feeling funny again. He'd been having strange thoughts about the true quality of the Dogman. It was a nice present but Morgan had stopped his smiling, and it wasn't the cold. The man hadn't needed to kill his Mam.

The tight silence was fractured by a flock of frightened blackbirds as they spluttered hard through the branches, cracking and whipping up with a force into the air. The hunter watched them squawk. He moved toward the point from which they came. Thirteen yards away he watched a fat ginger cat devour a small blackbird. The bird struggled and flapped its fragile wings in an attempt to try and get out of the cat's grip. In reaction to the waggling bird the cat shook its head from left to right and stood firm, waiting for its prey to give in. Morgan shivered in the cold, as he pointed his weapon at the cat. *Pop.*

He came out of the thicket and onto the brow of the hill, carrying the dead cat by its tail. Morgan looked back down the slope, across the dual carriageway, and up the Cwmgarw mountainside towards the farm. With one Red-beck pellet waiting in the air-rifle and one in his mouth, he was minutes away from finishing the challenge. He walked over to an abandoned fridge that lay on its side. He opened the door and peeked inside at his week's treasure of dead animals. He held the cat up. Face to face. Played with its hanging jaw. Felt the sharpness of its teeth. Grinned. He admired his rotting collection.

A sparkle of movement caught his eye. He was listening to a smooth rustling coming from the edge of the wood. He swung the cat over his shoulder, lifted the Shooter and waited. From behind the burnt out Nissan Warrior moved a massive black creature. The biggest cat Morgan had ever seen. A puma, a panther, a leopard maybe?

Morgan held the Shooter on the big cat. He looked down the thin, steel barrel tip, and up at the sleek blue sheen of the panther. From this distance, he knew if he fired the Shooter, it would only make the beast angry. The panther snarled at Morgan.

Morgan ran. He ran at pace. He ran across the footbridge going over the road and threw the dead ginger cat onto a stream of oncoming cars. He wondered whether he had failed the challenge. Naw. He had two pellets left. And he knew where he would put them. With a real purpose. He wouldn't miss.

Police Questions

One of the ceiling lights in the police station's toilet was faulty and Sergeant Barry Evans had been standing at the steel urinal having to put up with the flickering fluorescent beam. He brought his head down from looking up at the loose plastic tiles. He couldn't understand where all his piss was coming from that day. He was sure he hadn't had too much to drink last night. Maybe it was an infection of some kind. He lit another fag and yawned. The telephone number for Stars Dating Agency was scratched onto the white wall in front of him. And he didn't want to have to cancel his appointment. He had to get on.

Barry shook his cock dry, zipped and stepped away from the urinal. In the broken flicker he caught a sight of himself in the mirror. He threw the fag down and flattened some of his thin hair. Tightened his tie and rubbed at his bleary eyes. He stepped out of the toilet, into the corridor, and walked back to his desk. The place felt busy.

Most of the small police force were in a state of excited panic. It was a muddle. There were piles of standard forms scattered across every surface. Bits of kit resting on desktops, handcuffs, tagged evidence bags, utility belts. Rattling radios were whining and babbling away, the phone was constantly ringing and there was a general murmur amongst the officers sitting at their chipped formica desks. The heavy boots of uniformed men and women stepped through the room, wearing the thin blue carpet down into white streaks, and Barry watched the activity with a look of weary loathing on his face. He did not want to be amongst this lot, not this night.

The Chief Inspector appeared at his desk just as Barry spilt coffee over some of his own paperwork. He ignored the ringing desk phone and managed to soak up the tepid coffee with a tissue the Chief handed him.

– Did you speak to the media up at the petrol station? he asked.

– No, said Barry.

– Good. Don't. I've called a news conference for five forty p.m. We'll be keeping it simple. A positive line of inquiry.

– How's the girl doing?

– Fine, fine. Young fighter. Cwm hospital sorting it out. Lucky it wasn't your older brother, Nelson, doing one of his nights, eh? He laughed. Do we know whether the forensics people have finished up there yet?

– Naw, they were delayed getting there. Some git managed to steal the town council's new snow-gritter and got it jack-knifed in the tunnel, said Barry.

– Hah, Jesus. You know, I was saying the other day, the amount of traffic they have coming through now, there's no way it should still only be the two lanes. For ages the council been using the same excuses…

– Yeah. No-one can find the council man, what's his face? Gunter? He'll be manic when he hears some drunk nicked and burnt his new toy.

– True, true. So, what about the American couple? Anything decent?

– I don't think so. I should be done soon.

– Okay. Good. We've got to move on this. Let's not keep them too long. Are we still keeping the Hardy incident separate here?

– Yes. Definitely. Chances are this robbery is completely separate. This one's part of our recent string.

– Fine. You're not in tomorrow, right?

– Tomorrow afternoon. Got the official go-ahead to sort though that stuff with my son.

– Ok. You pick him up? Make sure to say hello to Jean from me.

The Inspector smirked and walked away in a sashaying manner to get a few laughs and upset Barry. He wouldn't be mentioning that flirty dirt bag's name to his ex. Barry tried to wipe at the coffee stain on his trouser leg. He gave up. The phone on his desk continued to ring. Probably nothing. He grabbed the stale white-bread sandwich from his desktop and ate. Ham and mustard. He was thinking of his date. She was meant to be good.

*

It was the first time Betty'd ever been inside a police station. The metallic room felt smaller than their hire car. Two plastic chairs facing each other. Her back ached. She couldn't cross her fat legs. She waited for Barry Evans to speak. He was reading hand-written notes. She watched him absent-mindedly flick at his stained tie and pat down his cotton shirt, trying to hide the filthy sweat circles under his arms. It wasn't as she'd imagined it, the police station. No. Ed had been with the Utah State Police Force all his working life and he'd never wanted her to be any part of it. No. Not his work. He didn't think it proper to mix his family with his work. They'd never had any real family. Sure, they'd tried. No. Family? It was the goddamned reason why they were in this small country.

– Mrs Evans…

– I've never…

– What?

– Uhh…

– Mrs Evans, if you have something more to say about the…

– Well… no, no, not really, sir, I was just going to say that, hah, I've never been in a police station before.

– Right…

– So this is it. First time, in a station…

– Okay, okay, so let's start at the beginning here, Mrs Evans. When exactly did you and your husband leave the United States?

– Uhh, Thursday, Officer. Yesterday…

Barry sat there and studied the large woman in front of him. Mrs Betty Evans, almost a classic example of the modern day shape. She was in her mid-sixties, with greying blonde hair of a feathery consistency. Her thighs and hips bulged over the edge of a tiny but firm plastic chair. She had massive breasts. He'd been trying not to look at them by pretending to study his notepad. He was worried he'd have to cancel his date and the bastards would charge him anyway. He'd used the agency before and had been thinking about Princess Lovelace. Barry let his eyes casually wander back to Mrs Betty Evans's ample chest. He imagined they'd had a few looks in their time.

– And you're on holiday?

– …we're not here on vacation, Officer. It's more of a business trip really. You see, when my husband retired he seemed to take a change for the worse. Ed went into himself. Wasn't how I imagined it to go. I thought it'd be a good thing? I was looking forward to it. Thought it'd bring us closer together? Hah, guess it hasn't really work out that way, yet. See, he'd been getting upset about some things. Just sitting at home, missing his buddies, missing the work, missing the investigation maybe. So, I had this wacky idea? I had the great notion, it'd be like an investigation, Ed'd be happy. And it'd be like a holiday, so I'd be happy. And we'd be together, so it'd be good for the both of us. It'd bring us back together again. A real kind of family bonding business. Over here, in Wales. Right?

– Right.

– Of course, Ed wasn't too keen on it from the beginning. But if the Osmond family could do it, why couldn't we? It was easily done. I managed to track down some of his parentage to a Nathan Evans who left the Welsh country in the mid-nineteenth century and moved over to America. Utah. Became part of the Church of Jesus Christ of the Latter-Day Saints.

– The what?

– Mormons, sir. We're Mormons.

Barry's eyes shot up. He hadn't realised they were Mormons.

– Right. So have you been in touch with them yet?

– Who?

– The relatives?

– No, of course not. We only just arrived, and then this happened up at the little petrol station. And, well, you see, I've been emailing the kind gentleman over in Texas-2 for the past few months now, but this was going to be a surprise visit. The family don't even know we're coming.

– Right. Why were you up at the petrol station?

– My husband got lost. We stayed on the road and went on through to the top of the valley without taking the turn into Cwmgarw and on towards Texas-2. He figured he'd find us a motel, somewhere.

– No. Pentrecoch. You'll find somewhere back down the valley. Pentrecoch.

– Huh?

Barry sat there with a blank face. He had to get out of the room. He squeezed at the biro he was holding. This was taking too long. Which idiot had even put these people in two separate rooms? He wondered why he'd even started with her. He closed his eyes. He slid his large hand up and over the back of his oily head. He should open his eyes. He knew he should open his eyes. He was nervous and he was sure this Mormon lady was still there.

When Barry left the room Mrs Evans got upset. She couldn't stop crying and Barry had to send in Sheila to try and calm her. Sheila was a uniformed officer who acted as a specially trained witness chaperone. She made tea. But Mrs Evans was upset. She didn't see why she was being kept at the police station. She wanted to see her husband.

Barry was looking at her husband. They were sitting in the room next door, trying to pretend they couldn't hear the muffled weeping of Mrs Evans. It wasn't easy. Every fifteen seconds the interview was punctured by a dramatic wail. Ed Evans leant across the desk, the thick veins almost bursting out of his rifted forehead.

– Disgraceful, he said.

The man was being a pain in the arse. Barry agreed.

– Okay, Mr Evans? You know I've been busy all day and I apologise for keeping you and your wife in separate...

– You're telling me the CCTV at that place was not even in operation?

– Yes, that's correct, sir.

– Disgraceful, he said.

– Yes.

– And you are telling me that you've not yet caught the gunman?

– That is correct, sir, yes.

Ed Evans leant back and shook his head. Barry had to speed this up.

– Okay, Mr Evans, let's go over just what happened at the petrol station, okay?

– Have you got a card, son? he said.

– A what?

– A card? A number?

– Uh, what for?

– In case I need to call you. Hell, in case I remember something else, after we're done in here. In case I see the dope wandering around on the streets and you country boys haven't yet picked him up yet. A card, Detective Evans, identification?

– Uh, yes of course, said Barry.

Barry tore off a scrap of paper from his notebook, wrote down the number for The Stars Dating Agency on it and handed it over to the red-faced American.

– Thank you.

Ed Evans folded the scrap of paper and placed it carefully in his jacket pocket.

– Barking, said Ed.

– Barking?

– I hope you're recording me, Detective Evans, because I'll say it just once more. Barking. Outside the gas station. Barking.

– Before the man entered the station?

– I heard the sound of a barking dog whilst the man was inside the store. The man was screaming like a woman. Clear he couldn't handle the homemade gun he was holding. Almost shot us by accident. Told us to get down on the floor. Then shot the poor kid by accident. Crapped himself and zoomed off, north. At a speed. Pathetic figure. Probably homosexual.

Barry had to speed this up. He did not want to miss his date. The American couple had been at the station for five hours. They weren't telling him anything new anymore. He should give them a break. Barry knew they weren't going to disappear.

Ed Evans tilted his head towards the fake, beech screen wall. He pointed and shouted above the crying wail of his wife.

– You know why? Why she brought me here?

– Uhh, yes. Your name.

– I DON'T GIVE A DAMN WHERE I GOT MY SURNAME, SON. I know where I came from. And it surely wasn't from around here. First frigging day in this Appalachian-like place and here I am. Held all day, in the weakest police box ever. Witness to a useless armed robbery, and questioned by a man who should actually be out there, looking for the psycho. FOOTWORK! Footwork is what we called it.

– Really?

– Yeah, really, said Ed.

The men looked at each other. Barry had to go. Ed seemed furious.

– You married, Detective Evans? asked Ed.

– Uhh, no, divorced. Look, it's getting late, I think we should leave it for today…

– You're lucky, son, because this one? My wife? She's been acting kind of weird recently. Gotten the idea that it'd be fun to have a vacation over here. Try and track down my past relatives. She's been emailing some fruitcake in this country, and I'm meant to meet up with him? All smiles? Say hello? I'm your long-lost great-uncle or something? I mean, shite, I've lived with that woman for a long time now, but how she talked me into this I'll never know.

– Oh.

– Yeah, *oh*. And that, Detective Evans, *that* is what a wife tends to do. WIVES. They sneak up on you, fast. They'll be talking about one thing? Always with another backed up in their twisted heads, ready to plant on you. Wives. Yes. Take you by surprise every dang time. You go out with the boys, perhaps? Go fishing for a week? Or a little hunting? And the wife? Flip, they'll make more of a thing out of it, kick it into such a fuss, you actually begin to feel goddamned guilty about it all. You begin to feel guilty about nothing. And they're doing it for a reason. They're doing it to make you feel you need to give them something back in return, so in the end you think you're sure doing some good. You give them the time? You buy them the pretty dress? You take them down the mall, to the expensive Italian Pizza house that their friends have just ate at? But you're just in the middle of their sneaky plan. They got it all figured from the first step. You see what I'm trying to tell you here, son?

– Right. But Evans is a Welsh name, isn't it?

– I DON'T GIVE A GOD DAMN WHERE I GOT MY NAME FROM!

Time to Return

– Tegretol? asked Doctor Crane.

  – Yep, said Hank.

  – Lamotrigine?

  – Yep.

  – Frisium?

  – Yep.

  – Topamax…

  – Uhh, yeah?

  – What about Diamox?

  – Yep. Rashes.

  – Okay… okay… let's try you on some Phenytoin. Yes. Let's see if this does anything for you. It's quite a strong neurological medication, Hank, so we'll begin at a low dosage for the first few weeks, whilst we try and ease you off the Pregabalin. We'll try and bring it up to 400mg by next spring. The tests we did here will take a few weeks to come through. However, simply looking at the MRI Scan we did, there doesn't seem to be any indication, any actual neurological stress to the brain that helps us here. Nothing much from the EEG video monitor, despite of course giving us the three seizures we needed. We're just going to have to keep on trying the drugs, Hank. Getting the right combination going. Juggling the routines.

  Hank observed the man. The doctor at the desk in front of him was one of those who reassured you they were in charge of the case, that they could handle the difficulties. He was also one of those who told you things without ever looking at your face. Always your feet. He was either obsessed with footwear, or the man was simply a bad liar.

Hank's body couldn't stop aching. He still had the EEG Unit attached to his head. And he hadn't been allowed to wash since he'd come in. He'd managed to damage his ankle in the fit that morning and the hospital wanted to keep him in for another week. Hank was determined to get out. He had many things to do tomorrow.

Hank worked secretly as the Pentrecoch Panda and he had an 'effing booking after the match in the Texas-2 community centre. Hank had been the Pentrecoch Panda for a couple of years now and it was work he disliked more than his insecure part-time slog at the petrol station. He was employed as a rugby mascot to entertain the home crowd. For eighty minutes he would have to walk around the rundown rugby stadium, waving and cheering at fans on the terrace. Doing his kung-fu moves. Dancing. Pretending he couldn't hear the laughter or drunken abuse often hurled at him from a forlorn home crowd.

Whenever play on the pitch became flat the Pentrecoch Panda was supposed to put some jubilation back into people's hearts. Truth of the matter was though, the panda mascot wasn't going to inspire anyone to come along and loudly cheer cock-a-hoop, as their home team got beaten once again on a windswept Wednesday night.

Hank was all too aware that the panda mascot had become a figure of distaste and ridicule, directly associated with the club's long line of failure. It was why he tried to keep his identity hidden. An underground militant group, calling themselves the *Pentrecoch Panda Assassins*, had even established themselves and had recently been sending hate mail through to the Pentre RFC, addressed to '*The Panda*'.

Hank once read a letter made from words cut out from a local newspaper: *'Panda bear, you insult our club. We will remove you'.* He'd shown it to the club's executives. The men had simply laughed.

For a bit more cash Hank and his panda costume would always get hired at a private event. The one after the game tomorrow was already making him wary. The kid was bloody Geronimo Evans. Cheyenne's dinky brother. Since he started seeing Cheyenne he let her in on his little secret and made her swear to almighty god that she kept it quiet. He didn't want his identity revealed to her rugby loving grandmother. Cheyenne had waved away his fears, she knew her Nan wouldn't even be able to make it to Geronimo's party. It would be rude of him to turn down the gig. He'd said yes, and Cheyenne couldn't stop winding him up. According to the stories she'd been telling him before he came into the hospital, Geronimo was a nasty little bugger. Apparently, he'd gone into the local shop only recently with a kitchen knife. Straight up to the till, said to Mr Gul, "I am the valleys villain. Your money or your life". Gul had hit the little shite and told him to piss off. But he had to chase Geronimo around the shop twice, just to get him out of the front door. He was an eight-year-old kid that liked to cause problems. And then there was Masaki to deal with. He would be Hank's other problem.

Hank hadn't been able to get in touch with his so-called producer, Masaki Hamamoto, and wanted to find out what was happening with his script. Masaki was a friend. They'd met at an amateur film club and when both men decided to quit the little group of second rate film-makers they arranged a partnership. Masaki claimed to be a producer and Hank claimed to be a writer. On the day before he went into the hospital Masaki had sent him a one-line email suggesting he had, at last, found the necessary finance money for their proposed joint feature film. Hank didn't trust this unlikely promise, certainly not before he spoke to Masaki in person. Shite, he knew he had to get out of the hospital.

– So I'm still an eppy then? he said.

– Hank, you'll always have epilepsy, said his doctor. It's odd. Some people start life as epileptics, others get it after a trauma to the brain like our regular fellows, Ivan and Carlton here, and then even more unexpectedly some people, hah, like yourself, get epilepsy, well, from nowhere. And unfortunately in these cases we can't actually ascertain the reason for the epilepsy, which occasionally makes it more difficult to control. We don't really understand epilepsy. Now that you have it, you don't get rid of it. No. You're an epileptic till the day you die, Hank.

– So what's the point of me sitting in here all week, having these tests?

– Ha, um, well because you're still having your, ah, seizures, Hank. Uh, on a more than regular basis. You're an educated young man, Hank, there's no reason to pretend otherwise, but you see, we still need to check up on you.

– So I can leave, right?

– Uh, are you working at the moment, Hank?

– No, Hank lied. He had three part-time jobs at the moment, but was desperately trying to claim some disability benefit.

– And you're still living by yourself, now?

– Yep.

– You know our recommendations about epileptics living alone, don't you, Hank? Don't bathe. Shower. Showers are better.

– Why?

– Just in case.

– Right.

– What about your cooking?

– Gas, said Hank.

– No. Shouldn't be cooking, Hank. No. Not on a stove. Microwaves, Hank.

– Right, said Hank.

– Yes. Microwaves, Hank. The microwave brought a future light of hope to the world of the single epileptic…

– So you're telling me I can't even fry an egg?

– Well just in case… as a precaution… um, what about partners?

– Look, can I leave now?

Hank gingerly stood up on the crutches he'd been given.

– Yes, let's get you going on the new medication and see what happens. Take it from there, but uhh, Hank, try not to let it get you down. *Formality*, Hank. *Routines*. As well as the new medication, Hank, you really should be working to a routine. A strict regular pattern should emerge in everything you do. Every day, stick to a routine. Picture everything in a square. *Framed*.

He watched as Doctor Crane framed him between his fingers. But the man wasn't directly looking at him, he was studying his feet.

– Blink, like a camera. Formalism, Hank. Yes, it helps. The routines.

Hank pointed to the EEG wires glued to his head.

– What about these?

*

Hank was only a few stops away from the estate. The bus had travelled up the valley and they were passing through Pentrecoch to Cwmgarw. They had dropped off the healed

69

and picked up the wounded. People were chattering about another robbery. Hank had tuned out. They passed over the bridge and went on.

Texas-2 was a peculiar mix of council houses built in the late fifties, two flat-roofed pubs and stubby blocks of flats all made in the seventies. In the eighties most of the piss-heads on the estate had a horse living in the back garden. It was argued a horse could be cheaper than the bus. The valley had a theme going on back then; it was all started by Cowboy Dan Jones, a local businessman who promoted Wild West Day. He told people to dress up in their best Wild West gear, all bought from his store, and celebrate. The Texas-2 estate sat beneath the bleakness of Cwmgarw mountain and crumbled daily, unattended, unloved and generally forgotten by the council. It was a place people even in the town of Cwmgarw, all of half a mile below, thought primitive. Texas-2 didn't even have a wrecked shopping mall, a bus centre, a Greggs, Peacocks or Woolworths. People in Texas-2 had a shabby police station. A hard pitched rugby ground. A few shops, featuring a chippie, a betting shop, and a cheap supermarket. The swanky people in the town below generally didn't like the Texas-2 estate. And the people in the estate didn't like the people who lived below. Hank had lived on the estate all his life.

After the 97B circular had dropped him off he limped and clattered across the estate and stopped in the middle of the square. The two shops were open. A three-legged dog outside Gogol's chippie sniffed its way through the rubbish. Hank lit a fag. Looked around. The boys were playing a loud game of soccer. Some bloke he didn't know staggered out of the betting shop. He looked at Hank on his metal crutches, raised his finger and shot at him. The man laughed and walked on by. In Hank's brain the noise of the footballers had become mixed with the cold whirring noise constantly looping around his skull. *New medication.* He limped on.

An old couple, Tash and her husband Bell, were sitting on a rotting sofa in the garden outside their house, drinking Super Kestrel. They'd never chucked the old sofa away when they bought the new one. Covered in a weatherworn, removable plastic sheet, Tash thought it'd be perfect for a kind of second living room, and a good place for her customers to wait if the queue was getting long. She was the local hairdresser on the estate, and her salon was in their front room.

Tash pulled at the heavy black coat she was wearing. She shivered. It used to belong to her dad. The fool had died when she was a child after setting himself alight in a failed insurance scam. Bell was wearing his special, insulated baseball cap. Tash had brought it back for him as a birthday present on her last trip to America. Her husband was about six-foot-three and would loom over the tiny Tash whenever the couple stood together. He was a gentle man, and she had always loved his more than generous size. Bell, or Belly as he was commonly known, was a little celebrity, and made some occasional money from any metropolitan media outlets who were delighted to document for shock purposes the sheer volume of the man. But his weight had become an issue. Personally he didn't like to think about a gastric band, and the thought of surgery had always terrified him. He wasn't looking forward to the health check Tash had arranged for him at the hospital tomorrow.

They often sat in the garden, in all weathers, waiting for her customers, watching the neighbours and friends walk past.

– Afternoon Hank, alright 'en? said Tash.

– Yeah. Tidy, like.

Hank scratched at the dried wire-glue, stuck solid in his

71

unwashed hair, and the wailing, warped sound of barking dogs trickled down the mountainside into his head. He looked up. Heavy clouds continued to loom. He reached the double doors of his block of flats and had to stop. The rain had started to fall properly. The rain was generating an enormous volume of unwanted noise inside his head. Hank started to shake again. The mixed sounds of barking dogs, and gallons of dead water falling, crashing, and bouncing up from the broken concrete peaked. It was followed by a deep silence inside his skull. Hank was holding onto the door and looking around. He could smell something. He could taste it coming. His eyes shut and he fell to the ground in an epileptic convulsion.

– Not cured him yet 'en, said Bell.

– Naw, said Tash. Never will.

Swords for Fun

Donna drove her car into Texas-2, a few miles below the Dogman's farm. They'd completed the first part of her plan and now they had to get the sword. The place was quiet. It looked a clutter. Some of the houses were boarded up, some burnt out. Cars parked in front of these houses were either a glistening colour with a big chrome-tipped exhaust or simply patched-up, rusted boxes. They were going to do it. They'd got the dog. And Donna was sure Leanne wasn't bothered by the killing. They both knew it would make the bastard weep. She believed the problem Leanne had with her plan was the idea that they would actually film the killing, to send it on to Boyd.

They had stopped at a junction and gave way to a naked man riding an enormous white cart-horse. The sound of the horse's hooves echoed through the stone cold streets, and was matched by the man, who was making some sub-human sound as he galloped past them at a clattering speed.

– Dogman knowse we're coming, yeah? said Leanne.

– What you on about? That wasn't the Dogman.

– Yeah, I know, I'm just wondering, like. You phoned him, the Dogman, yeah?

– Yeah, tried all week, said Donna.

– He ain't answerin? said Leanne.

– S'what I said.

– So what we doing now? said Leanne.

– We're just gonna visit him, get us a decent sword. And do it. Simple, said Donna.

– If you been trying all week, Donna, and he ain't answering, then he ain't in, is he? He could be in fucking Florida for all you know.

– He ain't in Florida is he? said Donna.

– How does you know?

– He ain't in Florida, said Donna.

– Might be, said Leanne.

– Yeah? Well I fucking hope not, cause I'm dying for a piss.

– Should've gone before we left, said Leanne.

– I did.

The sisters drove along the mountain road and took a turn onto the beaten track which led them through the woods to the farm. The sound of dogs, barking in a frenzy, became louder the nearer they got. Pinkie was covered with Donna's coat on the backseat because they didn't want the Dogman to know they'd already snatched him. They didn't want to take the risk. The Dogman would simply want the dog back. They pulled into a parking area and Donna put her car alongside someone's mud-splattered Astra. They saw the Dogman's Toyota Land Cruiser parked next to the concrete cabin. He wasn't in Florida.

Dogman was inside, asleep, hunched over the kitchen table. A long paper banner was crumpled underneath his hungover face. It was a sign which read: *Happy Birthday Morgan!!!* The floor of the cabin was covered in half-deflated rubber balloons and a bunch of dusty, party popper strings. There was a smell in the room of gently rotting dog food that came from the plastic boxes the Dogman had taken out from the chest freezer.

A prehistoric-sized bluebottle crawled across Dogman's stubbled chin and he pushed it off with his tongue. The fly landed on the dead screen of an old computer and flew out of the cabin door when the sisters walked in. They'd been in school with the Dogman. He was known as Dean then, and was the tall, older boy who always seemed to be playing amongst the younger children. Donna looked at him asleep. His nose was battered and he had two red marks on his forehead which were swollen and bleeding.

Donna quivered when she considered his coarse hands. She stepped towards him and punched his shoulder. The Dogman rose in fright, with the long paper sign stuck to the tip of his blood encrusted nose. His bloodshot eyes tried to take in the friendly shapes of the two sisters. He tried to smile. Donna tugged at the end of the draping birthday banner and pulled it off the tip of his broken nose.

– Aaaaaahhh.

The Dogman flung himself away, smacking his spine up against his chair. Donna held the four-foot paper banner up in the air and waved it in front of his face.

– Where's the toilet, Dean?

He raised his hand and waved it at the front door.

– Out there. On the left.

Donna was about to leave when the door was kicked open, only a foot from her face, and a wild looking boy holding an air-rifle bolted into the room. He ran towards Dogman, raised the air-rifle and pulled the trigger twice. The first pellet crunched into the wall behind Dogman's shoulder. The second pellet hit him in his arm and bounced off his shirt sleeve. Dogman let out a roar of pain and anger, he jumped towards the tiny boy, grabbed the air-rifle and threw it into the corner of the room and pulled the boy outside.

*

Dogman had calmed down and was drinking a beer. Donna partly told him what they were planning on doing, and why

75

they needed a sword to steal the hound. Once they had captured the dog, she would film Leanne pretending to slaughter the animal. Dogman liked the idea. Boyd Evans had been late with his monthly payments for the Newfoundland dog he'd bought from him. He offered the sisters tarpaulin sheeting if they needed. He believed it would give their film a more realistic tone. And after they had made the movie, he wanted his dog and his sword returned. He sat with Donna at the table going over the arms catalogue, *Swords For Fun*. There were numerous pictures of large, tanned, muscular men holding thin swords in aggressive poses. The Dogman claimed he had most of these weapons. But Donna didn't like what he was showing her. She wanted something better.

– Aw c'mon Deano, this is shite. Fucker's enormous.

– Yeah? So you wants something, what? Bit sturdier? said the Dogman. Well yeah, I got sturdier ones Donna. Expensive ones. I'll be doing you a real favour here won't I, for a sturdy one? What says you does me a little favour then in return for something big? Just in case it all gets fucked up.

Leanne had been trying to keep out of the way of it all. She was sipping on the can of warm lager, not really listening. It was her sister's plan. And her sister would be the one doing whatever favours Dean wanted to get a quality sword, not her. Leanne'd made this clear.

The strange little boy had snuck back into the room and was sitting alongside her in the corner. He was squashing beetles and anything else that crawled, with the tip of his empty air-rifle. After the attack, the sisters were wary when they were introduced to the boy. It looked as if he hadn't slept in forty-eight hours. Dogman told them that it had been his birthday only a week ago, and they hadn't yet tidied up the place after the party. The sisters knew Dean had been jailed years ago, for living in a flat with a woman who used to bottle feed her baby whisky. He'd told the police that he'd never really noticed the baby. The idea of an aggressive eleven-year-old child living in the care of the Dogman didn't seem right to the sisters.

Dogman had closed the catalogue. He'd been brought to the conclusion, quite easily by Donna, that she could take the best of his swords if she wished. He needed to brush aside the sordid events of the last few days. And the only way he'd be able to do this was sex. Donna knew this was her only choice. She was doing it for her sister. She knew he'd be easy. The physical act wouldn't last long. It was just the rank idea of allowing him that close to her flesh. She'd make him shower first. At least he had his arm bandaged because she didn't want his blood dripping on her top.

Leanne turned around and saw her sister sitting in thought whilst the Dogman left the room to get another can. Leanne wondered how much of a birthday treat she was really getting here. Destroying the dog as a birthday treat? Allowing Donna to shag the Dogman for a sword? It had to be wrong. Leanne didn't know what it was about.

– Listen, Donna, what if we changed the plan, here and now? What if we was just to keep little Pinkie? she said. Let's just go.

– No. Plan is, we kills his beast. We films it. And Boyd gets himself a movie.

– Boyd ain't gonna be too happy, is he? said Leanne.

– That's the fucking plan, Leanne, said Donna.

– Right, yeah.

– Yeah. We get home. Then we starts the party. And little Pinkie is more than invited. That man will cry. Trust me. So will this tosser.

Leanne turned back round to watch the boy. He was taking a break from killing things. He'd collected dead bits and pieces and shoved them into a pile. Leanne watched him as he fired up the small mass of splattered objects with a bic lighter. It looked like some kind of pagan burning ceremony. There was something creepy about the child. He looked up from the mini-blaze and saw he was being observed.

– Finding it difficult to speak, love, eh?

Dogman had returned to the room and was stroking her sister's hand. They were grinning. Inches apart. Leanne felt jittery. She turned back to Morgan, who'd shuffled up to her seat. He raised the empty air-rifle and pushed it against her forehead.

– I CUN FUCKING SPEAK. I JUST AIN'T SPEAKING TO SHITEHEAD NO-MORE, IS I?

Leanne shifted her eyes to the side to try and see if Donna and the Dogman had noticed what was happening. They weren't in the room anymore. Leanne heard a bedroom door slam somewhere behind her and her sister's false yelp of delight as she was thrown onto a squeaky mattress.

She looked at Morgan standing in front of her. He was wearing a filthy pair of pyjamas, his tiny hands gripping the air rifle, his face overcome with a twisted look of anger and delight at Leanne's predicament. Leanne placed her hand on the blue barrel of the rifle and slowly eased it away from her forehead. It had left a pink round mark on her skin. Morgan allowed her to lower the gun. She took a sip from her can of lager and offered the boy a drink. Morgan took the can of warm lager being offered. His face scrunched as he swallowed the brew.

– Tha's a nice dress, you got on, he said.

– Thanks, it's my work uniform, said Leanne.

– Why you wearing it on your birthday, 'en?

– I'll be changing soon, love.

– Does I look small to you? he said.

– I dunnoe, how old are you, love? said Leanne.

– Eleven.

Leanne looked at him.

– Maybe you should be in school, shouldn't you? said Leanne.

– S'pose, said Morgan.

– So tell us love, why ain't you speaking to Dogman anymore?

– Cause he won't let me torture Martin.

– Martin? Who's Martin?

– Mam's new boyfriend. Supposed to be my new dad, wan he? We got him locked up with the dogs.

– Oh, said Leanne. Where's your mam gone, love?

– He killed her, whispered Morgan. Put mam in Dead Man's Pool.

– Where's that?

– You know Lion's Rock?

– Yeah, I think so.

– It's below Lion's Rock, he whispered. Sunk her down with some metals.

– The Dogman really did this? said Leanne.

– Killed my mam with a real purpose, said Morgan.

– Oh…

– You wanna meet Martin?

Leanne anxiously looked behind her towards the bedroom. She hadn't come here to meet Morgan. And she certainly hadn't come here to meet a man in a cage.

*

Donna didn't want to talk about Dogman and the boy. Leanne had been getting increasingly agitated about what the boy'd said to her. He'd told Leanne it had been difficult for them both after the killing. Morgan claimed he knew the Dogman would be in trouble if he involved the police, so he had decided to try and take charge of the situation himself. Leanne didn't quite understand what he meant. Donna didn't quite understand why Leanne had switched into panic mode about all this. It was clear to her the boy had been taking the piss out of her sister. If a person is accidentally killed, and you've made the effort to hide the body, you don't go telling people about the accident, surely? Donna didn't want to know anymore. They'd come for a sword not a confession. They were not going to take part in some false murder investigation. She travelled on through the estate and kept her head in a straight line, determined not to listen to her sister rabbiting on beside her.

Leanne knew her sister wasn't listening. She'd noticed Donna had turned the car heater up, to try and please her, but she wasn't going to break easily. They couldn't dismiss what might've happened on the Dogman's farm. Someone had been killed. And she was sure the boy had told her about the killing in an attempt for help. It was more or less the first thing that came out of his mouth.

– Dogman killed his girlfriend, Donna, and is going to kill the poor man he's got locked up in a soddin' dog cage! We've gotta tell someone.

– No.

– The boy told me.

– No. We, I, *bought* a sword from the Dogman, that's all. We never killed no-one. All we're doing is killing us a dog, and that's different, said Donna.

– So you're going to ignore it all?

– Yep.

– Is that what Cagney'd do? Is it? Would Cagney ignore a murder case, hmm?

– I ain't Cagney. I'm Donna. It's what Donna'd do.

– It's not what Lacey'd do neither, is it? said Leanne.

– Yeah? Well, you never liked her, anyway, said Donna. I don't wanna play.

– No? Well if you ain't gonna be playing 'en I'm gonna be the cool cop for a change, said Leanne.

– You can't. You only just got the blonde highlights, and they don't count, said Donna.

– Come on Donna. We've gotta call the police, mun.

– No. Don't get involved. Nothing to do with us.

– Yes it is, said Leanne.

– NO.

– PULL OVER. I NEED TO PHONE THE POLICE.

– FINE, USE YOUR MOBILE.

– CAN'T. BATTERY'S GONE. PULL OVER.

Donna slammed her hand down on the steering wheel and smashed her foot hard onto the brake pedal. Pinkie made a grumbling sound. They'd stopped by the precinct, outside the estate's Costcutter shop, and Donna pointed at the smashed-up telephone box across the road. She was nodding her head in fury.

– FINE. PHONE 'EM, LACEY. GO MAKE A FRIGGING COMPLAINT.

– I will. And it ain't a complaint, is it? It's what any normal person'd do, innit?

– You are the *normal person*?

– More normal than you, Donna. You're a whore.

– I'm an escort, Leanne. It's professional work. And it's *you*, Leanne. A *normal person* would never have moved in with that Boyd and his dog.

Leanne had pulled the visor down and was touching her scraggy hair back into place. She moved her head from side to side, and pouted her lips to make sure last night's lipstick was still in place.

81

– Shite, come on. Speed it up. You're only phoning them fuckers, Leanne.

– Piss off, she said.

Leanne lowered her eyelashes and paused for a second to pose with a semi-sexy pout. She slowly winked at herself to try and annoy her sister even more. Donna struggled, watching her sister preen herself. Her fingers automatically touched her own lips. They'd left Dogman's farm in a rush, and whilst she'd managed to wash her face, she hadn't checked on her lips in his scratched bathroom mirror. She was certain her lip-gloss had probably come off.

– GET OUT OF MY CAR.

Leanne flipped the visor back into place and stepped outside the car. She looked up and down the street with her hands stroking the wrinkled pink uniform down over her thighs and back into place. She couldn't see anyone she knew. Her hands left her thighs and she shoved them deep into her skirt pockets as she ran across the road.

Donna had her handbag on her lap and her phone buzzed. She answered the call; it was from the Stars Dating Agency. She watched her frozen sister inside the phone box. She adjusted the rear view mirror and checked her own lips. She'd been right, they were looking dry and she automatically re-applied a light purple lip-gloss. She was brushing her hair down when Leanne came back into the car.

– There's no-one frigging there!

– Did you leave a message?

– Didn't even have the answer-phone on at the police station, did they?

– *The police. Phone the police. Phone 'em. Quick!* Hah, and they ain't even in!

– Shut it.

Lost Love

The Benzodiazepine tablets Boyd had bought from Mrs Sparrow would have taken the teeth out of the Iceman. He should have listened to his neighbour's advice and only taken one. Her GP had changed her prescription, the new type was double in strength. Boyd hadn't listened to her. He had taken three of them. He hadn't been able to move his legs all day.

When Mrs Sparrow saw his condition she'd immediately become a district nurse, and thought it her duty to check in on him. He'd known her all his life and since his mam died she was often poking her face through the back door. She'd been hovering around since early morning when he'd returned, and Boyd had been waiting for seven hours now to come off her bastard tablets. He sat on his brown Oakland two-seater-sofa, gazing at the TV. He wished Mrs Sparrow would piss off.

The ninety-year-old woman had been dancing to the sound of Michael Jackson for a long time. She had gone through a DVD collection Leanne had left behind and selected a suitable disc. Thought it might help Boyd. She managed to get the disk into the machine on a *repeat-play* action, but couldn't work the volume control. When she'd asked Boyd, he didn't seem capable of responding. He had simply gurgled and pointed his finger up towards the goldfish bowl. A loud Michael Jackson Live in Las Vegas sang and she danced all day. Boyd didn't know what to do. The sight of her withered hands clicking as she walked through the living room, the sight of her flapping legs under the flowery dress, her wriggling arse in some slow tempo beat, made him feel worse. He wasn't a fan, and he was sure Leanne'd think it disrespectful. You don't dance to Michael Jackson wearing cheap yellow slippers and a brown cardigan.

He'd been sobbing. Crying and thinking about his dog, Pinkie. Part of him felt he should be running to the police station and reporting the loss of his dog. Part of him felt he should be phoning Michael Jackson. If he'd lost his wife, one of them'd surely help. But he was uneasy about the police. And wondered whether Jackson was dead. He didn't want to risk it. Pinkie was not officially Boyd's partner. He knew those fuckers at the station wouldn't investigate the matter with any urgency. It felt unfair.

His left hand continually stroked at the chocolate coloured cushions where Pinkie would normally sit beside him. He'd decided there could be only two explanations: Pinkie had either managed to climb out of his car up at the petrol station, or someone had taken Pinkie. Stolen him. It was getting dark outside and he figured the strength of the drugs was finally weakening. He'd soon be able to look.

He heard Mrs Sparrow fumble around in his kitchen. She was looking for the sugar. She was always surprised at how clean Boyd's house was. The kitchen was all sharp silver metals, the living room all fluffy whites with a shade of brown. It was neat. Boyd had the heating on in here, and she'd had a good day despite her back aches. A better day than she would usually have, bored in her own freezing place next door, wrapped in a blanket, watching daytime telly. It was just unfortunate his house always smelt of dog.

She could see Boyd was coming off the drugs and she was glad he'd stopped his sobbing. She knew he'd been going through a hard patch recently. The poor man had been out of work a good few years since his dear mother had committed suicide, and recently that young bitch Leanne had simply left him. She'd always thought Leanne a peculiar one. And now it was his dog. It was difficult, and she kept on telling herself she was wrong to think this way, yet she couldn't help feeling pleased Pinkie had also left him. It was a large beast. Noisy. It would bark and whine for frantic moments every day. And during the night it could howl like a wolf. She felt sure she was being cruel, but she was glad.

Throughout the day she'd been listening to the voice of Michael Jackson. Listening to his voice for hours on end, she amazed herself with just how many of his songs she actually knew. The lyrics seemed to be programmed into her brain, stored in the back of her head in case of emergency, and they all came out rolling easily off her tongue. Maybe she'd learnt the songs from TV adverts. Maybe she'd heard them in films she'd forgotten. She didn't know, but she whistled in tune as fast as the man sang them.

And she'd impressed herself with her dancing. Fuck, she would've impressed Fred Astaire, she thought. She was mobile, despite her age. Certain to be one of those to receive a special birthday card from the Queen. She knew she'd always been a good dancer. Friday night at the Band club was a dance night, and she'd been a girl that could dance. She'd attained a lot of early boyfriends by her dancing skills. She'd been awarded the Cwmgarw Dancer of the Year for three years in a row back then. She still had the dainty, gold-plated cups on her mantelpiece. Bev, her late husband, had been one of the three judges on the competition board and the filthy rumour was she'd been given the prizes because of their relationship. But she was only thirteen years old back then, and they hadn't yet had a proper romantic relationship.

Boyd had had enough of Michael Jackson. He couldn't find

what Mrs Sparrow'd done with the remote. As the medication left his blood, the anger crept back in. Why would somebody steal Pinkie, he wondered. You don't steal another man's dog, surely? Everyone dreams about the bad things. He knew it was natural to wake in tears. But you don't steal dogs.

Mrs Sparrow came into his living room with the tea. She'd found the sugar. Boyd noticed the woman had changed. She was wearing a silvery cardigan and tight black trousers, too short for her bony legs. She wore white socks. She put the tray onto the table and sat. She let out a little gasp as her backside found the remote control and Michael Jackson disappeared from the TV screen. She pulled the remote out from under her and handed it over to Boyd.

– Ta, he said.

He picked up his cup of tea, took a sip and pointed the remote at the screen. Boyd and Mrs Sparrow sat and watched the afternoon news, drinking their tea. A report all about the robbery. All about the man who was becoming a media legend. The media had even christened the man: *The Valley's Villain*.

– *...the man who has robbed his way through numerous supermarkets and managed to avoid the police for over half a year, has apparently struck again. This time, seriously injuring a young shop assistant...*

It was a lie. He hadn't meant to shoot the girl. Boyd had become *The Valley's Villain*, and he hated the title. It made him sound like Lego man. *Voila, The Valley's Villain*. He hated the cheap alliteration of it. He was more than that. He wasn't the Welsh version of JohnfuckingDillinger and he wished he could tell them all the truth.

Mrs Sparrow sat, delicately brushing strands of her white hair across her scalp, nodding in dumb agreement with the news report. Boyd ground his teeth. It was difficult for him to watch. He turned the television off. The tears had started to stream down his cheeks again. He reached over to the bowl of fruit on the table and picked a dry green grape off its stalk. He rolled the small grape between his index finger and thumb and squeezed gently at its wrinkled skin. He wiped at the tears with the back of his hand, sniffed, and popped the grape into his mouth.

– You hungry, love? Mrs Sparrow asked. You want me to make you some tea, hmmm?

– No, no. I'm alright. I'm alright. I'm going out soon. I don't want my tea yet.

– Try not to start crying again though, yes? Come on, love, try. Be a big boy now.

– Hmmmm.

– Come on, don't cry. It's all people seem to do these days. I found this earlier, have a look.

Boyd looked down at the closed photo album she'd placed on his lap. The woman wasn't going to stop the tears rolling down his beaten face with this. She stood, leant over him, and turned the pages. She was trying to assure him it'd make him feel more relaxed. He knew it wouldn't help. The images of Mother and Father were making him feel worse. He slammed the book shut, firmly catching her finger.

– Mrs Sparrow, please. Would you sit back down. Please. This isn't helping me.

She sat, shaking her head.

– It's wha' I did when I lost my Bev. Makes you feel easier, she said.

– Your husband is dead. My dog ain't dead. Pinkie isn't dead!

– Pinkie's gone, love.

– Pinkie isn't dead!

– Come on now. Let him go. Live with the photos. It'll help in the end.

87

Boyd stood. It was dark and it was time to take the risk. He had to get outside and search for Pinkie. He had to look for his dog. He went into the kitchen to get his jacket. Mrs Sparrow was continuing to talk to him from the living room but she hadn't got up. She was mumbling. He found his jacket and grabbed Pinkie's leather leash. He walked back into the living room to see Mrs Sparrow sat on the sofa, holding a hand to her chest. She wasn't talking. She was trying to breathe. Boyd watched her a few seconds more as she let out an upset breath, and died.

– Aw shite.

A Hairdresser's Tale

Tash tightened the nylon cape around Hank's neck, placed her hands on his shoulders and looked at his weary reflection in the mirror. They had watched him stumble to his feet and he had looked too dazed to realise where he was, so they brought him into the salon for a trim.

– Right 'en, love. So wha's it to be? she asked.

– Uhh?

There was a slur in Hank's voice, and a dark sag beneath his eyes. He didn't know why he was sitting in Tash's place and his head was only just coming back to life. Again. And again. He knew he had been on his way home and hadn't planned to stop and get his hair cut. The decision had been made for him. Tash had told him that he needed his hair cut.

Hank stretched out his feet and looked down at his Adidas trainers. He wasn't wearing them. Clamped around the left foot was wet plaster wrapped in torn plastic. His right foot under a sodden sock. He realised he'd had a seizure. Earlier, when Tash and Bell had watched Hank lying there on the ground jerking in pain, a young man called Tetchy had appeared on his mini-motorbike and snatched at the opportunity. He had rifled through Hank's bag. They had watched him steal Hank's trainers: the one from his foot, the one from his bag. And then he casually left him twitching in the rain. She thought the haircut might please sweet Hank.

Tash had had her front room converted into a salon and she'd become the estate's official hairdresser. Hank had been coming to her salon since he was a boy. There was a white sink fitted into the wall where the TV should have been, rows of gleaming stainless steel cutting gadgets on display next to the sink and a fake red leather chair, its seat worn thin over the years. The room smelt of hairspray and cheap perfume, the orange, swirling patterned carpet covered in hair. Tash could cut your hair cheap, and quick. And everyone liked her. A woman in her early seventies, no higher than four-foot-nine, her face a mixture of crazy spiderlike cracks and the heavy make-up she always applied to fill in those lines. Her long white hair was pulled back into a pony tail, and she had those glittering green eyes that belonged to a cat.

Once you were placed on her red throne the stories began. Endless gossip about the estate would be shovelled into the customer's ear. And as a customer, you were expected to be returning tales for further consumption and later use. Hank didn't have any tales to tell. It was the new medication, perhaps. He tried to relax. He did need to get his hair cut. It'd been about a year since he'd last had it cut, and was looking long on both sides. Lank, Cheyenne had told him. He needed to get it cut.

– Heard about tha' Japanese bloke, love? One tha' manages the Relax-U-Backs business?

Tash turned her head to speak to a dapper little pensioner, the one who always sat in the corner of their living room.

– He's gorra glorious moustache, an' he, Lee?

– Yep.

Hank didn't know if Lee was family related, or simply lived in the corner. He was considered a fixture in the salon. Part of the interior design. The myth was that Tash and Bell employed him to bring an old-fashioned sense of the American Barbershop culture into her living room space. For years people actually felt sorry for the man. Little Lee in the corner would sit amongst Tash's immense selection of porcelain figurines, laughing at whatever fell from her mouth, endorsing her theories about life and the local stories as she interpreted them. It was his role to agree.

Tash patted Hank lightly on his shoulder, but he hadn't been listening. He brought his eyes up to the mirror and let them drift over the shelves covered in an ever growing cluster of Tash's porcelain. She had a thing for bright Hollywood bric-a-brac and was very smug about her collection. She had first travelled over to America in 1982, and had gone there every summer since. She would always leave her husband, Bell, in charge of the salon for seven days, mid-July. Holiday at Disney World and return with a tan, as well as at least five new statuettes. Fixed duty. She reckoned it was where she came from.

There were at least a hundred statues staring down at Hank. The laughing heads of Laurel and Hardy, Tom and Jerry, Chaplin, Mickey Mouse. A Tinkerbell standing next to a drunken Bugs Bunny. She had a thing for Betty Boop, had Betty all dolled up in different outfits: as a cowboy, as a glamour girl, a bathing Betty, a Betty out for a stroll, Betty doing a belly-dance. A two foot high statuette of Betty Boop in a white skirt, blowing around the top of her thighs. Hank let his eyes come to rest on the dancing elves. They looked dangerous. He shook his head. He thought he was going into one.

– Yeahhhh, Mister Masaki Hamamoto, mun? Your business colleague, in he?

His hair was a mangled entanglement from the hospital wire and glue. Tash pushed his head over the sink. She let the warm water flush over his glue-matted, hospital-dried hair. She took a wallop of shampoo and rubbed. Thoroughly.

– Urghhh…

– See, Mr Masaki? Used to be a real cheerful man. Sweet wife, you know? Beautiful. Geisha-like, porcelain. Daily wearing a silken apron and working the oven for his tender, Japanese stomach, and the sweet mouth of their child 'ey adores. Lives up in one of the nicer houses? On the Whiterock estate? The model family, love. Perfect, like. High-standard people.

– Urrggghh…

Hank thought he was drowning. He swallowed her shampoo and spat.

– Sorry, love. You okay? Apparently, tha' Masaki? He'd more or less twirl out their front door on his way to work. Every day of the year. And his wife? She'd be in tears. Crying, cause 'ey gorra part company for the day.

She pulled him out of the sink. Took a towel and patted the back of his skull. Why was she telling him this? Tash flattened his hair on the sides, picked up the brush and lightly combed the long hair back. She picked up the scissors, pulled at a strand of wet hair and showed Hank the proposed length. He nodded and let her start the cut. He shut his eyes and listened. He had to.

– The ideal family, love. Family values, see? Holds it all together, innit? They got praise for each other. See, story is, his sweet wife, well, she would clearly clean the shit from his arse…

Hank bounced himself out of the red throne. If he had to put up with listening to some story coming from Tash's stinking mouth, then it at least had to be a real one.

– Tash, his full name is *Gethin* Masaki Hamamoto. Gethin is only part Japanese. And his wife? Naw. She certainly isn't a sodding geisha. *Glynfuckinggraig,* is where she's from. A right nasty piece of work, by all counts. She doesn't tend to get on with her husband, *Gethin*, according to what he's told me.

Hank was standing, and tried not to wobble forward, his lank hair parted and half-cut on the one side. He was attempting to undo the cape from around his neck. Strands of wet hair had fallen onto the red seat and were slipping onto the floor next to his foot. He couldn't untie the cape. Tash must have put a double knot on it. He turned his back to her and blindly shoved his finger where he imagined the knot to be. She ignored his stubby action. She bent his finger away from the knot and pushed his weak frame back down into the seat and, with a gentle force, she patted his hair into place. He sighed.

– Alright, alright. Calm down, Hank, love. Not saying I know all the details, is I? Only heard it all from Mardy, like. Anyhow, family values? Tha's not the point, is it?

Hank sank. Tash massaged at his shoulders and combed his wet hair. He bent his head down to his chest and looked at the coffee coloured nylon cape, watching his breath create a dent in the light material. He felt embarrassed. He felt Tash's hand stroke at his hair which hung down the side behind his ear. He listened to the scissors make their crisp cut. He tried to ignore the voice telling him the story of Mr Masaki Hamamoto, and Hank again wondered why he was even sat there.

– He goes into work mega early, right? Wife's been giving him grief. See, Masaki, the Jap-man? He wasn't leading the sweet life no more, was he? No. Money problems. And this morning? It wasn't no better.

Hank held his hand up, and Tash stopped talking.

– Why're you telling me all this?

– Thought you'd like to hear it, love.

– How do you know exactly what happened to my associate, "the Jap-man", in his frigging office this morning?

– Podge told us. Came in today to get his own haircut,

before Mardy. Anyhow, that don't matter, does it? Masaki, he was sitting in his office behind the desk watching the phone ring when Kym, his personal assistant, trips in through the door. She never knew he'd even arrived yet. Straightens her pencil skirt and nods at his phone. And Masaki? He just gets up and scurries out his office like a worried rat. She legs it after him. Chases him down through the warehouse, past all the dodgy nightshift crew, and into that customer area. And Podge? His best salesman crawls up to him. Walks alongside Masaki and Kym, going, *"Morning, Mr Hamamoto. Moustache is looking tidy today"*. Masaki mind? Naw, he don't stop to talk. See, he got all them other things going on inside his head. Man reaches 'em electric shutters, covering the front window? And sets it on roll. Open. And Podge goes...

Hank couldn't stand it. He opened his eyes and shouted,

– TASH, you're speaking outtya fucking arse, mun! I KNOW THA' PLACE. Donnie is his number one man. Never heard of a Podge. Only Donnie. And I know Donnie. A right shite. Always wearing far too much aftershave, and giving you one of them meaningful smiles. Looks like he painted his teeth with Tipp-Ex.

Tash massaged his shoulders again and Hank sat there, rigid.

– So, anyhow. Masaki, see? He's gorra leg-it outta work. Fast, innit? So, he pushes past people and out the building. Kym's running after him, and tha' horrid sales assistant, Donnie, appears out the darkness, like a vampire or something. Right ghoul. Wearing too much perfume. Never like you, love, naawww. Donnie, all smiling like his teeth been Tipp-Exed. And 'ey all steps out into the car park together, with Masaki going up to his car. Them two behind him. Standing there, with frowns on their faces. And Masaki? He goes, *"I'm going home. I don't feel well"*.

94

Hank opened his eyes once more and saw Tash standing behind him with the scissors in one hand and a comb in the other. She was looking at the electric razor by the sink. She had stopped cutting at his hair and their eyes met. Hank bent his head backwards to speak to her.

– Is that it? he said.

– Wha'? No! No, mun. Course not!

– Not much of a story, eh? Hehehe, *I'm going home. I feel sick.*
Tash tapped at the back of his head with the comb and said,

– Listen, mun. Tha's just the starting bit, innit?

*

Masaki Hamamoto felt sick. He was going home. It was going to be an important day, and he'd made the foolish error of bothering to go in to work. He'd wanted to get away from his wife, Carol, and left the house without breakfast to try and find some peace at his workplace. He had sat behind his office desk for minutes and as soon as he heard the telephones start to ring he had to leave. He needed to compose himself, and was not going to be able to do so at the office. It was an important day.

Masaki drove with the reassuring thought that his wife would have left the house by now. He felt tense. Cold white fields sped past the window and disappeared behind him. It was absurd, but he could not stop thinking of the film *Psycho*. Marion Crane's large eyes, flickering in black and white. Left to right, as she raced on down the highway. Masaki didn't have forty thousand dollars and he wasn't running away to marry his boyfriend. Hell, he didn't have a boyfriend. What Masaki did have was a short list of troubles. Problems which had been nagging him for far too long a period. And today? Today was the day to resolve his worries. His burdens, arranged alphabetically inside his balding head, were listed as: –

1. Hair; 2. Hank; 3. Production meeting.

For years now, Masaki felt it unfair that his Japanese hair had been failing him. He had grown his moustache in order to distract the customer from noticing his balding scalp, but recently he'd noticed the moustache simply wasn't working. The customer's curious eye would often study his thinning black hair before even looking at the Relax-U-Back product on display in his hands. Masaki had decided to take control of his hair condition. He would visit the hospital for his private appointment with the hair transplanter. He was nervous of course, but knew his hair appointment was his minor worry. He was going to get the full works: the Rooney.

Today was the day his colleague, Hank Evans, was to return. Masaki had been avoiding Hank. He'd not visited him nor had he returned any of his repeated phone calls. He knew Hank would be desperate to know what the situation was with the script and whether Masaki as a part-time producer had actually succeeded in truly getting any of the necessary financial interest for their film.

Masaki carried on driving down the dual carriageway, and loosened his clamped grip on the steering wheel. He found the car mints and peeled the wrapper from one to feed himself. He liked mints. They were good for his driving. For the past week, since Hank went into the hospital, Masaki had indeed managed to get the financial interest secured. The film was going to be made and he was due to meet the investors later that day.

Masaki Hamamoto was a man who had adored film since he was a child. For hours Masaki could sit in Cinema B, open-mouthed and intoxicated by the splendour of *La Dolce Vita* and the talent of Federico Fellini, whilst his elder brothers would settle down in Cannon's Cinema A to watch *Friday the 13th*, not a worry to trouble their bothered faces, in the knowledge that their ten-year-old brother was next door. They knew Masaki was a scatterbrain. Every trip to the cinema made Masaki grow up knowing he wanted to be a filmmaker.

As a young man he moved away from the family restaurant business and started work for *Relax U Backs* with the full, inner knowledge that it was only to be for a short while. As an older man, however, he was still there. Deep from within a warehouse unit over in Pentre, Masaki promoted whatever cheap, massaging devices had been designed that year. To this day, he was amazed at the international market for these lightweight domestic toys. He had never stopped wanting to get out of the back business and into films.

The dual carriageway took him past the mountain and Masaki noticed a teenager, on some kind of motorbike, appear behind him. It was Tetchy, now on the hard shoulder and speeding right alongside Masaki, riding a two feet tall mini-motorbike. Masaki swerved slightly when he caught sight of the danger. Tetchy was wearing his headphones and screaming along to some music, barefooted and freewheeling it down the left hand side of the car, with his shoeless feet stuck out on either side of his roaring bike.

– Fucking arsehole, said Masaki.

He would be home shortly, and could calm himself for the production meeting. He believed there to be a new problem he'd now have to face with the film financiers. Masaki didn't want to trouble Hank at the hospital, he knew he would certainly agree with him on the matter, and was determined to phone him today. He told himself he was a strong man.

When Masaki came to the bridge a black shape tumbled out of the skies above and landed on his windscreen. The screen shattered. The car shuddered. A large ginger cat slid off the blood-smeared windscreen and Masaki's car came to a gentle stop.

Traffic swiftly eased into a slow stream of cars which travelled past Masaki in his still vehicle. A ready-made audience of onlookers gaped at the man in his broken-down car, making malicious faces at the pathetic figure. They flowed past. Slow and indifferent.

*

Masaki parked the car outside his house. Although the windscreen had shattered it was still firmly in place. He needed the car that day and could get the windscreen replaced tomorrow. He had managed to wipe most of the blood off the glass and believed he would still be able to see through the broken cobweb of lines. A curtain in the upstairs bedroom parted. Carol peered down at him. Masaki was annoyed his wife hadn't left yet.

They had never really got on, and he increasingly wondered why they had ever married. Their neighbours always thought they were a funny couple. Last summer he had joined the weekly Film Club. She told him it was the beginning of a mid-life-crisis. He chose to ignore her. It was at the Film Club he met up with Hank.

Hank was a writer, edgily willing to talk about promoting the script he'd recently finished. Masaki had immediately claimed he was a producer. They had found themselves in agreement when it came to choosing what films were suitable to watch at the club. Neither of the men believed *Ramboner II* to be a bad film, they simply felt it more appropriate to be watching something a little less explicit. The seven other members in the club had their minds set.

The two new members' friendship had formed that very first night. They'd both responded to an internet advert which stated the club was the place to meet other local men and women who were interested in watching and making film. Neither Masaki nor Hank had realised the Film Club only watched and made porn. They weren't fans of porn so they left. During the summer months that followed Masaki found himself working with Hank on a number of short film projects.

Masaki learnt Hank had given up trying to get financial backing for his feature film script, *Lilies of the West*. It was a script that didn't seem to be able to move past the lazy hands and minds of its few readers. Masaki took it away and read it in one sitting. He thought it was outstanding. He said so to Hank. A script that should be made, he told him. A film of honour which needed to be made. A film set to remind people of the dangers of Americana.

He produced a contract for Hank to sign. And Hank signed. It was a golden contract. A moral pledge between himself and Hank to make their noble film. A film neither crass nor esoteric. A film that was pioneering and vital. A film that would shine in the face of the vulgar, commercial shite being churned out. The script was now legally owned by both men. *Lilies of the West* was a romantic drama about the folly and the sins which existed deep within the history and practice of Welsh Mormonism through to the present day. It would rock the market, re-define what a commercial venture in film might be. Others didn't see it that way, and claimed the film didn't have any commercial weight to gain backing. Masaki insisted they go ahead and make the film cheap on DV-Cam. He was desperate.

Then, as if from nowhere, Masaki had been contacted by a local businessman who claimed to have read the script on the net, and was hooked. Masaki was flummoxed. He didn't understand how the script was on the internet in the first, or any place, because he knew Hank was keen to keep the script and the copyright firm to his chest. He wanted to ask Hank how this could have happened but it didn't seem correct to ask, and so it was maybe because of a residual sense of Japanese propriety that Masaki had taken a step in the wrong direction. Without talking to the writer, it was the producer who had met with a local businessman, Caradoc Johnson, a young millionaire with investments in various projects stretching from South Wales to London. A man who, indeed, was known to have a passion for film, and commercial return, and as soon as the words Welsh Mormonism had jumped at him from the pages of the script, Caradoc wanted involvement.

Caradoc Johnson had business links with an American media company based in Utah, and knew at once that he could sell such a film package. An American business partner who practised Mormonism and was married to a woman of Welsh heritage meant that Hank's script would receive the superior funding necessary, as long as small changes were to be allowed. Masaki was keen. Of course, minor changes could be made.

Masaki kept the deal strictly confidential. He would only tell Hank about their success when he was sure it was sealed. Caradoc Johnson stormed ahead and employed a group of Mormon writers to make the necessary changes to Hank's original script. And within days of Hank being in the hospital, Caradoc and his team of investors went to work. *Lilies of the West* became *Bloodwood.* A money winner.

Masaki had argued with Caradoc and the Americans but they dismissed his concerns. They wanted to meet him. He had to take control of the situation. His adam's apple bounced and Masaki felt a sob rise to his dry throat. He left his broken car on the driveway and entered his home. A small, curly-haired, poodle-type dog could not stop barking at his appearance. The dog sat at Masaki's feet in the living room and he tried to ignore the questioning squeaks coming from the manufactured dog's mouth. He leant forward in his armchair, stretched his cramped back, and rubbed at his neck.

Carol banged around in the kitchen. She hadn't liked his explanation of what happened to the car. She didn't believe him. She didn't believe cats jumped off bridges. She had liked the idea of the hair transplant, despite the cost. It could be done in a day and a half and, in her eyes, Gethin would then look far more appropriate as a member of the business community.

Their ten-year-old daughter, Vicki, walked into the room. She was pale. She stopped a few feet away from the side of Masaki's head and stared into his ear as he curled his back against the pain. Masaki shouted to his wife.

– Why haven't you taken her in to school this morning?

– She said she didn't feel well.

– She looks alright.

– Yeah? Well, she said she felt sick. Maybe she has what you have.

Masaki held his position, his face firm. He didn't turn to his daughter.

– Do you feel sick?

Vicki nodded at her father.

– Well, maybe she's not well.

– That's what I said.

Carol came into the room and slapped Vicki on the back of her head. Her head jumped forward with the blow.

– Mind, you never can tell with lying little Vicki, here. Just like her daddy, eh?

Vicki glared at her mam. She paused and said,

– Owwwwwww.

Carol turned to Masaki.

– What you doing? said Carol.

– Nothing. Um, I'm still a little shaken up… Has anyone phoned the house this morning?

Carol took her coat and her own car keys and moved towards the front door.

– I'm going out. You look after Sicky Vicki.

The phone started to ring. Carol picked it up. She listened then handed it to her husband and slammed the front door. Masaki knew the Southern drawl was that of the American investor, the one found by Caradoc Johnson. It seemed the man had more or less taken over the film project. Caradoc had become the second man. And, Masaki knew, he'd become the man they wanted to erase.

– Hi there? Is that a Mr Marsarkey Hamamoto?

– Yes, yes. Who, umm, who's this?

– My name is Joel Miller. You don't know me, Mr Marsarkey, we haven't met yet. But hey, you'd be foolish to pretend you didn't know what this was all about now, wouldn't you sir?

– Uhmm, yes of course I…

– In fact, you'd be darn foolish, if you weren't sitting there expecting our call this morning.

– Yes. I wanted to talk to someone about that… the meeting, you see…

Masaki turned away from his daughter, who was eagerly watching him speak, and whispered into the phone.

– You see, I'd prefer it, um, if you or Mr Johnson didn't ring my office. And definitely not here, no, not at my home…

– Ha, and just how are we meant to get hold of you, Mr Marsarkey? You don't seem to be answering our calls. Or

102

email. This is being stretched to the limit here, sir. And we haven't got a business deal going on here, Mr Marsarkey. You know, we are not equal partners on this anymore. We moved our money into your account recently.

– Yes. I know. I'm sorry. I am trying to deal with that, but you see…

– Well, I'm sorry too, Mr Marsarkey, but from our perspective things just aren't moving speedy enough. No. We need to assess the state of play here.

– Yes, um, yes we do.

Masaki felt his chest jump and he took the phone away from his ear. He had it pressed against his thigh and found himself rubbing at the pain in his neck, trying to ignore the cushioned American voice coming from the phone.

– …we are going to meet today, sir, as planned. Move this on. There is a deal to be struck between us here, Mr Marsarkey, and it involves more money, lots of greenbacks, bud, for both yourself and Hank Evans. Mr Marsarkey? Hello? Are you there, Marsarkey…?

Vicki watched her father stand and let the phone fall onto the chair. He left the room with his hand on the back of his neck. The dog raced after him and sprinted upstairs. Vicki nervously picked up the phone. She could hear a whiney voice.

– Mr Marsarkey?

– No. It's Vicki. My daddy's not here. He's gone somewhere.

– The heck's your father gone, sweetheart?

– Spain.

Vicky quickly pushed the red button on the receiver and put the phone back in its cradle. She gave the dead phone her middle finger and turned to find her father.

Vicky sat on the bed alongside her sobbing father. She

didn't know what to do. The poodle-type dog was on the bed close to Masaki and watched Vicki with a suspicious glare. Vicki placed her arm around her dad's shoulder. The jealous dog placed its head onto Masaki's lap. They sat like that for a long time, Masaki with his head bent forward, his babbling face hidden in his hands. Her dad couldn't stop crying.

Vicki got bored. She patted him on the back and stood. Masaki raised his head and when he saw his daughter in front of him he let out a stifled wail of horror and delight and started to sob again. Vicki shrugged. She turned on her heel and left him. She went into the living room and turned the TV on to watch *Animals at Work*. When the phone started to ring, the phone didn't stop ringing.

It had been ringing for an hour and Masaki chose to ignore it. He lay on his bed with the dog beside him. He could not meet these people. He could not cheat on his good friend. When Vicki walked into the room the dog barked and Masaki raised his reddened eyes and flinched when he met the steady gaze of his daughter.

– Do you want me to answer the phone, dad?

– NO. No, sweetheart don't, don't answer the phone. No.

– Should I unplug it, dad?

Masaki was dumbstruck. He had assumed he couldn't stop the phone ringing all morning but his daughter was a genius. When the phone stopped, the stillness was strange. They looked at each other. Vicki showed her teeth. They had won. She held her fisted arms up high in triumph. The family poodle-type started its bark. Masaki looked towards the open doorway and drank in the thick wave of beautiful silence. He wondered. His mobile phone started to ring. He looked at his daughter and said,

– Sorry.

Masaki had stopped sobbing. He felt ashamed to have been in that state in front of his daughter. He was a strong father. A strong man. And, he was trying to tell himself, he could deal with this. He would meet these people.

*

Tash had finished the haircut. She prodded at the back of Hank's shoulder with her electric shaver. He hadn't been listening. He was asleep.

– Tha's it, 'en love, she said. All done.

Hank opened his eyes. He studied himself in her mirror. He held onto the one arm of his broken glasses and moved his head to the side. Left and right. Tash had shaved his hair dead short all over, and he didn't like it. He had become a skinhead.

– This isn't too short for my head, is it? said Hank.

– Naw mun, perfect, said Tash.

He could only hope Cheyenne would think it made him look better.

*

With one last shove Hank managed to open the swollen door to his flat and stood there in the doorway, bent and breathing heavily, a drugged body not used to the new medication it was taking. Before his haircut, he knew he'd been outside, immobile, and lying in the rain for a while. His seizures made him lifeless for minutes, only just aware of people shyly stepping over him. Or of the one kicking him. The kids taking his hospital crutches to fight with. And wondering if somebody had pissed on him. Some bastard had definitely stolen his trainers. The sodden cast that covered his left foot had been written on: *'Fuck you Spacca. Love, Tetchy'*. Hank knew the moron. And he would get his frigging trainers back.

Cutting through the stagnant air in his flat he heard the cold beep of his answer-phone. He scanned the week-long supply of damp envelopes stacked by his bare foot, held the doorframe for support and shoved the brown bills to one side. With difficulty he wriggled his fingers toward the edge of a large envelope and managed to grab the heavy package. Holding on, he tried to pull himself back up but his left arm didn't have the strength. He lost balance and slammed against the stinking carpet.

The determined electronic beep that came from his answer phone was making him shaky. Hank felt a tingle in his leg. It wasn't going to turn itself off. He'd fade out before the battery would. He left the envelope on the floor and limped over to the phone to press the flashing button. The electric voice told him,

– *You have five new messages...*

His father sounded drunk. Lonely. Hank limped past the counter into the kitchen. He checked the rusty gas stove. He hadn't bothered to clean it when he left for the hospital and the brown bacon grease between the two burners needed a wipe. He turned it on and listened for any stream of gas. The phone beeped and played the second message. The voice sounded more drunk. Shouting to itself, mumbling to itself about mam going in and a possible washing machine crisis. It was hard. They had both loved her so much. Hank remembered how dad had reacted when his mother received the fatal news from the hospital. Since she went, his dad had been letting his emotion out with the bottle. Day by day. Week by week.

Hank wiped his face and hands with a manky tea towel and opened the door of his fridge. One egg. He opened the freezer. Green peas. Findus. They sat in a frozen white frame. He hadn't turned the fridge off. He put a pan of water on and stood by the stove to watch it boil.

– *...pick up the phone, Hank. Hank? I know you're there, son? Hank? I visited her today. Maybe I'll pop in tomorrow. You heard what happened? Hank?*

– *End of message.*

The phone beeped and he listened to the third frantic message.

– *Hank, it's Masaki. Listen, we need to talk, my friend. I'm sorry I've not been in touch. Bit too busy. I know this sounds odd, yet we have us a minor problem. I'd like to talk, to meet with you on this. You will agree.*

– *End of message.*

Masaki had sobbed on the line for what seemed like a minute or two. The phone beeped again. All he could hear was the sound of his father, breathing heavily across the line. Hank couldn't stop thinking about Masaki.

– *End of message.*

Hank twitched and watched the swirling water boil steadily in the saucepan. He found a frying pan. The telephone beeped once more and played the final message. It was from his third part-time job.

– *This is a message for Hank Evans, from Mr Lee Cape, assistant Chief Manager of Family-Land. This is a formal message, Hank, that terminates your employment at the store. We request that you return our Family-Land uniforms fully cleansed. If you have further enquiries about this, please get in touch.*

Hank limped to the phone and deleted the messages.

– Routines. Stick to the routines, he said.

The phone rang. Hank strove to disregard it. He felt weary and hungry. His shiny new medication was making him dizzy. Across the counter was his scattered collection of pills standing in their various coloured cartons. These were the routines he had been told to follow.

By the side of his kitchen was the bathroom. Hank stood by the gas cooker. A blue flame scorched the bottom of the frying pan about to contain the egg. Hank looked at the bathroom door. He hadn't been able to wash all week at the hospital because of the EEG Unit.

In the bathroom he pulled off his clothes. He stood in his underwear and looked at the empty, pale green bath-tub. He turned and looked at his reflection in the mirror. His skinny body was white with red welts and scratches created by his recent fits. His hair had been shaved a No.2 by Tash. He looked into the sink at the smallest bar of pink soap in the world. Held his hands up to his face and pictured the soap through his framed fingers. He looked at the bath. He didn't have a shower. He wasn't allowed to bathe.

Hank stood at the sink trying to wash his body. Armpits. Cock. Face. He was at the sink with his head under the tap trying to get any remaining EEG glue out from behind his ears. He washed his teeth. Stood at the sink and looked at himself in the mirror.

– Routines.

He was running the bath. He had swallowed the new medication again. The bath was full. He carefully got in, letting his fractured foot rest on the side. He put his broken glasses onto the chair and let his frame sink beneath the water. Eyes closed. Tight. Underwater. He struggled to hold his breath.

There was a ringing noise. Hank heard the ringing noise. Hank ignored the ringing. He knew it wasn't Cheyenne. He lay there. Then felt the water vibrate. Pulse in his ears. He choked. He burst. Spluttering. Coughing. Breathing hard, Hank slurped the air in.

Hank had had two fits in one day. He was exhausted and knew he would be for many more days to come. It had been hell. How on earth did he think he'd be able to manage the panda nonsense tomorrow? He was in his bedroom and had taken the large panda head off the desk and placed it on top of his folded costume. He noticed there was a clump of dried earth above the ear and that most of the white fur patches across the back of the costume were splattered with crushed grass and tiny flecks of brown mud. The crowd had roared when he slipped during a game the week before he went into hospital. Parts of his back hurt him after that particular fall, with the skin on his elbows turning a pinkish red. He flicked at a patch of mud and watched it drop onto the carpet.

– Bugger.

Hank sighed and bent over to brush the specks of mud across the woven fibre. He frowned. He knew the Pentrecoch Panda had become the town clown. His dad loved to tell him that the mascot was a figure of mockery from Pentre to Cwm. He liked to tease and tell him that, never mind, at least he had actually become a man *in* the entertainment industry. Hank stroked a stain on the back of the costume.

He was on the sofa. Dry. His phone was still ringing. Was it Cheyenne? He was staring at the blank TV screen. He looked at the plate on his lap. A plate of boiled green peas and an egg. He turned the TV on and began to eat his supper. The phone had stopped ringing. The room was quiet and Hank sat there and listened for a moment.

The monotonous noise of the TV brought him back in. The local news flashed edited images of a robbed petrol station on the screen. It looked like Hardy's petrol station. Police. Onlookers. An ambulance. The faded family photo of a teenage girl in school uniform. It was Cheyenne. He turned the volume up as the picture snapped to the weather forecast. Hank shook his head. It couldn't have been Cheyenne.

Hank switched channels and let his eyes move to the wall behind the warm black box. The peas were cold. His head leaned to the side. He swallowed and steadied himself. He was tired. He was too tired to deal with Masaki. Hank sat there and waited. He moved his mind away from these broken images he hadn't really seen.

Hank rubbed his shaven head. The last time he'd had a haircut like this, he must've been about ten. A bullied ten-year-old at primary school. The identikit red-brick Victorian school containing the basic five classrooms through which passed, generation after generation, the children of the area. A large playground was moulded to let them maul each other. And the worn pine floor of the Assembly Hall, scene of the ritual of daily worship before education.

Hank wiped the dried spittle from the side of his mouth. He sat in his dressing gown, listening to silence. An hour later and he still hadn't moved. It was cold in the room but he didn't get up and turn the electric fire on. Would tomorrow be just as bad as today?

Pinkie and the Ladies

Pinkie sat alone in Donna's flat, panting in a whispery way, with his head hung low. The sisters had brought the dog to the back-end of a cold town miles down the valley, on a torn street that faced a bitter wind. Donna's flat used to be part of a Bed & Breakfast called Sunny Nights. The place was sold on years ago when the owner was imprisoned for assault on a customer who had refused to pay his bills. Sunny Nights was auctioned by the local authority, and the house had been split into seven flats which managed to contain the same seventies style furniture and designs of the late unlamented B & B it once was.

The big dog raised his head when the sound of a crying baby sprang out from behind a closed front door and drifted along the damp corridor. He jumped when the noise of a neighbour's television vibrated from the floor beneath his heavy body. Pinkie moved his nose about the room and raised himself. He sniffed at the thin mattress flipped by Donna onto the floor for Leanne, and prowled past the nicotine-stained, white leather settee. Red carpet was spread throughout every room. In the kitchen the red had become a dark brown grease that coated a Valor Bistro cooker set only inches away from Donna's foul smelling bathroom. The dog sniffed at black rubber straps tied to the end of a double bed in Donna's bedroom, and idly stepped back into the living room. He stood looking at the laughing plastic skull on the mantelpiece, a lipstick-smeared pint glass on the table, half-melted black candles on the sideboard, and the dripping gold star painted on the wall. He sniffed at the bowl of brown water and stepped away. He looked up at the Samurai sword Donna had balanced on the mantelpiece and sat down again next to the door. It was late.

Donna was in the bathroom fixing her hair and putting her face on for her appointment when she heard loud crashing noises. She raced into the living room only to find an enraged dog sniffing and biting at the cardboard boxes. He had leapt onto the sofa, chewed at pillows, jumped down and knocked over her boxes, scattering teacups, tea-towels and saucepans. Donna snatched at the Samurai sword. She figured it must have been the first time Pinkie had seen the sword in her hand, and he instinctively barked louder when Donna started to wave it at him.

– What're you doing? Stop. STOP IT.

Pinkie was a large dog. His head was level to Donna's bellybutton. He showed his teeth as Donna moved nearer, snatched at the hem of her dressing gown and tore viciously, ripping it from her body as she leapt backwards onto the glass table to gain height.

– What's the matter with you, eh? You've showed me you can chew? Well, you can't chew metal, can you love, eh? COME ON, TRY IT SCOOBY.

Donna was more or less trapped, standing above him with the sword pointed downward. Naked. Her tanned orange frame was covered in colourful tattoos. The doorbell rang. Leanne had been to the shop to buy food for the dog and was outside standing in the corridor. The ringing doorbell instinctively stopped Pinkie barking. He turned, and Donna saw it as her chance. She made a break and jumped off the table to answer the door. She'd swung the sword around and caught Pinkie on the side. The sword made more of a slap than a cut and the dog reacted quickly, moving away from the weaving blade. Leanne stepped into the room and looked at the shambles. Pinkie sat in a corner, terrified. Her sister casually swung the sword around.

– What the hell's happening in here? said Leanne.

– Nothing. Just practising a few moves with little Pinkie. I look good doing this?

– Yeah, like a right fucking dragon slayer. What's with all the make-up?

– I've got a job tonight, said Donna.

– You're kidding me, right?

– It's what I do, Leanne.

– You've got a customer? Coming round here, tonight?

– Naw, mun. My Mistress X character doesn't have this bouffant hairspray style, does she? No. He's not one of my regular clients. I'm doing the Stars Dating Agency a brief favour. They gave us a call, out of the blue.

– What? Who the hell are you meant to look like?

– Dunno, really. Did a quick search on the web. It's some British reality TV star. Princess Loveluck? Got famous on the TV series when she had the luck to pluck another one of the contestants, Shelvey B, the millionaire American DJ. He fell in love with her on telly and they married. I never heard of her. The Agency reckoned their usual escort can't make it tonight and I said I'd take it on. I'm gonna travel back up and over to the Mountain Meadows Hotel.

– And this is my birthday party treat, is it? Me and Pinkie here, celebrating alone?

– No, no, don't worry. It's a quick booking. We'll be having our celebratory drinks later, Leanne.

A Night in the
Mountain Meadows Motel

Ed sat on the edge of the bed sneezing, fiddling with the remote, trying to get a stable picture out of the TV. He wanted to watch a news report on the morning crime. He couldn't find any tissues. He couldn't find any picture, and was getting increasingly annoyed with the old box. Ed and Betty had been released from the local police station and Officer Sheila Davies had informed them that the girl was in a stable condition at the hospital. She'd also said the nearest place to stay would be the Mountain Meadows motel. When they first unlocked the heavy electronic door to enter room 151, Betty had cheered. Ed almost puked. The room was filled with a dense plastic odour from a can of air-freshener that must have been sprayed dry. Its sticky fragrance sank into his pores and he hadn't been able to stop sneezing. His wife was in the bathroom, singing to herself. Unlike him she'd been wearing her pleasant face ever since they'd entered the bargain double bedroom.

Ed stood smoking, thinking he hadn't seen rain like it. He had to guess it was a signal. It was hitting the road and getting sprayed across the streets outside like a Cleveland Gatling gun, creating fresh potholes and soaking the side of the building. Maybe that was why he couldn't get the television set to work. He pulled the thin brown curtains shut, stepped away from the window and sat back down onto the bed. He stared at the fuzzy grey grains bobbling around on the small screen in front of him whilst listening to his wife sing.

Ed knew there was something happening between himself and his wife. He just didn't know what. Ed had been a cop for forty-five years and since he'd retired they had developed something queer between themselves. He felt it was cold, hollow. She'd say things to him and he wouldn't respond. He wasn't going deaf, he just couldn't react. She believed he was going nuts. She told him so. She'd asked him what was happening. He had to wake up. His wife was worried they were getting old. They were old. It happens. His wife was worried their marriage was falling apart. It was falling apart. Ed sneezed. It was his fault. He could accept that. It wasn't Betty's fault they were where they were.

With his big toe Ed picked at the twist in the scrubbed carpet and sneezed. It was *his* fault they were in this goddamn country. It was his branch of the family that had run away from this godforsaken place. They sure didn't like it back then, and, hell, had they ran. He knew what his great granddaddy had done. Hell, it was why he'd distanced himself from them. Unlike his wife, he knew all about the Mountain Meadows Massacre and the Mormon militia. But he was never a man who was gonna go on national television to apologise to a bunch of red Indians and corpses. He'd always thought the Meadows Massacre nothing more than a law-abiding skirmish.

He didn't want to be in this shabby small-town country, discussing the history of his kinsfolk with some goofball claiming to be related to him, but what choice did he have? What could he say? It was his fault. She didn't have a family. He knew he had to change. He had retired, and they had to re-start. He could do that without being on vacation in this concrete dump. Ed's toenail snapped as he dug it into the carpet and the blood sank into the nylon twist. Dang, he didn't like this place. He sneezed and watched as the snot sprayed across his ivory coloured foot. It was his fault they were in this country.

– Come on, you piece of shit.

Ed slapped the remote control onto the blanket covering the bed and glared at the TV. Betty yelled from behind the bathroom door.

– Ed? Ed, you okay, honey?

He took a step up to the TV and steadied himself in front of it.

– Yeah.

– The receptionist said they always serve a delicious meal. We better get going if we want to eat our supper, honey. You ready to eat, Ed?

Ed mumbled in response, put his hands on the top of the television set and leaned over the back. He studied the cables shooting out of the back of the foreign set and spotted what he thought was the aerial.

– What's the matter with this little country?

The wiry aerial was attached to the television with a piece of Sellotape and as Ed sneezed again, he yanked it off. He held the broken aerial in his hand and examined it. The aerial was a hand-crafted object. A coat-hanger. He threw it on the floor and took a step back from the TV. He wasn't surprised when he saw the picture was less fuzzy.

– Ed? You listening to me? Honey?

Ed sat back down on the edge of the bed as Betty came out of the bathroom and was startled at the ritzy appearance of his wife. Betty had bathed and dressed for the cheap supper at the Diner and Ed noticed she'd even put make-up on. He didn't think his wife owned any.

– Well? Are you coming down, honey?

– Uhh, yeah...

Betty was staring at her husband sitting on the bed in his

tracksuit trousers and yellow T-shirt, waving a remote control in his hand, pointing it at the TV set. Ed hadn't washed or changed since they'd got into the motel. He was continually rubbing his nose and trying to sneeze. Betty stood there in her new skirt and cardigan and watched him watch her. She'd put a bit of purple lipstick on for fun, and was worried she looked like a clown.

– So, you're not coming down?

– Uhhhhh, yeah, I'll be down in a minute. I just want to see this first.

Betty glanced at the small TV screen and spun on her heel.

– FINE.

His wife walked out of the room and slammed the door. The glass vase swayed on the sideboard. He flinched at her departure. That was his fault. He turned back to the TV. He couldn't get any other channel. He sat there and watched *The Simpsons*, massaging his reddened, raw nose. He had to accept change. He had to smile, godammit.

The muzak was filtered through the speakers hidden in the plastic plants situated around seating areas. Betty walked through the bar leading to the dining area. The place was almost empty. In one corner sat a young couple. Alone at the bar was an attractive lady and a few tables down from her sat a large blond man talking to another gentleman. Betty heard his American accent and she could see he was upset with something. He was finding it difficult not to shout.

Betty sat at a table unaccompanied, eating a wet salad. On the large white golden-rimmed plate opposite her was Ed's steak and fries, going cold. She picked at it now and again. It was on the day Ed retired from his job at the local police station she decided he had changed. The man couldn't smile anymore. He'd stare. He could stare. But he'd stopped smiling. And sure, Betty knew they'd grown apart over the years. She was hoping this little trip would've been fun. She had dreamt it could bring them together again. She sighed as she placed a cold potato fry onto her tongue. She'd been wrong.

*

A raven sat on the bonnet of his car. He waved his arms to scare it away and got in with Vicki. Masaki turned the engine on and reversed a few feet down his short drive, out onto the street. He softly revved the engine and listened, then sped along in his shattered car with Vicki, his wife having gone out for the night. They found the Mountain Meadows Hotel. Two stars. Large, with its own crazy golf course. Masaki drove into the car park, past a line of polished shiny vehicles. He noticed the entire car park was layered with a pale gravel, and he could feel his tyre roll and delicately crunch upon these stones.

Inside the hotel the young staff wore neat uniforms of a vibrant red. Masaki entered and stopped to take a deep breath, allowing the fragrant, chemically perfumed air to coat his face. Vicki pushed her father forward. She would not stay in the car. She urged him towards the almost lifeless hotel bar, where Caradoc Johnson and Joel Miller sat. They were at a table with a brown package placed in the middle. Masaki stiffened and then walked towards them. Joel Miller stood with a hand outstretched. Masaki shook the tight grip of a six foot tall American Mormon. The man held Masaki's hand for far too long.

– Mr Marsarkey! You made it. Please join us, and we'll get through the deal. Fast.

Caradoc Johnson clicked his tongue and shoved a finger in the direction of Vicki.

– Um, yes, that's my daughter. Vicki. She was not feeling well earlier, so I…

Caradoc scowled. Miller beamed at Masaki. The blond, blue-eyed giant was making Masaki's hand hurt. Miller let go of Masaki's crushed hand and said,

– Intelligent men know the family is very important. And you, Mr Marsarkey, you know what we want. What I want. I am the key figure. This is a business meeting, not a family gathering, I'm afraid.

Vicki placed a finger on her father's wrist. He smiled at his bright young daughter. She nodded at him, and went across the room to the bar. She sat next to a young woman who had patted the empty stool beside her. And from a few feet away Vicki watched her nervous father and the two men talk together at the table.

Miller had told Masaki to sit. Masaki remembered what he had decided to do. He eased himself onto a chair, shook his head, and asked,

– With respect, sir, what if I did not wish to take part in this? If I did not sign? If I did not take your filthy money, on principal. I believe Hank Evans, the writer, would have the moral courage not to sign. And if that were the case, I will not sign, either.

Miller glanced at Caradoc.

– This is what I've had to deal with over the last month, Jo. This nonsense.

– Okay, okay. Now I understand, you and Caradoc here have been having a little argument over the last few weeks. And these are truly engaging questions, Mr Marsarkey, that often pull strings. But I am not one to adjust once my offer is made. And, to continue, I don't care what you two boys have got going between you, I'm moving on with the project. I like the new script. We are making *BloodWood*. So all we need from you, Mr Marsarkey, is to sign. We're offering you and Hank Evans a fantastic deal here. We've sent him a copy of the script, and we've sent him an agreement to sign.

– What? You should not have sent him anything, said Masaki.

– Get in touch with the young boy. Take the money and run. The complete hand-over, okay? Done.

Masaki didn't have a single thought in his head. Miller picked up the form for him to sign and passed it to him across the table. Masaki snatched it from him and put it into his jacket pocket. Joel Miller threw his large hands into the air in pretence of applause at Masaki's actions. Caradoc Johnson looked like he was enjoying himself. Miller patted the script that was in the middle of the table and Masaki looked down at it.

– No.

– You would be making a mistake.

– No, he wouldn't.

The three men were startled when they heard the voice of Vicki. She had slipped away from the bar to remind them she was in the room and had been listening. She stepped forward and put her hands on her father's shoulders.

– I am here to represent my dad. You two've got ears. My dad is saying no.

– Ha, you don't want to be representing your papa, sweetheart.

– I'm here to represent my very strong-willed father.

– Ain't worth it sweetheart, said Miller.

– Yes it is. My daughter has faith in me. I do not wish to take your money. I'm a man of morals, said Masaki.

– Aw, Jesus.

– And I will return the advance payments you provided, as soon as I can, said Masaki. Our meeting is over gentlemen.

– Closed, said Vicki.

– Where are you going? asked Miller.

– I am going to get my hair restored.

– He's getting it done over in Spain, said Vicki.

*

Barry had managed to get out of the police station for his date and was searching around him inside the Mountain Meadows hotel bar. He couldn't see anyone he knew and when he focused on a woman sat at its far end he felt a touch annoyed. Donna just let him study her. For the five minutes he'd been there she was chatting to a small girl. The girl had jumped off her high stool and snuck over to a table to grab the hand and shoulders of a Japanese bloke who Barry assumed was her father. They left the place holding hands.

He looked at the bar in front of him then back down its length towards a formidable looking blonde escort. He didn't understand it. He guessed she was in her late twenties, in a tight red dress and sipping on a pint of lager in a bored, almost detached manner. Donna blew him a kiss and gave him a casual wink that somehow suggested she was not the least interested in her customer. He shuffled up to her and tried to smile.

– Hi, said Barry. I'm Brendan.

– I know, said Donna. And I am the Princess.

Donna opened her arms out in a wide display and grinned at the man in front of her.

– I don't normally do it like this, she said. I mean, s'usually in my place, like. But they'd checked you out. Said you was alright to meet, like. So…

– You were sent from The Stars Agency, right?

– Well, yeah. As I say, freelance. But also works with 'em sometimes, dun I?

121

– You're the Princess, right?

– Yep.

Barry rubbed his sausage-shaped fingers across his forehead and took a sip from his pint of bitter. Donna pulled at the top of her red dress. She tugged it down into place across the top of her chest.

– When I phoned the company, earlier? When I phoned them? The girl… she uh, she asked me who, who I wanted to… you know… which star… which actress or singer it was, I wanted to…

– Fuck, said Donna.

– Well, yes, yes, he said.

– S'alright.

– I know. But you see, my problem is… you see, I said to the girl on the phone, I said, when she asked me, who it was I wanted to…

– Fuck.

– Well, yes, said Barry. Exactly. And you? Well, you don't look like her, do you?

– Some people reckons I do.

Barry frowned and shook his head in disbelief. He almost laughed.

– No. I wouldn't say that, said Barry. No. You don't.

– Some people does.

– No.

– Well, others say I look like her.

– Ha, no, you? You don't look like the famous Motown singer, Princess Lovelace that I ordered. She isn't blonde.

Either Donna or the sodding phone operator had misheard which star this old sod had wanted to meet. In her head Donna certainly wasn't going to be taking the blame for the slip-up. And wasn't going to be informing Brendan that she was actually trying to look more like some Princess Loveluck, rather than the glamorous singer he'd booked, Princess Lovelace.

– Listen love, she said. You wanna do this or not? Cause I dun have to be sitting here chatting, does I?

Barry coughed and took another sip from his pint. The company must've misunderstood him. She wasn't bad looking. Maybe it wasn't a big offence. He'd already booked the room. He pulled at the tip of his nose and nodded at her.

– Okay.

– Good, she said.

*

Ed entered the motel bar wearing his pale blue suit and tie. He spotted Betty sitting in the restaurant and went straight on through. She was waving at him and pointing down to his cold golden plate. He walked up and joined her.

– I ordered your steak.

– Thanks, honey.

Ed sat and prodded at the thin piece of meat with his fork, picked up his knife and tried to cut it. His wife watched him yank a piece of meat from one end and put it into his mouth. He chewed slowly, and managed to swallow. Ed then managed to smile at her.

– You look cute tonight, he said.

– Thanks.

– Betty?

– What?

– This morning? In the car?

– Forget it, she said.

– I was foolish. I was stupid not to speak. I love you, honey. I've always loved you. You know that, sugar, don't you?

Ed stopped eating the shrivelled steak and looked at his

wife. He did love this woman. She was a part of him. A part of him he was fortunate to be able to share. He knew he needed to get out of the darn rut he'd fallen into. His mind was racing. Hell, he was thinking back to the last time they were even in a motel together. It was in Scranton, Pennsylvania. Seventeen years ago.

– Great steak here, honey.

Ed pointed at his dry steak. He smiled again.

– I need to change, I know. Maybe all this will help.

– What the hell are you playing at, Ed? I know you didn't want to come here. Didn't even know where Wales was until I showed you the map. Now you're telling me…

Betty had lowered her eyebrows. Her husband was still sadly smiling at her. Did she really believe a piece of cold meat could change him? No.

– It's been a long day, Ed.

– Yes. You're right. And tomorrow? Tomorrow will always be a better day.

Princess Loveluck

They ambled down the long, dimly lit corridor toward the hotel room. Donna had her arm half curled around Barry's waist. She tickled at the fat under his thin shirt. Her sharp fingernails scratched his pale skin. Her perfume was intense and its chintzy scent matched the quilted purple wall-paper. Barry counted doors on his right as they stretched on toward their room. Donna was whispering up into his ear. Her slight weight on his side was setting him off-balance. And she was beginning to sound sly.

– I know you from somewhere, dunnae? she asked.

– No, he said.

– Yes I does.

– I'm not from around here, Princess. Salesman. Travelling.

Donna kissed Barry lightly on his cheek. She let her tongue slide down to lick his neck and she laughed as he jumped away in quick fright. He had stopped walking, turned and pushed her to the side of the wall. She giggled softly and snuggled against his grip. At the end of the corridor Barry had spotted the two people who stood against the door next to his own booked room. They hadn't seen him and Barry glanced as Ed took his hand away from his wife's shoulders and opened the electric door to enter their room. She followed him in with a croaky laugh and a shake of the head.

*

Donna was lying in her panties on the double bed. She was looking up at the wall behind her which was almost covered by an enormous photographic mural of a Swiss mountain scene. Idyllic blue skies, and swathes of green pine trees, scattered across a snow-coated mountainside. Barry was sat on a chair. Dressed. Drinking. He wasn't going to be able to do anything else with those two next door.

– You think tha's a painting, love? asked Donna.

– No, said Barry.

– Thought not. Too detailed, innit? Nice though. Pretty like. Tidy hotel this, innit? My sister Leanne'd like it. Could live here, couldn't you? If you was rich, like? If you had enough money and was travelling round a lot. Tha's what some people does, innit, Brendan? That what you does, love?

– No.

– What d'you think it's like, then? she asked.

– What?

– You know, being rich?

– Being happy, I suppose, said Barry.

– Really? I dunno, cause I mean, say you was rich, right? But you had no friends. No-one tha' loved you, like? No-one tha' cared for you? No-one to talk to? No family, like? Wouldn't be happy 'en would you, Brendan?

– No, said Barry.

– You got any family? Anyone you has to look after, like? I'm looking after my dopy sister, right now.

– Not really.

– Oh. See the way I sees it is, you doesn't need to be rich to be happy, does you? Naw.

Barry took another drink. Donna raised her legs into the air and pulled her satin black panties down. She tossed them over her head towards Barry. He watched as she massaged her tanned tits and ran a finger leisurely down over her tattooed belly to the top of her shaved pussy.

– Right, 'en. Three rules, Brendan. Always with a rubber. No kissing. No anal. You ready?

– Ah, you, uh, you mind if we, if we just talk? Keep talking for a little bit? he said.

– You doesn't wanna fuck me? she asked.

– I don't think so. I mean, if that's alright with you? I've changed my mind, here. It's just… I just… I don't feel quite right, right now.

– Don't worry about tha', Brendan. I'll get you hard. It's my job, innit?

– No. I'd prefer to talk. If that's okay? he said.

– Okay. I can talk if you wants to talk, Brendan. Yep, can talk, alright. If tha's what you prefers to do. Talking's easy, innit? Talking. Yep. If tha's what you wants to pay me for, fine. Suit yourself, like. Yeah. Talk away, love.

– Thanks, he said.

Donna lay back down on the bed. Barry remained sat in the chair and took another sip from his glass of whisky. Speechless. Donna picked her head up from the pillow and looked at the wall. There was an enormous muffled bang next door. It sounded like two elephants stomping around the room and leaping onto a creaky bed. Donna looked over at Barry. She pointed at the wall.

– You married, Brendan? she asked.

– No. Divorced.

– So, wha' you wanna talk about, Brendan?

– It's Barry, he said.

– Who's he? she asked.

– The name. My name. It's Barry. Not Brendan. I lied.

– Oh. Right. Don't matter. You rich, Barry?

– Ha, police men around here aren't fucking rich.

Donna bounced up from the bed.

– Ha. Knew it. Knew I knew you. Works down the station, don't you?

She slipped over to the drinks cabinet and opened a mini-bottle of vodka. She was disturbed. She was thinking of her sister. She'd want her to mention *things*. Barry took a sip from his glass of whisky and threw his head back against the chair.

– My sister's been trying to get hold of someone down at that station all afternoon, said Donna. Anything exciting been going on?

– It's been a busy day. What's your sister's problem?

– Oh, she just wanted… look, it was nothing, really. I'm sure she'll get over it. But she wanted to… well she… she's the one that… maybe she'll try again…

Barry took her black panties off the end of his crossed leg. He held his arm out and handed her back her underwear.

– I'm going to have to quit this one, Princess. Thanks for the meet.

He took out his personal mobile phone card and email address and gave it to Donna.

– Please, give this to your sister. If she needs any immediate help. This is my number. Tell her to phone me. I'd be happy to speak to her. Or you.

Change of Plan

Donna had shot back down the valley and pulled Leanne out of her flat for the birthday drinks she'd promised. She hadn't even changed out of her tight red dress and heels and felt slightly out of place in the pub. The sisters were in The Greyhound, and they'd chosen the grubby pub to try and spite each other. Leanne had refused to go to Spangles, so Donna'd suggested The Greyhound instead. She was surprised when her sister agreed. The pub was a wreck. The customers were the same men that'd been coming in every night for the past thirty-five years, and the sight of the sisters, especially Donna, was unusual to their eyes.

The duo had been drinking and arguing for two hours and were beginning to feel the strain. They were supposed to be celebrating. They had made the snatch. But simply seeing the large, sad-looking dog in the flat when Donna was out doing her job had shoved Leanne right over to the other side. She did not want to kill Pinkie. It was not going to happen. Donna was furious. She drained her pint glass and slammed it back onto the sticky, beer-ringed table in front of her. She tapped her sister's knee and shrugged at the bar.

– Want another, 'en?

– Spose.

Donna got up, tried to steady herself, and hobbled across the room. Her high heels cut into the beer-rotten carpet. Nine men in the dimly lit pub all watched Donna stretch her tight, risen skirt back down and stumble to the bar. She could hear the gentle whistling and laughter again but couldn't be bothered to turn around. The sisters had been getting the stick since they'd walked in through the doors.

– Whooooeeeeeee Calamity!

– Nice fuckin arse, girl!

– Bet Clint would 'ave 'ad a shot in there, love, eh?

Donna stood at the bar with her back to the noise and waited to be served. Leanne was thinking she should have agreed to go to Spangles. She watched her raw-boned sister turn at the bar with two brimming pints of cider and a packet of peanuts hanging from her mouth. She was hoping the bitch'd trip. She was being applauded and cheered across the room back to their table. Donna shoved the pints down, spat the packet of peanuts onto the table and tugged her skirt further down her legs. She turned to the room with a scowl on her face.

– Keep it calm, Calamity, said the barman. Keep it calm.

– Ta, D, said Leanne.

– Yeah, cheers.

Donna sat. The sisters both took a long swig and Leanne opened the packet of peanuts. Donna scanned the dingy room with her snake eyes and swigged at her warm pint, but she got no response from the group of beer-bellied drinkers who averted their faces and downed their brown pints with a smug glee. They knew they had to be careful, they didn't want to tip their luck and have the young girls leave. Naked legs and perfumed hair was adding a bloody welcome glamour to their local pub.

A droopy looking git in a dirty brown suit had shuffled up to the table besides them and slumped himself down. He poked his tongue out of his mouth and wiggled it in their direction. The girls didn't bother to look at the drunken fool.

– Alright 'en ladies, mind if I joins you both? Name's Ivan.

– It ain't gonna happen, said Leanne.

– Yes, it is, said Donna.

– Donna, we've cocked this up. It's a dog. I'm not a dog killer.

– We didn't go all the way up the valley, nick his dog, screw the Dogman for a sword, and come back, not to kill it. Naw, we're making a blockbuster here Leanne, and Pinkie is gonna be the star.

– I ain't killing a dog, said Leanne.

– You don't have to kill it. I'll kill it. You simply record it, on the mobile. And we send it on to tha' fucker Boyd. It's revenge, Leanne. Revenge.

– I ain't killing no dog.

– Fucks sake, mun. It's a dog, said Donna.

– No. I ain't killing him, D, said Leanne.

Donna stroked at the tattoo of a dragon on her arm and felt the goose-pimples rise. She had the cop's card in her handbag and had thought it would be an extra gift to hand it over to Leanne after they'd completed the job. But her sister's stubborn nature on actually completing the task was unbelievably irritating. Her sister's flat-mate was a psycho. A man who liked to screw his dog, and who had viciously beaten her. Donna loathed the man more than she did and couldn't understand why Leanne didn't want to hurt him. To punish the man. Leanne patted down her hair, took a drink and stood.

– Where you going? said Donna.

– Uhh, take a piss?

Donna watched the back of her scrawny sister walk to the ladies' room. There were blue and yellow bruises on the back of her white legs and on the top of her feet where Boyd had smashed the heel of his boots down onto her ankles.

Leanne was looking in the toilet mirror. The make-up on

her face couldn't conceal the punch marks left from Boyd's fist. She turned away. They hadn't seen another woman in the pub all night and Leanne thought the toilet was looking cleaner than the one in her sister's new flat. It probably wasn't used that much. Since getting back, she'd made the phone call to the police three times and no bastard had answered. She couldn't be bothered to call them again. If no-one was answering she wasn't gonna be telling them all about Dogman and his boy.

She didn't know how many times she'd have to tell her sister she didn't want to kill the dog. Sure, it would hurt Boyd, but she didn't think it much of a birthday treat. It was in Cwmgarw park when she'd first met Boyd and Pinkie. Leanne had been sitting on a bench with her bags besides her. She'd been moved out of the council flats over in Tonfach. They were about to tear the damn things apart and the only people to be re-housed were the ones with family. Donna had been urging her to leave the valley. To move on down like she had. But Leanne felt she was due a break from her sister. She'd been thinking about the army. If only she got a bit more muscle in her arms maybe they'd accept her.

She was surprised when the odd looking fella and his enormous hound had stopped to sit and have a chat. She wanted to ignore the stranger, and did, until he started talking about his sixty-eight-year-old mam who'd recently committed suicide. Apparently the suicide note he'd found didn't consist of any lines of love and forgiveness, just a cold statement of malice and anger which placed her son and his dog at the centre of her death.

Leanne remembered she hadn't felt sorry for the man. She'd simply sat there on the bench as he talked on and on about his mother. He'd obviously noticed her bags were full of clothing and junk she'd carried from her flat and seemed to quickly realise her situation with the council accommodation. She'd only started to listen to Boyd when he suggested she wouldn't need any cash to rent the empty room over in his place, that is if she did need somewhere to stay. As long as she would cook for him, and keep the house tidy, she'd be able to stay there for free. He'd assured her they'd remain physically separate beings, but if any one did ask she'd always have to behave as if she was his partner. Leanne figured she was brave enough to take a look.

Boyd Evans hadn't seemed a nasty man. Leanne knew nasty men. She'd been with nasty men. Boyd was different. And he was excited by the fact Leanne had come to live in his home. He'd believed Leanne's presence made him appear rather more settled within the small community. Even if she was ten years younger than him, his neighbours, who were mostly all friends of his dead mother, were pleased to see he'd taken a step away from his dim life and managed to attract a woman.

Behind the curtains, though, Boyd had felt he had to teach Leanne basic lessons about his home and himself. It was only a few weeks after she'd moved in there that he let her into his darkest secret. He was a criminal – the 'Valley's Villain'. Leanne didn't like it. She'd learnt that Boyd was finding it difficult to make his payments on the large hound and so had come up with his robbery scheme. Leanne had tried to suggest it wasn't worth taking the risk. He didn't listen. And, Leanne told herself, she was living there for free so he could do what he wanted to do. They'd lived their separate lives without any trouble and Leanne had become comfortable in the place. She'd do the shopping, buy the food for the dog and the butcher shop meats for the man. It was only some nights ago that things had changed.

Leanne had returned from the supermarket that afternoon

whistling in the breeze. She'd walked in through the front door and into the living room to catch the sight of Boyd, naked and drunk, standing behind his massive dog. They were howling in what seemed like a celebratory unison. Boyd patted and stroked the head of Pinkie, as the dog slurped and licked. Time froze. Leanne dropped the two shopping bags to the floor and raised her hands to her face and screamed at the hideous image of Boyd manipulating his barking dog.

Boyd went into some wild drunken rage. She couldn't escape his assault. Stamping and punching followed. She passed out. She woke in a mangled bloody tangle lying in pain on the living room floor. Boyd and his dog were asleep on the living room settee. Leanne wiped her hair from her face and noticed a letter had been placed on her belly. Boyd had written it. It was her suicide note. Next to her feet she saw the rope. He was going to hang her. She quietly got up. He slept drunkenly with his legs wide open. She stood in front of him and pulled her foot as far back as she could.

She could hear the man wailing in hysterical pain at the end of the street. When she appeared on her sister's doorstep, miles down the valley, she looked a battered, bloody wreck. Leanne knew the look in her sister's eye would've frightened both Boyd and his dog.

Donna downed her pint and kept her attention away from the arsehole sitting at the table next to her. He was out of his head and for some reason couldn't stop waving at her. Every now and again his annoying hand would flick across the corner of her eye as he twiddled his fingers into her vision. Leanne came back to the table.

– Come on. Let's go.

– We ain't going nowhere, Leanne. Not till we sort this out.

– It's sorted. We ain't killing the dog, said Leanne.

Donna was dismayed to hear the news. Her younger sister had taken control.

– Seems like we got ourselves into a bit of a situation here, said Donna.

– It ain't any situation. I ain't into killing animals, said Leanne. It's where I stand. It's a dog. He was manipulated as much as I was.

– Fine. Well we could just go get us someone to beat the freaky shite into a bleeding pulp. Know people who'd enjoy it.

– No, no. I should have gone directly to the police. I shouldn't have run sobbing to you. I shouldn't have brought you into my mess. This man is dangerous, Donna.

– Well sure, you're right. And we also know how much the perverted prick likes his dog. Fact is, we got us his dog, said Donna. Bit of a problem, maybe?

– You're right. So here is what we do. I've been thinking it over. We just need to change the plan.

– You wha'? said Donna.

– We're still gonna make us a little film Donna. And we're still gonna be sending it on up to the freak. But, it ain't a snuff flick, is it? Naw, we don't kill us the dog, Donna. No.

– Then what?

– We just use it, as ransom, like. Happening all over the U.S.A., innit? It's called dog-napping. We claim we'll execute the dog. Cut it into little pieces. Chop off its hind legs. Cut off its tail. Scissor off the ears. Yank out the tongue and poke out the two eyes. We'll do it all, lest the shite comes back fast. With the cash. He's got money. It's a ransom demand, innit? Revenge. Punishment. Right?

– So we don't kill Pinkie? said Donna.

– S'right, said Leanne.

The sisters were mute.

135

– Okay. Great, said Donna.

– Good, said Leanne. Come on, I've had enough of this place.

– Bet you'd both like to see it though, eh? said the forgotten old man at the table nearby. Go on, I dares you.

The drunken man waved at them and pointed at his groin. His trousers looked as if he hadn't washed them for the last fifteen years he'd worn them. Dark marks spread across his thighs and the broken zip was pulled only half way. The drunk peeped up and gave Leanne a wicked wink. Donna glanced at her sister. Leanne smiled. The two sisters faced the fool, raised an arm towards him and together they delicately pushed him on either side of his chest to watch him sprawl and tumble backwards onto the floor. They gave each other a high-five, laughed, and left.

DAY TWO

Past Lives

Ed lay snoring beside Betty and she gently eased herself out of bed. She stood and walked to the motel bathroom with a long feeling of regret bubbling up in her stomach. She sleepily sighed. She knew they should never have come to this country. And it was to be her fault. A weary heaviness swamped her chest, ready to burst free in sobbing angst. She nervously took a large breath, scratched at her earlobe and sighed. She was perplexed. Had she really done the right thing? Was Ed actually ready to change? This was what the big man had at least suggested he'd try to do last night.

She found her toothbrush and began to clean her brittle teeth and swollen gums. It hadn't seem long ago when she'd first noticed Ed, *changing*. And it was for the worse. He'd wake and sit in his chair every day. Barely moving his head in the heat. Waiting for his lunch, his dinner, and his bedtime. She couldn't stand being stuck in the same room as the immobile man. The house used to be her space. Then Ed retired, and she realised they weren't holding hands. They were different.

Betty's friends assured her Ed wasn't developing a medical condition. The same thing had happened to Martha's husband, Al. It was a passing mental stretch caused by the act of retirement. He'd be back to normal in a good few weeks, she was told. Those weeks dragged into months, and then about a year, and Betty got lost. She spat the toothpaste and her blood into the sink and rinsed her mouth with tap water.

For years the couple hadn't been one hundred percent practising Mormons. They simply didn't have the immediate family like all the others. But, living in Salt Lake City, it was often impossible not to be aware of the latest Mormon fad. After the Osmond family did it on National TV, most Mormon families across the whole state of Utah were eager to trace their damned origins. The Church of Jesus Christ of the Latter Day Saints had stacked up the largest genealogical database archive in operation. Some computer whizz-kid had managed to save and place the names and dates of every Mormon since time began onto their website. If you had Mormon blood in you, and a few dollars in your pocket, you'd be able to surf their system online or visit the Central Library and trawl through the archive. Betty's best friend and her husband had already done it. They'd gone to the library with a dusty package containing forgotten family details and came out skipping in delight. Her friend found out her kinsfolk used to be English landowners from a place near Southampton. It was a marvellous result and she bragged about it to all her pals, at every coffee-drop, shopping trip and telephone call, in what was becoming an increasingly annoying English accent.

Betty took another sip of tap water. It was early in the morning. There was barely any noise in the motel and Ed still hadn't moved. She moved from the sink, pulled the end of her nightgown up over her thighs and waddled over to the toilet. She was ready to burst. She remembered that she had told herself back then she wasn't being jealous of her friend's success and would only try out the 'family-search' malarkey as a small-time hobby. It was something to help take her mind off the Ed situation. She knew Ed wouldn't have approved of it if she'd told him what she planned to do. So she didn't.

The box-shaped library built near Temple Square always seemed to be full of family members searching for their past.

When she had walked into the hushed building there was a flutter of excitement in her palms, though she found the archive department slightly daunting with the lines of faces staring at silent screens. Serious teenagers whispering to their wide-eyed parents. People sat in front of computers, or dark microfilm sets, many of them with earplugs attached and hands covering their mouths. They were like a bunch of NASA flight controllers, waiting for the big news.

A young library worker had been quick to scurry up to Betty and introduce herself. She was one of the seventy strong team of LDS church members who volunteered on a daily basis to help the new customer at the library. She thrust her brown-sleeved arm out at Betty.

– Good morning, Ma'am, I'm Nephilia, how may I help?

Her volunteer had been disappointed when Betty told her she hadn't brought any official documents with her to the library. She didn't have any. She was even more disappointed when she couldn't seem to find a written word about Betty's darn maiden name. Yendell? They both felt she'd failed. For an hour Betty had paid her excited assistant to search on the computer, trawling through thousands of digitised archives. Her own surname, Yendell, didn't even exist. And Betty wouldn't waste another dollar on the damn hoax. She was upset. The Mormon Family Website wasn't producing the information she'd expected. Her forlorn assistant suggested they carry on and do another search, to try and find another link. Betty's marital surname. Her husband's family. Evans.

– Be a ducky surprise for him, surely? she said.

It was her own family she wanted to find. Betty was less interested in the Family Tree on Ed's side, and she wasn't going to be investigating details about Ed's heritage as part of some kind of crazy hobby. But she weakened, and gave the insistent woman what she knew of Ed's background.

141

She was soon being told about Ed's great-grand-daddy, a Nathan Evans. A faithful man who had travelled far from a beautiful, spiritual world, a country called Wales. He was one of the ten thousand Mormons who emigrated from south Wales in the 1840s. He'd travelled across the States and became a minor figure in Utah law enforcement.

Back home that day Betty sat in the kitchen opposite a mute Ed, having just finished their evening meal. She'd left the library knowing she would not be making a return. Betty did not want to tell Ed. She stirred her coffee, saw a brown hair floating in the tepid drink, and pulled it out of the mug. They'd eaten the fried chicken and white gravy dish from her Weight Watchers guide book. And she sat, picking at the dried onion rings stuck to the table top, half wondering where the hair had come from. She'd tried to wipe the table clean before they sat, but the dried onion wouldn't budge. The plastic cloth on Ed's side was even worse but she knew he didn't care. Ed stood and robotically picked up the empty plates. Betty watched him and listened to the metallic echo as the old man started to wash and bang their dishes clean in the stainless steel sink.

After four days of keeping a guilty silence Betty changed her mind. Sure she couldn't just tell Ed, he probably knew his family history and her trivial research would only irritate him, but she guessed if she were to do a bit more research, she might be able to interest the big man. A retired man often had a hobby. Could it become his hobby? She'd find out a few more details and hand them over to him, an unfinished project to try and propel his attention forward. He might even thank her.

She didn't want to meet up with the stale scent of the library again. What she did instead was turn on the ancient Apple Mac computer they had in the spare room. Betty decided she could dodge the official family software package buried in Salt Lake's Family Library. And so what Betty did was put out an ad in every on-line newspaper operating in the country of Wales to ask if there was anyone out there related to a distant Nathan Evans. She was delighted when she got the immediate response: *Yes*.

It was an email from the Evans family in the Cwmgarw area. A Clayton Evans, who was the son of Michael Evans, who was the son of a Burton Evans, who was the son of Joseph Evans who was the elder brother of Nathan Evans, who was the father of George, who became the father of Ed Senior, who had left Ed Junior as a young boy alone with his dying mom in the Mormon Orphanage in Tuba City, Utah, circa 1939.

For the next four months Betty and Clayton emailed each other every Tuesday afternoon. Betty would sneak into the spare room, turn the dusty computer on and wait for three minutes with her hands resting around a large mug of coffee set on the table in front of her. Ed didn't know what she was doing, and she assured herself that she was only doing it for him. She'd often notice her reflection in the green computer screen and try to dismiss the fact that she was wearing one of her most expensive blouses with a newly bought skirt to match.

History had never been Betty's favourite High School subject as a kid. It was a class taught by Miss Waltstein and she'd rather spend the hour watching a black fly crawl across the windowsill than listen to her whiny voice. And so it was from her Welsh mystery man that Betty began to learn fascinating new snippets of Mormon history. Apparently, Ed's ancient Welsh relative, Nathan, was a man fortunate enough, favoured even, to have personally met the famous Elder, Captain Dan Jones. Clayton emailed her:

from:clay.ev@hotmail.co.uk
to: ElizabethEvansmormon-info-search@gmail.com
subject:evansmormonfamilyhistory

Hi Betty,

How's Ed? Hope your both feeling a little better t'day after
the flu problems. not had it myself yetthis time round – tho u
alwasy now it'll come. Right?!!

Anyhow,

__bit of detail here about the Grrreat Danny Jones – (amazed
they didn't teach you this stuff at High School!!!!!!!!) – me and
my cousin, Hank been knowing it always. for years. anyway
– Capt Jones – Man was a Mississippi Steamboat Captain –
afloat the boat – Maid of Iowa – became the finest Mormon
Preacher ever!!!! And all cause he met up with (and wait for
it...................some aclaimed mudered???) the
original founder of The Mormon Church, th egolden-boy...
.... Joseph Smith!!! The 2 men met in the Iowa State
prison, back circa1844 (Danny J for selling items they didn't
like inthe State ofIowa__and JoS because the townsfolk hate
d the growing religious trend of hisMormonism). !

Sneaky Jo managed to convert – CptDan – to the religion
ofour Mormon faithood. He thought Dan had good voice on
him and would make a great preacher. told him it was hislife
duty to become an Elder of the Mormon Faith. Bingo!Dan
converted a nd Jo Smith instructed him_

""it is uor immediate responsibility to do take the trip. The
journey. To go from AmericaUSA-to the small state ofWales-
from where Captain Dan had originally come. ""

It was theCptn's hjob to comeand convince, and convrt, the
Welsh peoples. To Get th em into MormonChurch. Build up

the weight in numbers. (Minor Point here, Betty – JosephSmith was once played by VincentPrice in the terrific 1940 movie, Young Frontiersman! – if you ever get a chance to see it – has all the details – not CormanHorror stuff but good) – anyway…

Clayton had researched the origin of his family in micro detail, and he was delighted to be able to give Betty all the information he could via almost indecipherable e-mails. Ed's relative was a young man who had joined the Mormon road-show on a simmering-hot summer night in south Wales way back in 1844. And like many in the rough and raw Aberdare audience of miners and ironworkers, he was a suffering man. A drunkard who had lost his faith and preferred to attend one of the fast growing public houses rather than one of the recently built chapels in the area.

The Zion Trumpet taught him of the glorious healing aspects, hidden in the new faith of Mormonism, and he had listened with sober intent to the short-arsed Minister Dan Jones who preached with a fiery vision from the stage. Like many others in the audience Nathan cowered in shame and fear, and when ordered up on stage by this little man he did so in awe. He was to voice his own, individual concerns aloud and for the public ear, and was seductively told by the inspirational Minister that he, Nathan Evans, would need to join the long queue for the Induction Ceremony for the short trip to Salvation, aka America.

Three days later a hungover Nathan awoke aboard a packed boat leaving Liverpool docks. He found out that his immediate conversion had placed him in the Mormon Tabernacle Choir, and he was expected to be one of the hundreds of impressive Welsh voices in that throng. Nathan was slightly disturbed by the speed of the Mormon Church but the converted group were already set on their long mission to join their hymn-singing brethren far away, across the Great Plains of America. They started singing in fear and hope against wild seas and raging winds.

They travelled across America for days, singing together for comfort in their creaking wagons. For miles the sound of these men and women, singing with a hidden dread, would float across the dry new land. The muscles in their stiff jaws and upright bodies adjusted to the bounce and wobble of the hard wooden seats, and the pulchritudinous songs that came out of their open mouths became harmonised on the tough trail West.

Native Americans were perplexed by this musical outfit and mainly ignored them. The ignorant travellers would often pass by, singing out, unaware they were being watched. The dusty Welsh settlers became a sort of national American institution in their ability to sing and travel, oddly unharmed by the warring tribes of the plains. The thought of the un-loved wife and bullying elder brother that he'd left behind in Wales only added to Nathan's happiness and his sense of a new-found destiny. A manifest destiny in a new-found land.

Betty flushed the toilet and walked back to the bedroom. Ed hadn't moved. His snoring had ceased and she believed he'd wake shortly. She stood by the window and looked out. A thin light was beginning to trickle through a gloomy sky. Today was the day. For months Betty had wondered what Clayton looked like and whether they could perhaps ever meet. He was family, after all. Betty had been getting to the point where she thought she should tell her husband about her internet correspondence. To travel to Wales to meet up with Clayton Evans would be a delight, yet she knew it would be a difficult task, perhaps impossible even, to persuade him. He wouldn't care for all this flat history. But

146

the day Clayton wrote to her about the Mountain Meadows Massacre in 1857 was the day Betty knew she'd have something with which to influence Ed. He was a lawman after all, surely he'd be keen to learn about his family's past involvement in that famous crime.

from:clay.ev@hotmail.co.uk
to: ElizabethEvansmormon-info-search@gmail.com
subject:familyhistory-mountainmeadows

Hi, Betty,
You never heard about the Mountain Medows stuff???!!! Wow!
i'm amazed. The Massacre? – the Mountain Meadows!? Never!No? It's been something hung ovr our heads for years!! that's justin Wales. ! and u don't know anything about it! M.M!!!!!!!!!!!??????

O.K. See, it all happened in1857, when a number of Christian-Dutch settlers – (that's wht they called them then, but they were basically 'Deutchies' – dangerousGermans))!!! it was these men, women and children – they were toldd by the American Governmet to find settlingland in u'r sweetMormon State of Utah. it was a bit of a nasty political decision by those high lions in charge

American president, James Buchanan and his comrades came up with a wicked plan – a decision made for the sole puirpose of breaking up the disliked and then hated brand of growwwing Mormon popularity. See, at first AmericanChristians admired the bravery of these Mormon settlers. could only laugh at the fictional Book of Mormon 9cheekyb*st*rds)!! But the growing wealthand size of theMormon State? – began to disturb American governmnts. .when the innosent Dutchie settlers arrived. in the USA? They were sent by those officials to what they were told was a free state. UTAH!! They were told, they could make it their own!! Course not, causewhen they got there Mormon Elders were not a happy bunch! and they had the cleverbrains to come up with a sweetplan of their own!!!! The Fight Back!

Now this next bit Betty, this really is theCormanhorror stuff11!!!, so take a break. habe a breath.Please. i do not wish to upset you with it all – If you do not wish to read this, then please, turn away : – !!!

These Deutchie people settlers were allbrutally murdered by a group of Mormon Militia!!! – all disguisede as Native Americans!
And it was the Welshman, Nathan Evans – our pastrealtiveand and his new Mormon family unite – who took charge of all the massacres. discharged them all. Slaughtered bodies were simply left to decompose and rot on the open plains of the Utah State for two longyears.

Clayton was astounded his American relatives did not know about their past connection to the bloody Massacre. According to Clayton, it was the Mayor of Salt Lake City himself who, a while ago, had asked all those Mormon families with the surname Evans to stand up in public and apologise on national television.

They knew all about the massacre in Cwmgarw. The Evans family had suffered the guilt and the humiliation for a long period. Some Evans's had even changed their surname. Betty had to explain she didn't know anything about her husband's involvement in the massacre, whereas Clayton claimed his own family had borne the brunt of it all their lives. They thought it part of their ancestral duty.

Clayton was eager to meet over the issue. He gave Betty his address. He sent her photos of himself and other members of his family and Betty exchanged images of herself and Ed. The gentleman invited Betty and her husband to make the trip. It would be a joy to meet a section of his family. Betty was pushed to the edge and finally fell. She brought herself to show her husband the truth. To tell him about her secret search. This was who he was. And now they were here, in Wales. They had come to south Wales. And they had not even told Clayton they were going to be there. Ed and Betty were to turn up as a surprise. She watched as Ed opened his eyes. He noticed her looking at him. Today he would meet his distant family. It was Ed's family, it was Betty's idea.

Daily Routines

Hank blinked. When he had got out of bed that morning he'd been pleased with himself. He had a boner that would've impressed a silverback gorilla. But by ten he was getting irritated. The bugger wouldn't leave. The new medication was making him giddy. And almost every muscle and tendon in his body seemed to ache. Things got worse when he answered his father's mumbling hungover phone call and he learned about the shooting yesterday up at the station.

His dad had heard about Cheyenne and the terrible incident at the petrol station when his younger brother, Hank's uncle Barry, had phoned in from the police station. His dad knew Hank was coming out of the hospital yesterday and hadn't dared call him. He'd try and see him later. Hank told him not to. He had a lot of things to do. Cheyenne was lucky, and in a stable condition up at the hospital. Hank's heart seemed to flap when he realised he'd have to return there. He didn't want to be hobbling across town with a pole between his legs but he swiftly took his jacket and rushed to leave the flat. He paused inside the front door when he once again noticed the large brown envelope lying on the doormat.

Hank should never have sat back down. For an hour he sat reading *Bloodwood*. The script had been sent by an American producer who was offering both himself and Masaki a small amount of money to sign a legal agreement which detached themselves from any copyright issue. *Bloodwood*. Hank was furious with Masaki. He sat turning pages, to read scenes that simply did not exist in his *Lilies of the West*. He didn't know what deal Masaki had got them into but Hank knew this was not his script.

He ran his hand over his shaved scalp and groaned in fury. He believed his original script was a sombre but fictional romantic tale. It was to be set in the Mormon State of Utah just days before the Mayor of that city was supposed to have made an apology on national TV for the Mountain Meadows Massacre of 1857. It was about a local historian, Tom Evans, who falls in love with a Native American woman, Martha. From what Hank could tell it had been re-written as an overblown comedy, the historical detail re-jigged, the moral tale removed, and then sold, with random blood and violence, as *BloodWood*. It was now more of a harum scarum historical romp rather than the artistic masterpiece he believed it once was. All he had to do was sign.

BloodWood. It contained Hank's characters and a number of key scenes from his script but his own sorrowful transatlantic drama, replete with historical meaning and contemporary relevance, had been torn up and mangled into a rambling tale, grotesque and leering and written to expose the hideous nature of the Victorian Welsh and their industrial hell of an existence from which, half crazed and criminal, they had to escape. It was a script written to lay the horror of the Mountain Meadows bloodshed and barbarity directly, and only, at the feet of the transplanted Welsh converts to Mormonism.

His own script had started out, after his film course had ended, as a self-reflexive parody of the many trashy Westerns put on American television back in the early sixties and seventies. Hank himself had studied those shows and it was those black and white TV serials which his own central character would later remember in a string of distorting nightmares. He becomes an historian, one involved in researching the bloodthirsty work of the Mormon settlers. *BloodWood*, however, used his character to look back in time at a world which is presented as a cross between *Blazing Saddles* and *Back to the Future*.

He thought he knew Masaki. He believed him to be his friend. He didn't understand how Masaki could have committed this betrayal. He wanted to phone Masaki, to know the reason why this new script had come about. It was Masaki who had told him he adored his script. Hank had believed the cheap bastard.

He pushed his second pair of old glasses up and rubbed his closed eyes as the searing hurt of the betrayal deepened inside him. He stood abruptly and yelped at the pain that shot up from his ankle, and looked bitterly at the plaster casing around his left foot. He wouldn't let that fool Tetchy get away with stealing his trainers. He limped to the kitchen. He had to visit Cheyenne. Things to be done, as well as his 'effing panda duties that afternoon. Could he do them? He wasn't superman. Yesterday he'd had a fit-fest. He felt bad. Real bad. The sodding things would normally occur once every two or three weeks. After he took the plunge, if he could spend days tired and lying down in his bed, he would. And then there was the foot. Or the ankle, or whatever he had broken, split or strained. That in itself was painful, there was certainly a good reason they had put the plaster on it up at the Cwm hospital. He knew if he was to try and do all his tasks, it'd certainly be a tough fucking day.

He saw his new tablets and swallowed a couple more, only to immediately panic. He wondered, had he already taken his morning dosage? Shite, he knew he had. These fucking pills were strong. He tried to tell himself he hadn't touched them that morning, and tried to breathe calmly. Should he try and puke? He noticed there was water left in the kettle and turned it on. He looked at the telephone. He wouldn't speak to Masaki over the phone. He was going to meet the treacherous bastard. He listened to the kettle boil. He watched the kettle boil. When it had boiled he made himself an instant coffee. He picked up the mug. He sipped at it. He waited for it to cool.

Cheyenne would agree with his new-found aims, all of them, from Tetchy to Masaki to the panda. He would deal with everything. He would not allow his ailment to restrain him. Hank Evans was an epileptic. He was not a weak person, he would indeed stand tall amongst them. This was his chance. He was clear about it. His mother would have been proud. And he would leave this forlorn valley, this unpleasant land and all of the black sheep who were its forsaken inhabitants. There was no other way. On his way back to his chair he stopped by the film contract. Took a pen from the table and signed.

Mormons Meet the Family

They left the motel early, wearing their Sunday best as they prepared to meet the unseen and unknown. Ed was in his pale blue suit and tie, standing tall. Hair and moustache glistening, a fixed smile on his mouth. Betty had the lipstick on again. Flowers on her lap. She was pleased with her husband. He'd washed and groomed himself properly that morning. Yesterday's rain had turned into snow overnight and now a cold white sun was happily burning away. The curling terraces in the valley beneath them were shining in the morning light.

– What do you think of this place, Ed?

– I wouldn't want to go knocking on doors round here.

– When was the last time you did that, honey?

– Ha yeah, guess so, sugar. Them young cops these days, huh? They probably all do it via the net anyway. Googlesearch. No need to knock on doors. Ain't no footwork necessary.

Betty was restless after last night. Confused. Maybe it was the event in the petrol station that had brought them together or was it simply being in a foreign land? She knew they were closer now than they'd been in a long while, and it seemed curious. Ed had made advances in his life last night. Betty saw Ed had become eager to step away from his anxieties. She was certain he could accept his new position. That of a retired man. A man who faced the black hole. Yet dang, he could face his future with his loving wife besides him also. He was ready to do that.

The hire car Ed drove had lost its rattle. He leaned towards the door and listened tentatively, expecting to hear the metallic noise in his ear. Nothing. He was upset. It had been part of the journey coming up to the place and he'd grown used to it. The car felt different without the noise. He was sure he had heard it yesterday. It was part of the car. Ed straightened up. He wiped the frown from his face and smiled. He didn't need to hear a loose screw rolling around inside a car door. He could talk to his wife.

– You nervous, Ed? said Betty.

– Hah, no.

– Don't worry, I bet they're nervous too.

– What?!

– Clayton and his family, sugar.

– Oh, yeah, sure, said Ed. They didn't know we were over here, right?

– They soon will.

The motel receptionist had given Ed directions on how to get to the Bevan Estate, or Texas-2 as the locals had liked to name it. They were a couple of miles away from the motel and it seemed a gentle ride, despite the light snow falling. It was only when Ed came to the edge of the fragile estate that he began to strain behind the wheel. The car seemed too big as it crept on through the narrow streets. Streets full of screaming, red-faced kids waiting for a bus, and suspicious parents who stood inquisitive on doorsteps and watched the unfamiliar car as it worked its way awkwardly past their homes. Ed squeezed the car between a line of vehicles parked on either side of the road. Betty saw the tip of her husband's tongue pressing out against his upper lip. They turned onto the wider main street and Ed relaxed. He gestured towards Betty's big handbag on her lap.

– Oh Ed, come on sweetheart. We've been over this already, she said.

– I know, I know, I'd just like to make sure. Get it straight.

– Okay.

Betty took out the photograph which Clayton had sent to her. It was an old Polaroid of his family, sitting around a Christmas dinner table. She held the photo up and Ed glimpsed at it.

– Right, okay, okay, so the one in his thirties on the left with the blue sweater on, that's Clayton, right?

– Yes.

– And in the yellow, with the pink hat on her head, that's the wife. Jean? said Ed.

– Yes. And the fat young boy at the end there, is their son. Marshall. The one sitting next to him is his cousin, said Betty. He's called Hank.

– That's an old photo though, that must have been taken a long while ago, right? Why did they send us that one?

– Maybe it's because they all look so happy.

– What did you send them of us?

– Oh, a few snapshots, holiday stuff mainly. The one of you on the boat with Rob, the day you caught that fish. The one of me, after I'd been on my diet, oh, and our wedding day photo.

– Our wedding day photo? Why?

Betty put the Polaroid back into her bag and pointed at the small roundabout at the end of the main road. Ed hadn't been able to get the Sat-Nav working properly and simply agreed.

– I think this is it, she said. We turn right at the roundabout. We get onto the road below the Bevan estate and take the first turn on the left, just a hundred yards, take another left and it's 57 Orchard Close.

– Okay. Got it. Here we go, said Ed.

They were like travellers crossing the frontier. The lights turned green and Ed drove into a section of the rundown estate built alongside the Cwm mountain. The grey street was

156

covered in litter blown about from an upturned bin. Clayton had told Betty that his estate lived in shadow almost every day because it had been built only metres away from the enormous mountain behind it. The residents lived in a lingering darkness. Betty pointed at a turn on the road in front of them.

– Orchard Close. Over there, said Betty.

– Ok. Seen it. Not exactly pretty, huh?

– Ed, behave, come on.

Ed pulled the car up outside the house, turned the engine off, and peeked out of the window. He rubbed at his brow and felt Betty's hand touch his arm.

– I'd better get their presents out of the boot.

He opened his door and stepped out of the car onto the icy pavement, holding the door tightly to keep his balance. He gave the door a shake. The rattle had truly disappeared. The screw must have gotten stuck somewhere. Ed shook his head and slammed the door shut. Betty joined him on the pavement. She pointed towards the newly painted house. The house seemed to stand out in the street above the rest. The garden was neat. Their fence wasn't broken. The house next door had a goat tethered to a stick on its front lawn. The one next door to that had a burnt out car lying on its side in the yard. Clayton's looked neat. Betty rang the doorbell with a sense of excitement and a woman in her fifties, wearing a pink dressing gown, answered. She looked at them. Betty stepped towards her and smiled.

– Uh, Jean? Jean Evans?

– Yeah?

– Hi. I'm Betty. Betty Evans, and this here is my husband, Ed Jr. We are the long lost family, all the way from the U.S. of A.

Jean Evans turned around and screamed into the house.

– Marshall. GET YOUR ARSE DOWN HERE, NOW.

157

Ed and Betty were sitting on a sofa with cups of cold tea. There was a plate of biscuits on the table in front of them, which they hadn't touched. A dainty white Christmas tree was next to the TV, and tinsel hung around the four walls. Jean and her teenage son, Marshall, sat on the chairs opposite. Marshall's fat stomach strained against the T-shirt he wore. It was too small. His head was pointing downward and his anxious mother was trying to hold onto her panic.

– He's not a stupid boy, she said.

– He's a man, said Ed.

– He's a mathematical genius. A wizard on the computer. Trying to follow his cousin, Hank. Get a place in university, like. They reckoned Marshall could've basically chosen any career from about the age of six, if it wasn't for his social problems, like.

– Yeah, his problems. You listening to this, Marshall? Your problems, said Ed.

– Yes, sir.

– Good. Cause *your* problems are basically our problems now, aren't they?

– Ed, please.

– Betty, the genius sitting over there has made us cross the goddamned world, to this spot, in order to meet up with a family that don't even exist.

– Ed. Please don't swear in front of Jean and Marshall here.

– Your son ever tricked people before, Jean?

– Oh yes, Ed. He's been in the bloody papers hasn't he? Embarrassing me and his dad. He's doing his community services today. Working this afternoon. Has to go round doors, knocking. Giving people information. For the council.

– They let him knock on their doors?

– It's punishment, said Jean.

– All because he tricks people?

– Yes. People looking into their past mainly, searching for the family links. Americans. Always Americans. Lots of Welsh Americans, see. Giving them all this false info about their family trees, like. Mainly Mormons, it is. It's a criminal obsession. Him and his cousin. Hank's done a script. Marshall here, he was the one put it on the net, don't think Hank knows anything about it like, but Marshall got them the finance for the film going. Yeah, them two. Got a real thing about the Mormons. It's the school, see.

– So, you've had people come over before?

– You're the first ones that've actually visited, Ed.

Ed looked at his wife and back at Jean. He wasn't smiling.

– Have you ever been to Wales before? said Marshall.

Ed stared at the young man. There was a stillness in the room.

– This is our first time, said Betty.

Ed took out a cigarette and started to light up.

– Do you mind if I smoke, Jean?

– YES.

– Oh.

– …I mean, yes. It's jus tha' I'd prefer it if you'd do it outside, like. It's my own habit. I'm trying to quit, you see, Ed.

Celebrity Status

Cheyenne was right pissed off with Hank. She had to remind the nerd, after the TV people had come round, that they were there to film her. Not him. This was her chance. Not his. It was her arm the bullet had gone through. Smashing into her flesh. Tearing through her skin and jumping out into the cigarette packets. The bullet had taken off her best tattoo. She'd had a three hour operation. Fifteen inches of stitching. And half a breast left. And everyone was saying how lucky she was. Well, she wasn't smiling. It hadn't happened to them, had it? It was her.

She'd been lying in the hospital for thirty-seven hours and it wasn't like anything she'd seen on TV. The pain in her arm and side was monster. Hank had made it worse. The doctors had sorted it, given her all the medication, and left her. She felt dumped. They believed if Cheyenne hadn't been wearing her silicone tit lifters the bastard's bullet would have gone right from her arm and straight into the middle of her chest. Killed her. Bone dead. Instant. Instead, the lead travelled up her arm, ricocheted into the silicone and bounced out past her head. The big American fella had told her she'd been lucky.

After the operation yesterday morning, the police wanted her in an isolation unit at the back of the hospital. And she was lying there with a numb throbbing coming from her bandaged parts. A pain that was writhing itself around her body, from her arm down to her little feet, like a worm.

She was pleased when her mam and dinky brother had

come by yesterday. And pleased they hadn't brought her smug-faced nan, dressed in her lacy, best funereal garments, but a copy of *Hello*. Her nan was apparently seething. She claimed it should have been Nelson or the Pentrecoch Panda in hospital, not her grand-daughter. She was looking forward to the game to hurl abuse at the pathetic mascot figure. There was a new job interview over at Family-Land, so Cheyenne's mam wouldn't come in today. After her interview, she'd have to make sure Coleen, her best mate, had everything in place for Geronimo's party. Cheyenne knew her dad wasn't going to appear. He wouldn't even know it had happened. The arsehole didn't like coming off the mountain. Playing his games. Barking. Her dad wouldn't know about her fame. She didn't care.

When her mam had left, her brother had managed to hide. Cheyenne only knew he was in the room when something started beeping and a nurse had to run in. Geronimo had detached electric wires at the back of the hospital monitor next to her bed and it started flashing to the accompanying noise of some hysterical danger wail. The nurse was enraged with her brother. She'd made him stand there crying whilst holding the copy of *Hello* up for Cheyenne to read. The size of the plastic tits on those models was beautiful.

It was the main reason she had to thank the shite for shooting her. 32A to a 36D. Both her mam and Cheyenne had agreed, long ago, that her tits weren't really big enough for her body. She wasn't going to grow them anymore. She needed the boob job. It was what a celebrity did. But four grand was a lot of money. So they saw this as a great opportunity to try and get it sorted. They'd stitched her shot tit back together, but it wasn't the proper shape anymore. A second operation was due. And Cheyenne wanted the silicone implants. Her problem was the doctors weren't willing to enhance them both. The NHS didn't do things like that. It'd have to be done private.

Her mam'd been arguing with the doctors all day yesterday, and believed they were beginning to break. She explained how it would be better for her daughter. How a mini boob job would boost her psychologically after the trauma. Whenever the doctors came round to check on Cheyenne, her mam told her to burst into her acting mode. Tears. Wailing about her tits. Her mam said she'd get the local paper involved. They'd be keen to do a piece about *the lucky, local girl – spited by a nasty NHS*.

And Cheyenne was going to be pleased with the attention. It'd boost her well into the spotlight. When the film people turned up earlier today, Cheyenne knew she was onto a winner. And she now lay in bed, eating her Toblerone, waiting for the local TV news. When Hank had appeared in the morning he was being a right smeg and she'd told him to sod off. Cheyenne figured she was moving way above him. A true celebrity. She was moving on. But Cheyenne shuddered when she thought of what she'd actually done after he left.

The Family Tree

Ed was standing in the back garden with Marshall, smoking. They were on a patio that had only been half-finished and forgotten about twenty years ago. A garden lay a couple of feet away from the pile of unused square slabs of faded pink patio. Overgrown tufts of grass and cat shit. Their garden was surrounded on two sides by gigantic leylandii trees. And above the gate was the back of Cwmgarw mountain. The huge mountain shadow and the trees were making sure that Ed and Marshall stood almost in a dark box.

– I thought Mormons couldn't smoke?

– They can't, said Ed.

Ed looked down at the plump Marshall; he dropped his cigarette and slapped the boy hard across his head. Marshall yelped and staggered backwards in fright as Ed grabbed him and slapped him again. Marshall tripped, Ed caught him, held him firmly in his grip and slapped him again. A line of blood came from Marshall's nostril and he gasped in surprise. Ed pushed Marshall away, reached into his jacket pocket, took out another cigarette and lit it up.

Marshall steadied himself and scratched his head with a bewildered expression on his face. He brought his hand up to the end of his nose and touched at the trickle of blood that came from his left nostril. He let his hand come down to rub his little moustache. He had forgotten to put his shoes on when he followed Ed outside and his feet were getting icy. Ed held his head up and casually exhaled a line of blue cigarette smoke. There was not a flower in sight. He studied the enormous snow-coated trees that fenced the back garden. He shouldn't have hit this boy.

– These are interesting trees you've got here, Marshall.

– Thank you, said Marshall.

– They seem to be quite popular in your area.

– You seen them around?

– Yeah. They can get quite big, can't they?

– Two hundred feet tall, sir, said Marshall.

– It was nice meeting you, Marshall. My wife, she thought you were a likeable fellow on the internet, she thought Clayton Evans was an intelligent man. A man who wanted to help us.

– I wasn't telling lies about the Nathan Evans family.

– Maybe. But we're certainly not related.

– I did want to meet you both.

– Well, we've met, son.

– Are you upset with me?

– I thought I'd failed yesterday. I was the one making the apologies. No, after this it's my wife. She's gonna have to apologise to me, son. Maybe I've regained my status as the man in charge, here. Maybe I've regained my ground. Maybe, it was worth the trip, after all.

The Pleasures of Celebrity

When Hank got to the Cwm hospital he was out of his head on his new medication. Breathing heavily. He floated down the rubbery corridor, waving an ice cold bar of Toblerone in front of him, and weaved from side to side checking the room numbers on the long line of doors. It was an enormous Toblerone and it weighed a ton. It was one of those two-foot long Toblerone bars. One of the special ones. The mega-big ones you only get as duty-free. He stopped outside the room five doors down from Cheyenne and crazily threw it open.

The family around the dying man inside turned their heads in shock to watch a young man enter their room waving a bar of Toblerone above his head. He had his eyes half-closed and was grinning as he shuffled himself further into their room. He opened his eyes and realised he was in the wrong room.

– Sorry. Thought you were Cheyenne…

– Get the fuck out, you fucking wanker.

– Of course…

– GET OUT.

– Sorr…

Hank quickly hobbled back to the door. He held the bar out and prodded it at the space in front of him. He leaned against the corridor wall and sucked in the hospital air. He knew he had to get his new crutches, but would try and visit Cheyenne first. He calmly asked a nurse in the corridor for Cheyenne's room number and found the right door. When he stepped in he could see she was asleep and gingerly came up to the bed.

He wondered whether he should wake her. He didn't want to just leave the Toblerone on her bed. She wouldn't know who it was from. And he didn't trust them up there. If he left it in the room it'd be sticking out.

Cheyenne wasn't asleep. She'd heard the door clatter open. She knew it was him. Hank. She could smell the oily sod. Load of Old Spice put on to impress her. She opened her eyes and flipped Hank the middle finger, accidentally driving it under his glasses. She almost caught his eye with her nail. She pointed at her disabled arm.

– I only got us one arm, Hank. How'm I meant to eat tha'?

– Hah, we're a perfect match. I've only got one leg.

– You frigging flid.

– Oooh, the charm of Cheyenne.

Hank put his skinny arse down onto the plastic orange chair, a guilty grin stretched across his cheeks. The bar of Toblerone stuck out between his thighs. He rubbed at his newly shaved head, waiting for Cheyenne to notice the cut.

– Fucking idiot, she said.

– Don't worry, mun. Look, I can break it up for you, can't I?

A regal Cheyenne lying in her bed, pretending to be angry with him. Truth was, she was glad he'd come along. Maybe lighten up her day. Entertain her, like. She knew he'd want to. It was only when she looked down and saw the mess he was making, trying to break up the giant bar of chocolate with a plastered foot he'd badly wrapped in a plastic shopping bag, did she actually get angry with the geek.

The strain in his face. The tendons in his neck, bulged, ready to burst. Did he not have the strength? Cheyenne watched with horror, menace forming on her brow. He desperately tried to snap triangular chunks of Toblerone into edible chunks. He just couldn't do it. He didn't have the strength.

– Wha's the matter with it? she said.

166

– Aaaaww, it's frigging solid, mun. It's like a rock, Cheyenne. Frozen.

– Wha'?

Hank had got himself up and belted the bar down against the back of the chair. Crack. The bar didn't hit the chair full on. It came out of his hands. He slipped on the lino and slid against the chair. The new medication. He could hear Cheyenne laughing at him in the distance as he lay slouched. He spotted the damaged Toblerone bar under her bed and crawled to get a broken piece.

He appeared triumphantly and slid a piece of chocolate into Cheyenne's open mouth. Picked up the tumbled chair and sat on it.

– Feeling any better now? he said.

They ate pieces of chocolate in a romantic hush. He was surprised that Cheyenne hadn't mentioned his new haircut. Or noticed his plastered foot. She was half out of it, but he thought she at least might've noticed that his ponytail had disappeared.

– You're looking great, he said.

Hank looked at her pink carnations and the jumbo Get Well card he'd dutifully bought at the hospital shop. He romantically told her he would bring her a gift every time he visited the hospital. Cheyenne groggily told him not to bring her any more flowers. Her room was full of them and she was beginning to feel like a dead bee in the garden centre. She hadn't liked the Monsoon perfume either. And thought the raspberry Gummi Bears were too chewy.

– How're you feeling? he asked.

– Knackered.

– Hah, me too. It's this toxic new medicine they put me on.

Hank bent in half and jolted upright, showing his sharp teeth. Grinning like a rodent.

– I've had some good news though, love, he said.

– I'm the one in fucking hospital, Hank. I don't want to hear your great news, do I?

– Thought it'd make you feel a bit better.

– I'm in agony.

Hank realised he had made a small mistake. She had her eyes shut and her head faced the far wall. He should've realised how much she might be hurting. He briefly examined the morphine drip attached to her arm. He could gently turn the plastic nozzle to the plus sign and release a heavier dose of the fluid. It might make her feel a little better.

– Wha' the fuck're you doing? Don't touch tha'. Get away from there.

Hank shrugged his shoulders. He picked up a smashed chunk of Toblerone from the floor and broke off a triangle to eat. The door opened and in walked two people. A woman, highly perfumed and dressed in the tight-fitting, black striped suit normally worn by the High Street estate agent. She was followed by a bald, large-shouldered man with a black beard and a tripod slung over his shoulders. The woman scanned the room, inspected Hank's position and raised her hand.

– There? she said.

The cameraman simply nodded in response. He walked over to Hank and pushed him in the seat four feet backwards to the corner of the room. He dropped his bag and started to set up the camera. The woman moved to the bed with her hand outstretched towards the disappointingly plain-looking girl lying there.

– Cheyenne Evans, yes?

– Yeah? said Cheyenne.

– Hi Cheyenne, I'm Sam. Sam Parry. And this is Colin, my cameraman.

Colin waved his hand behind his back whilst he bent over

the tripod. He pulled out the rigid legs to the right height and took his camera out of the bag. Sam widened her sparkly eyes and flashed her teeth, broadening the shape of her tanned equine face. She looked like a delighted horse that'd just won the Grand National.

– Ever been on TV before, Cheyenne?

– TV?

– We're from the Evening News. Wondering whether we could speak to you, Cheyenne? asked Sam.

– TV?

– Yes, said Sam. Do a little piece perhaps? Talk about what happened to you over at the petrol station? The trauma of being shot? The pain it involved? The agony of the robbery…

– Wha', now? said Cheyenne.

– Yes. If you can. I mean, if you feel like you could. Say a few words, I mean obviously, I'd understand it, if you felt…

Cheyenne quickly raised herself in bed.

– Yeah, course, mun.

– Great. Okay, Colin. You ready?

– Just a sec, he said.

– This gonna be Sky News? asked Cheyenne.

– Well, no, no. But we're hoping. Yes. Colin and I think we have good chances on this one, don't we, Colin?

– Bring us some attention, said Colin. Get all of those lot paying us some attention. They've had it all up North. Should be bored of the stories running out of those murderous seaside resorts. Bit of publicity for us, this one. From our part of the country. We got our stories to tell down here, haven't we? This is it.

– Wha'? Lying here? Like this?

– Cheyenne, you look beautiful, said Hank.

– Piss off. I look bloody terrible like this. I've seen myself. I've not had a shower in a day. I've not got any frigging make-

169

up on, have I? I've not even got my bloody hair extensions in! Not a fucking chance. No way. Not like this.

Colin had the Sony 900 DV Cam set up and was looking down the view finder at a greasy-faced young girl shouting at him. He took his eye away from the camera and winced up at Samantha.

– What do you think? she said.

He shrugged his shoulders in agreement with a distressed Cheyenne.

– We've got time. It should help.

Sam bent over the camera and checked Cheyenne through the view finder. She looked a wreck. Both Colin and Sam were thinking about selling parts of the interview to an online tabloid. It could be viral. Profit-making.

– Okay, okay. Let's work speedily on this. We'll give you a face scrub and fix the hair.

Colin dipped into his large black bag and came up with the make-up kit, a see-through plastic bag that contained basic blushers and studio creams. The lighting in the room was too bright and he knew Cheyenne's skin would shine without a proper rubdown. He gave the bag to Samantha who placed it on the edge of the bed and took out the facial wipes, the foundation, the blusher, lip gloss, eye-liner and the fake tan cream. Cheyenne was looking annoyed. These were very basic products. Sam snatched at the grubby towel from the bag and went to work. She spotted the sink in the corner of the room next to a doped Hank.

– What's your boyfriend's name, Cheyenne? she said.

– Hank?

– Hank, said Hank.

– He's not my fucking boyfriend, said Cheyenne.

Hank was in a dazed stupor. After the explosion, the new medicine had somehow re-worked its way through his arteries at a higher strength and speed. Spaced-out and smiling, he hadn't been listening to the conversation in the room. He'd been trying to tick off boxes in his brain. Making sure he'd done his deeds for the day... He'd given Cheyenne her gift... they'd had their romantic moment... he'd got rid of Mister Stiffy... he'd...

Someone'd been shouting his name, so he got up and looked around. He was nervously thinking his boner was having a second coming as soon as his eyes focused on Sam Parry. Hank had never heard of a day-long hard-on before. Sam asked Cheyenne whether he'd been taking anything unusual.

Cheyenne and Sam Parry had told him to get the bowl. But he couldn't find what it was the women were ordering him to do. He felt a large hand on his back push him into the sink and he spotted a bowl.

– Thanks, said Colin.

Sam had washed Cheyenne's face and was leaning over to use the soaked cotton wool to wipe the *Fake Bake* tan cream into her pores. Cheyenne had noticed the size of Sam's chest and was fairly impressed. They were perfectly round and looked beautifully firm.

– You had the boobs done, Sam?

– Yeah, about a year ago now. Better for TV, like.

– I'm trying to get mine done in here.

– Yes, we know, she said. It's a good topic.

– Yeah?

– Plan is we're going to use that as well, she said. It'll be a decent story for our online piece, Cheyenne.

They all nodded in agreement. Cheyenne was keen. This was celebrity. They'd be able to get the photos. It would be her chance. Sam stood back to admire her work. Colin was standing behind her examining how Cheyenne would look for the camera. Cheyenne had the mirror in her hand and believed she was looking sexy. TV-like.

– So what's the deal 'en? Wha' should I say about the bastard? I'll do anything you wants me to, said Cheyenne.

– Well, this is it, see, Cheyenne. We were thinking about the interview. What would be the best story for us all. What could bring the most attention to our piece. And you see, we were wondering whether you could actually forgive the man that shot you.

– You wha'?

– Have you heard of the Valley's Villain, Cheyenne? said Sam.

– Wha'? Yeah, course.

– The man that's held up and robbed five supermarkets, eleven petrol stations, fifteen corner shops and a train? The man that has shamed the South Wales Police Force for over a year now?

– Well, yeah. It's the Valley's Villain, innit?

– Well, he is also the man that shot you, Cheyenne.

– Oh.

– Yes. An accident we believe. It's not a killing. No. But he did shoot you. And we think it is enough to get us some national coverage. So, we were wondering if you could forgive him for us, said Sam.

– What? Why?

– Stir things up a bit. Publicity. Get our faces shown. And, course, there is the money, she said. We sell this story and you're going to be getting the money as well as us.

– Well, yeah, said Cheyenne. Sure.

Hank had trickled out of his skull and managed to tune into all this. He was in the corner biting on his thumb. He couldn't believe what he was hearing. This was his girlfriend, the man almost killed her. His girlfriend. And these people wanted Cheyenne to forgive the man? She couldn't do that, surely not. He clawed at the back of his shaved head.

– They want you to *thank* this man? he yelled.

They'd paid no attention to the doped Hank and were surprised by his rampant announcement. He started shouting with his fist in the air and Colin automatically swivelled the camera onto him. The boy was furious.

– I'm gonna fucking find him! Not forgive him!

This was good. This was subplot. They all knew it. Hank could work to their advantage here. The forgiving girl and the raging bespectacled skinhead boyfriend. It wasn't a cliché. They didn't have to worry about her face. They could sell all this, despite her face. People would like this. They'd love it.

*

Cheyenne'd been lying on the hospital bed for hours afterwards. Lying there, waiting for the evening news to come on, still nibbling on a piece of her chocolate. The pain had left her body and she felt like she was adrift. She'd told Hank to piss off after the TV people left. She'd terrified him. She warned him to leave before she started spreading her own news about her knowledge of panda bears. She knew her Nan would be interested to know. She wasn't happy with her interview and couldn't believe the nonsense coming out of Hank's gob. Hank was going on about how he was going to be the man standing up for his girlfriend. He would catch the thief that shot her. Well, he wasn't her boyfriend anymore. And maybe she even had herself another man. Tetchy, perhaps? Sam and Colin were rubbing their hands. These TV people had come to film her. Not him. It was her story. Not his. Hank left. Cheyenne was furious with him.

173

Let's Do It

– Never smother a man with love, Leanne. It's not how it works. You never treats a man like a king.

Donna took a long drag on her Menthol Malboro and raised an eyebrow above her sunglasses. If Leanne needed advice on how to control the man then she was more than happy to give it. She knew the tale. She knew the tricks. It was her job.

– Cruelty is the key. Let them learn the pain. Earn it.

The two women had been out walking the stolen dog. And when the drizzle turned to a heavy rain they stopped at the empty Wimpy to sit and discuss the subject of men. Donna placed her knuckle firmly against her fanny and scratched hard. She sniffed the motionless cafe air and wondered whether she really wanted a bacon sandwich.

Jesse, the obese waitress, came back to the counter from the kitchen. Her rich red Wimpy uniform stood out against the stark white interior of the place. They were trying to upgrade the burger bar. Make it look more American like McDonalds down the road, and so they'd also recently changed their uniforms.

– Does you think the red suits me? she said.

– No, said Donna.

– Better than the pink I got, said Leanne.

– Spose, said the waitress. Anyhow, what'd you two want?

They were eating the breakfast special. Blinking at the white plastic tables and chairs in the sharp morning light.

Donna ate like she was eating in a competition. She ate at a spectacular speed, wiping the last of the egg yolk and baked beans up with the crust of the white sliced bread and sipping on her sugary tea with a slight contempt for the slowness of her sister. She let out a little burp as Leanne sulkily pushed a slice of bacon around her jumbo plate of unwanted food. She had gotten bored with her sister's supposed knowledge of men, and the way they should be treated.

Leanne watched the movement of shoppers icily drift past the cafe's front window. They were both suffering after last night's drinking session, and she was sure her headache must've been pounding at a faster pace having to sit and listen to the natter of her sister.

– Got a call from Tash this morning, said Donna.

– Who? said Leanne.

– You know, Tash. Aunt Aggie's friend, Tash? Tash and Bell? Tash, mun, said Donna. One with the moustache?

– Oh yeah, said Leanne. The hairdresser in Texas.

– Anyhow, she phoned us, said Donna.

– She alright? said Leanne.

– What? Yeah, she's alright. Course she's alright, mun. Ain't about her.

– Thought her stomach was bad?

– What? No, it's not her. That's Belly, innit? said Donna.

– Oh, right.

– Anyhow, Tash, she told us this morning about our Boyd. Man's well upset, apparently. Been seen wandering all round town, putting up his posters like, innit?

– His posters? said Leanne.

– Yep. His 'Missing Dog' posters. Hehehe. Man's been in tears. But it seems like we got ourselves another thing here, said Donna. You remembers our second cousin? Aunt Aggie and mam's youngest sister's daughter's daughter? Cheyenne?

175

– Sort of, said Leanne.

– Girl was working up there at the petrol station yesterday, wannit? Fucker shot down our own blood relative. Tash told us. She's gone into hospital.

– Jesus. The sod.

– Yep. It happened, said Donna.

As soon as the rain stopped, they were going to be making their ransom film. Leanne looked out of the window at Pinkie. They'd tied him to a lamp post, his fluffy, dark fur soaked by the rain. He looked like some docile brown bear they'd put on a leash, and Leanne immediately felt sorry for this enormous thing. Donna had been giving him little kicks and punches all morning, telling him what they would do if Boyd didn't respond in time with the ransom money. Leanne saw the dog raise its head against the downpour, peering against the rain to look inside the warm cafe.

– Now, I ain't into killing animals, said Leanne. I told you that.

– I know, said Donna. You changed the plan.

– That's right. Dog didn't hurt me, did it?

– Fine, said Donna.

– Fine. But, for what he did to me, like? And what he did to poor Cheyenne? That man does deserve his punishment. Right?

– Good. We just uses the dog as ransom, like. Revenge, love. Punishment. Right? said Donna.

– Yes. Soon as this sodding rain disappears, we is up and out.

– Good.

Donna took a dry sip of tea from her empty cup and placed it on her saucer. The rain continued to splutter down and the women sat. Waiting. Neither of them wanted to get wet. Donna looked across at Leanne, at her face with the yellow punch marks left by Boyd's right hand. Leanne looked under the plastic table at her skinny legs. She turned them to the side and could see the bruises stand out against her pale skin.

– When we gets the dog back to the flat, I needs to change, said Donna.

– Wha' you on about?

– Well, feeling a bit like Jungle woman now in this, in I?

Donna was pointing at her leopard skin jacket and shiny leggings. Leanne let out a groan.

– Reckons I need to get a better outfit on, like. For our video.

– But *you* ain't gonna be *in* the frigging video Donna, is you? We're gonna be filming the dog, mun. You're just gonna be the voice-over, innit? The voice, the picture behind the picture, like.

– I know, I know, but I'd be a much better, more menacing voice, if I was dressed up in a better outfit.

– What?

– Bit of black rubber, like? said Donna.

– Awww, come on, mun. We're not faffing about here, Donna!

– Naw! I needs changing, Leanne. It won't take long. I've got the outfit. It's the one I wear for a regular of mine on a Tuesday.

– It ain't a Tuesday!

Donna had her fingers splayed in front of her face, and was studying her nine gold rings. She let her eyes drift finger to finger as she turned her hands over and examined the rings with forensic scrutiny for scratch marks or dirt. She grabbed the rings one by one and with nine heavy pauses managed to tug each of the nine rings off her fingers. She laid them in a line on the table top. Each of her tight fingers with a band of white that marked the spot where the ring had rested.

– I loves gold, she said. Don't it feel weird when you takes 'em off your fingers? Real lush. Takes them off, and they always feels light. Weird. Mind, I always gotta keep my necklace on. Never touches tha'. No.

Donna pulled out the side of her T-shirt and used it to start polishing her rings. She picked up the largest one to polish. It was a chunky band of fourteen carat gold. Donna wouldn't tell anyone where she'd got it. Leanne leaned over to help her and picked up the one she liked best, blew the grains of caster sugar off the side, and rolled it between her thumb and forefinger. She slipped it onto her own finger. It was a beautiful ring. Medallion style with a fierce Welsh dragon cut into it. Leanne always thought it was a man's ring, but Donna claimed it wasn't. Reckoned it didn't matter whether it was a man's ring, or a woman's ring, long as it fitted her finger.

Leanne held the ring up to the window. She closed one eye and stared through the ring at the dripping dog outside. The rain had tapered. Donna looked at her sister. She pushed her empty plate to the middle of the table and stubbed out her cigarette.

– Right 'en, said Leanne. Let's do it.

A Little Walk

Hank saw the bus jumble to a stop. It had stopped two hundred yards away from the front of the hospital bus station. The exhaust of the 97A circular let out a long cough and a hot spurt of black diesel dribbled into the mountain air. Four passengers dutifully thanked their driver and stepped easily off the cosy vehicle into the bleak light. The bus was early. The pain from Hank's swollen foot spread uncontrollably across his face as he rammed it down onto the snow-covered pavement and moved as fast as he could towards the back end of the bus. He scurried forwards, dragging his plaster-cast foot along. A lone man already waiting at the bus stop had danced on ahead of him up the steps of the zippy single-decker. He scratched at the growth on the side of his neck and sniggered lovingly at the driver.

– You're early today 'en, love?

– Yep. Treats. Christmas, innit? said the driver. Come on.

With every step Hank patted the metal side of the bus with his hand as he finally got to the open doors and grabbed at the step-bars for balance.

– Come on peg-leg, carry your arse in! Sit down. Don't wanna be missing the Pentre kick-off today, do we? said the driver.

Hank got up the steps into the stomach of the warm bus as the electric doors clicked close on his back. It would take the direct route back to town. They pulled away from the pavement, and with an explosive *cha-chunggg*, shot off.

*

He was looking at the worn shoe on his right foot. And the cast that covered his other foot with Tetchy's signature on it. He'd tried to coat the plaster with a bag to stop it getting wet but it was already half hanging off. He pulled the carrier bag from around the cast and placed it under the seat. Cheyenne wouldn't tell her Nan about his panda act, surely. She wasn't that silly. Had Cheyenne actually been serious? The name Tetchy had slipped off her tongue and Hank hadn't been able to think straight. They'd grown up together, Tetchy and his older brother. They had moved into the house next door to Marshall, Hank's cousin.

Tetchy's brother was considered a bit twp. Couldn't read. Couldn't write. He'd been put into one of the special classes in school. There were three of the special classes. G.a, G.b, and G.c. They were called the G-Force. It was where Hank really got to know him. Hank never liked school, he used to mitch a lot. And when he was in school the teachers often kept an eye on him, watching, expecting trouble to happen. He once got into a fight with Wyatt Evans over the rules of Chucking. Hank was sure you won if your opponent's plastic lid flipped over, even if it landed closest to the wall. Wyatt disagreed. The fight lasted the full fifteen minutes of the morning break and was cheered on by a large crowd of boys. It was only when the bell rang and a lot of the audience didn't return to class that the slack teacher on break realised something had happened.

Hank and Wyatt were given the dap by the Headmaster. Five illegal slaps of hard leather against their thigh. And as an extra they were put into G-Force for a year. Both boys liked it there. It didn't involve work. The young teacher in charge of the boys with learning difficulties, Mr Webb, thought it ridiculous these two had been put into his class as a punishment. He argued with the authoritarian head of the school, but to no avail. The Headmaster dismissed any counter-argument. It was his choice. Mr Webb put the two boys at the back of his class behind Tetchy's brother and gave them books to read.

The books handed over to Hank and his fighting partner were ones Mr Webb had in his own bag. Two American detective novels he was returning to the library. Wyatt didn't bother touching his book but Hank was immediately caught by the cover photo on his. A dead woman, bleeding from the head, lying on a silver gun as large as her naked body. He sat and he read. He was gutted when class ended and the teacher asked for the books back. They were overdue. That evening Hank was ready and waiting in the library when Mr Webb came in to hand his books over.

Hank sat in the class and regularly read the American novels Mr Webb offered. He was absorbed with the fiction. It was why he'd bother to turn up. It was just a shame Tetchy's brother could so easily disturb him. He could get the boys in G-Force laughing over the smallest burping noise he made. He could get Mr Webb laughing with his daft remarks about the red ants who could save the planet from the aliens. He'd just learnt the alphabet and teased Hank about his name when he learnt he could magically create something mega-brainy from it. He'd drop the H and call Hank *Wank*. Hank had *Wank* written all over his bag, his pencil case and his books. *Wank*. The bastards laughed for a year every time it came out of Tetchy brother's wet mouth. Wank. Tetchy's brother left comprehensive school early and then spent a long time in jail. Hank laughed for years at that.

He did hate his name, though. Hank was part of a generation of children in the area who had been brought up by parents who were enthralled with everything to do with the American West. When pits closed, Cowboy Dan came along with a magnificent proposal as to how a down-trodden community could make money. You just turn an unemployed town into a cowboy theme park. You get state funding and go to work within the tourist industry. Most people living in the area thought this crazy idea was sleek. They formed a co-operative and proceeded to write letters to their MP in an attempt to officially re-name the Bevan housing estate and the nearby town of Cwmgarw *Texas-2*. It was explained to the community that Texas was actually a state in the US of A, and therefore neither Cwmgarw nor the Bevan estate could officially be 'twinned' with Texas. They ignored this advice.

Cowboy Dan was a local builder who claimed he'd been living in America for years as a rancher, and came back with enough moolah to buy a large amount of derelict land. He also bought an old farmhouse on the side of the Cwm mountain and rebuilt it into the massive 'White Ranch'. He'd often be seen riding through town on the back of his stallion, dressed in his Wild West gear and inviting people up to his ranch. Urging them to join the 'D Western Society'.

Some traditionalists living in the area thought the idea would be damaging to whatever small businesses still existed. But the cowboy theme-town had a lot of support. It was almost a cult thing for some, based purely on people's love and longing for the American Wild West, at least for the one they saw on TV and film. *Bonanza* was big. And David Carradine had just burst into everyone's living room.

Cowboy Dan promoted a weekly Wild West Day. Every week people would dress up in their best Wild West gear, all bought in his shop, and they would party. Dan would spend hours teaching kids how to shoot, showing them how to use the lasso and ride a pony, whilst their parents would lounge about and drink in the Golden Nugget saloon. It was a former pub which cowboy Dan had bought for a song. He smashed out its brick frontage and replaced it all with an enormous single pane of glass. There was a long wooden bar inside and a loosely fitting boardwalk balanced on the pavement outside. You entered through wooden covered half-doors that swung open and shut, just like they did in the Pictures. They even had a spittoon you could use.

Cowboy Dan and his fans were laughed at by the media and ignored by the government. Their official plea to get the estate's name altered was dismissed. And the hordes of intrigued tourists they were hoping to attract never did manage to make it. People finally began to sober up and realise their strategy for a cowboy theme town was not going to work, especially when the longstanding rumours about Cowboy Dan were found out to be true.

People learnt he'd left America after spending fifteen years in a Nashville jail on charges of pederasty. Cowboy Dan fled the valley. His ranch burned down, and parents gradually started to name their babies in a more conventional fashion. There were some that still had the aspiration. Hank read only last year of a baby who'd been christened Tonto, but nowadays it was mostly a John or a Janet.

*

Hank stumbled through the streets leaving a trail of shit behind him. He'd stepped in fresh dog shit at the main Cwm bus stop and went on without noticing the stinking brown marks which his heavy plaster-cast foot had been leaving on the frosted pavements.

He'd been annoyed all morning. Small things, mini things had been building up inside him since he'd returned from visiting Cheyenne at the hospital. He had forgotten to ask for his new crutches. The sodding bus had terminated in town and he had to walk on through Cwmgarw just to get to another sodding stop to take him home. He could feel the tiny things pestering him. Electric things inside his brain, nervously tapping at his skull. He was trying to hold back. He didn't want to have another one. He should have stayed indoors. But he couldn't help himself. He could deal with Cheyenne, yet he wasn't prepared to let a sod like Tetchy take his trainers as well. And then there was Masaki. Hank was going to pay him a visit. He needed to see him. And then he had the rugby match to work, followed by the bloody party.

He knew he should calm down. Relax. He didn't want to spark something. They weren't the best trainers you could buy. But they were *his* trainers. And they had been for five years. He felt attached to them. They were moulded to the shape of his foot. He could have been wearing one of them that morning instead of his work shoe. Mind, with the shoe in place he'd be able to give Tetchy a decent kicking. If Tetchy was dumb enough to sign his plaster cast and admit to the crime then Hank was going to thump him for it.

Hank figured he'd be able to catch a bus from a stop near Masaki's place, then head back over to the estate to sort out Tetchy. Grab the panda outfit and get down to Pentre for the match. It was do-able, he was sure. Perfect. Masaki, then Tetchy, then the panda for the rugby and Geronimo's do. He had to carry on. He was supposed to be taking it easy, letting the new drugs work through his knackered body. Doctor had told him. Relax. Watch daytime TV. Read a book. He'd tried. The only thing he'd read was the film script he'd been sent and the contract he had signed. He could take their money and run. He would. He'd show Cheyenne. It would be a new start. He could move from this area and begin. Yet his mind was full of questions he needed to ask Masaki. Who were these people? How had they received his original script? Why had Masaki agreed to their wishes, to the way they could adapt and transform his brilliance into their steaming crap?

Hank crossed the bridge into Cwm Park and tried not to look at the steady flow of dark water beneath him. He had to stop. Relax. He kept his head angled and breathed slowly. It had been a foolish idea to walk to Masaki's house. He leant upright against the railing. Beneath him the banks of the river were still white, covered in a rich, unpolluted snow. Hank noticed the movement of the river had crept into his ears and ballooned inside his head. He ached.

He had trouble breathing. His legs felt as if a heavy stone had been tied to each one. They had developed a weird weightiness and he was finding it difficult to pick one up and move on forward. He couldn't fucking walk. The micron-sized nerve cells in his brain were loving it. They were ready to explode. Hassling each other, flickering on the brink of going bananas. Hank had to steady himself. He stared at the scattered footprints in the blackened snow, tracks covering the path in front of him. People had walked along that path already.

He stood on the edge of the park inside the gates. The thin white snow covering the grass gave the Victorian trees an enormous presence. Lilliputian squirrels scrambled past his sealed feet, squealing in delight at his discomfort. The path was scattered with slippery leaves, hundreds of the tiny fuckers. The line of immense dark tree trunks was black against the grey sky and white grass. And underneath the leafless bony trees were the greedy worms, living amongst the rot. Hank was giddy and a little pulse in one ear was making him blink. New medication.

He had to sit. Someone was on the bench directly in front of him. Hank looked further up the path towards the next bench. It was a burnt couple of wooden legs. He looked further on, but there was no other bench after that. He had to sit down. Now.

He sat on the edge of the broken, icy bench, not wanting to disturb the scabby looking little boy who sat at the other end. The boy, Morgan, had come down from the mountaintop for a wander dressed in his school uniform, a matching thin blazer and tie under his blue Parka. Hank let his head roll back and breathed out. He was angry with himself. Why the fuck had he thought he could walk to Masaki's house? He let the giddiness float from his head down through his nostrils and out. He trembled. There was a strong smell of shit in the cold air, and he wondered whether the smell could be a blocked sewer somewhere.

Hank opened his eyes and looked up at the naked trees. A line of hanging Christmas lights dangled from tree to tree. Amongst the council's Christmas decorations hung shit bags. The shit bags would be thrown up by an angry dog owner who refused to use the dog-bin. An idiot's protest. They'd *clean up* their dog's shit alright, but because they disagreed with the council's authority to impose a law of actually placing shit into the dog bin, they'd show their disagreement by hauling their shit bags up and away into the air. Hank shook his head and looked towards the river. He sniffed.

Morgan was leaning forward and continually spitting between his dangling legs. He had created a spit-puddle. A round, bowl-shaped puddle of spit that had melted the snow on either side. Hank spat. He had little saliva in his own dry mouth. He looked at the boy's spit puddle with a feeling of envy. Morgan looked at Hank and sniggered. Both sat and contemplated the round puddle of spit Morgan had created. Hank looked at the boy who was staring back at him and pointing at his shit-smeared plaster-cast foot.

– You've trod in shit, said Morgan.

– What're you spitting for? said Hank.

Morgan sniffed loudly as an answer then spat again. A long, drawn out greenie stream that almost made Hank retch.

– Stop spitting, you little prick, said Hank.

The boy sniffed again. Loudly. And spat.

– If you don't know why you're spitting for then why don't you stop it?

The boy sniffed dejectedly.

– What's that meant to mean? said Hank.

The boy sniffed again.

– What're you spitting for?

– I dunno, said Morgan.

– Stop it then.

Morgan looked down at his spit puddle.

– I gorra lotta spit in my mouth. Needs clearing out, dunnit? he said.

– Use a frigging toothbrush then.

Morgan looked at Hank. Sniffed. Then spat. An enormous amount of phlegm hit the ground. Hank turned his head. A miserable-faced magpie landed on the path in front of them. Morgan spat at it.

– You're an idiot walking without crutches. Wha' you doing, walking without crutches en, eh? said Morgan. Stop it.

– I know, thanks for the advice. It's difficult, said Hank.

– Can't walk without crutches on, can you? Bloke two doors down from me and mam's old place, he lost his foot. On crutches all the time, he was. Learnt to do tricks on 'em. Waiting for his special leg to come, like.

– Fascinating.

– Yeah, said Morgan. You still gorra foot?

– Yes.

– Did the army not give you the crutches, then?

– They were stolen, said Hank.

– Tha's not right, is it? Shouldn't nick the crutches, should 'ey?

– Nope.

– Mind, shouldn't be walkin' without 'em either, like.

– I know, said Hank. Thanks.

– Naw. Could use a zimmer I spose, said Morgan.

– I haven't got one, said Hank.

– My nan uses one. Uses it round 'er house. She's speedy on it. Calls it the chariot.

– Fascinating, said Hank.

– Yeah, said Morgan.

Hank wasn't sure whether he felt better or not, but he knew he had to carry walking onwards. Crutches or no crutches. He wasn't going to listen to this little boy jabber. His legs felt dead and his cold arse didn't want to move. But it'd be pointless turning around now. The boy started spitting again. Hank told himself to get up. He stretched and yawned.

– Where you going 'en? said Morgan.

– None of your fucking business, is it?

– Only tryin' to help you, innit?

– Then shut the fuck up, said Hank.

They watched an old woman in a bearskin brown overcoat walk slowly on down the melting slush towards them. She was talking to her leashed dog, straining to pull it back, as the mongrel eagerly sniffed the air along the strands of dead grass on the edge of the path. She grappled with the lead and held tightly onto a small blue shopping bag. Hank hugged his jacket round his chest. The woman stopped to let her dog shit on the path and passed the two people on the bench. The boy spat. The boy spat and rubbed his legs. Hank copied him. His spit landed on the toe of his plaster-cast foot and took off a fleck of dog shit.

188

– Naw, shouldn't be out walkin' with tha' foot, mun. You don't go wanderin' bout town with a large bit of plaster on the foot, does you? How're you gonna get all the shite off, eh? Thought of tha'? Hehehe. Can't waddle into the house an just take the plaster off, cun you? Ain't a shoe, like? Gonna be gettin into bed with all tha'. Hehehe.

The muscle in Hank's forearm twitched. His shoulder jerked and his arm rose into the air for a moment. They both watched the movement. The hovering arm rested and dropped down, back onto his trembling leg. Hank touched his arm. He held it in place. Had he had one?

– Yeah, everyone needs their feet, don't they? said Morgan. Spose we all needs our feet, and our toes, like. They're there for something, innit? Dunno nobody without no toes. Mind, never see the point of 'em really. Less you just dies without 'em. Explodes, like, or something, innit? Toes, eh? What do we do with our toes, when we goes? Is they important to anyone? Hurt to come off won't they? You could collect thousands of toes. Not too nasty, neither. Is only the toes, after all.

– Aren't you meant to be in school? said Hank.

– I ain't going to school, is I?

– Why not?

– I'm thinking 'bout feet. And dogs. And leaving this place.

– Well. It's what everyone wants to do. If you ever get the chance to do it, do it.

Hank stood. He was large over the small boy. He ground his plaster cast foot slowly in the spit puddle, managing to wipe off most of the dog shit. The boy moaned when the smell of soaked dog shit and phlegm reached his nostrils. Hank was determined to get to Masaki's. It was part of his personal pilgrimage that day. He was going to get there.

Zoophilia

Boyd stood on the edge of the Texas shopping precinct watching a three-legged dog rummage through a bag of discarded chips. He was feeling ashamed of himself and had tried to look elsewhere but the sight of this beautiful beast put him in a bubble of ecstasy. His eyes fixed on the wet snout of this hungry hound as its pink tongue constantly licked at the remains of a dried curry sauce and vinegar-stained newspaper wrap, nudging it over and over the snow-coated ground. It made his weakened blood tinkle between his legs. Boyd was a man who couldn't deny his sexual fetish. He was a man who loved dogs.

He'd loved dogs for years. Always believed there was a special bond between himself and the canine being. A bond not entirely attached to the physical enjoyment both he and the animal would receive. No. His passion had always been based on the relationship itself. It was a romantic bond.

At least that's what he told himself. He knew it was illegal in the UK, but he wasn't somebody to be bound by convention and the injustice of an old-fashioned British law. He was a stubborn man. A man who loved dogs. He didn't abuse dogs. And he didn't regard it as a problem. No, and as he stood there in a part of the small ex-mining town, his immediate problem was far more painful. Boyd was a man who had lost his dog.

He watched as the three-legged hound ate and his thoughts flicked once more to what had happened to Pinkie. A day spent weeping without his dog and Boyd knew for sure that he was a lonely man.

He would spend most of the day continuing to walk through the cold streets in Cwmgarw and a further mile down south in Pentrecoch wearing his black rubber snow shoes, searching and stapling Missing Dog posters onto boarded shop windows, gluing them to the sides of shaking plastic bus shelters and tying them around lamp posts, all with the forlorn hope that some charitable angel would call his number. He knew it was unlikely.

He was upset so many people were out walking already. The Cwm park was like a circus. Some of them didn't even have a dog. They walked as an exercise. Despite the cold they were out, walking and talking. Every person he passed always had something to say. The words hit his elephantine ears like a stick. He didn't want to hear the broken parts of misunderstood conversations but the people he passed didn't stop talking.

– …he's taking the team down. Pentrecoch club shouldn't even 'ave a fucking mascot… Could use a zimmer. Nan's got one… Listen, honey, if we're going back tomorrow, maybe we should visit the girl… Alright, mam, I'll be there. I get Geronimo a birthday card… The panda… We ain't got no seagull problems up 'ere. Should bring him back… Can't keep phoning her. Not for three weeks… Same as the last time… Uh?… It was wrong, wrong mun… His dad? Now he cun fucking paint… Goldfish…

The faster he walked, the more people he passed. He got zapped by their monotonous voices. They were out to shop, they were out to play in the snow, they were out to walk and talk. None of them out to help him. And the words they spoke were blown through his head like poisoned jungle darts. He had felt wretched all day. He began to feel that what he was doing was pointless.

It'd been difficult for him to smile. It was one of those things he knew he had to do, and had always found difficult. The idea you should smile at some unknown person had always troubled him. As a teenager when he walked Cujo, the family dog, his mam had always slapped him for not putting on a false smile. You passed a fellow walker and you smiled. Some even said "Hello". You took a walk, and you had to fake a smile. Part of the task.

He had to smile at anybody he met. To greet passers-by with a nod and politely ask them whether they'd seen his missing dog. He walked alone, and put up the posters featuring a photo of Pinkie displaying his thirteen-stone of Newfoundland flesh. A quality photo of a hound he believed Crufts would have accepted. It was an image which made tears roll down Boyd's pink face every time he stopped to display a poster.

He had returned to Texas-2 with only six of the thirty-seven Missing Dog posters he'd made. He had to get more. And when he came across this three-legged dog in the precinct and stopped to watch he cursed himself aloud, he couldn't move away from the sight of the little beauty.

Wind caught the laminated sheets he held in his gloved hand and Boyd held them tighter to his heart as this stray glanced at him for a second with a wooden curiosity. Boyd pursed his lips and made a wet clicking sound in an attempt to comfort the three-legged dog. He had a light voice that sounded as if it hadn't wanted to mature from childhood. The dog studied him.

Tash and Bell fumbled along pushing a low-slung shopping trolley on which rested a large mattress. The three-legged dog heard them before Boyd did and bounced away from the squeak of the turning wheels. Boyd came out of his bubble and felt knackered. He hoped Tash and Bell would carry on past him but knew they wouldn't. They'd stop and chat. It was what the old couple did.

When Tash saw him she let go of the trolley to give him a wave, and slipped on the ice. She shoved her husband forward and his elderly hands struggled to bring the slithering trolley to a stop on the snow-coated pavement. Boyd had put out his foot to help and Bell leant gasping against the mattress. Tash was brushing snow off the side of her shoe and coughing. She pointed at the posters in Boyd's hand.

– Alright 'en love, still putting 'em up 'en, is you?

– Naw, said Boyd. Done these, just on my way home. Get some more. Not seen the little fellow, have you?

– Naw, love. We've jus' cum back from yours, 'aven't we? Went round there to see your bloody neighbour, dear Mrs Sparrow. Gonna give her a real treat, our spare mattress here, wasn't it? Reckoned her back'd been playing up. Too much dancing, like. Always been a decent dancer, Mrs Sparrow. Mind, sodding typical, goes round there, and the senile fucking scag ain't in, is it? You 'aven't seen her, have you?

– Naw.

– Only spoke to her the other day. Oh well, if you sees her, like, tell her we've got a comfier bed than her old one. It'll come cheap an all, said Tash.

– Yeah, and if you sees Pinkie...

– Yeah, jus' saying to Belly 'ere, wasn't I? When was it? Two hours ago?

– Wha'? said Bell.

– Jus' saying it, wasn't I, Belly?

– Yeah, said Bell.

– The dogs. 'em dogs, Dogman's, like. Seems sodding quiet, dunnit? Snow, is it? Bit weird.

– Yeah, said Bell.

– Strange, like, innit? You loses yours, and Deano Dogman's up on the farm, all goes shush, like?

– Yeah, said Bell. Weird.

– Yep, said Tash. It's the cold, is it?

Boyd looked up at the mountain and listened. He couldn't hear a thing. The noise from the wailing caged puppies and dogs Dean Evans kept on his farm had been ricocheting around the shabby streets of the Bevan Estate for fifteen years. Today there wasn't a whine or a bark or a growl to be heard. Boyd didn't know why he hadn't noticed the gap. His stupid ears had seemingly switched off. He felt a crawling trauma race down his back.

– Anyhow love, if you does see your neighbour, Mrs Sparrow, you know…

– Yeah, right, said Boyd. I will.

– Tara, 'en.

Tash and Bell squeaked away with their trolley and Boyd was left there to stand looking up at the Cwm mountain. He knew where his fucking dog must've gone. Why had he been so fucking blind not to have figured it out. It was natural. Boyd felt like a fucking moron. He'd been in such a state of anxiety, hoping and believing Pinkie had simply wandered out of his car. No. His dog wasn't lost. His dog wouldn't leave him. His dog had been taken. Dogman had stolen his dog.

Boyd came into his kitchen and slapped the posters into the bin. He shoved his head into the sink and screamed against the metal drum. He had bought his dog from the farm a year ago and he still owed the Dogman money. Boyd went to the kitchen drawer and took out the gun. He would find his stolen dog. They would be re-united.

*

194

Tash and Bell were on the sofa drinking cans of Kestrel superstrength. They'd left the mattress in the low trolley a few feet away in their garden and a girl had come round to play on it. They sat watching her bounce. Bell let out a weak burp and rubbed his stomach with a look of agony flashing across his face.

– You alright, love? asked Tash. Belly hurting, is it?

– Yeah.

– Don't worry. Be round the hospital for the appointment later.

– Yeah.

They heard a thunderous bang from the woods above. An echo travelled down the mountainside onto the estate with speed. Mountain trees shook and crows jolted into the sharp grey skies. The small girl squealed in fright as she jumped harder onto the mattress.

A Little Ride

Hank was in the back of a cheap taxi. The boy was right, walking had been a problem. He felt his time was running out. At least he'd managed to scrape the shit off his foot. The depressing sod driving the car hadn't said a word since he'd got in. The filthy stretch of cotton-covering placed on the back seat of the car looked as if it hadn't been washed since the day it was put on, and the smell of sick coming from the floor matting made Hank cough as he thought about his dad's late-night drinking sessions.

He was feeling better. Less giddy, but still knackered. He kept on thinking he should say something, make small talk with the glum-looking man driving the car. Comment on the weather or ask if he was going to watch the rugby game that day. Ask why his taxi had a tannoy attached to its roof. The kind of polite meaningless exchanges you might make with the hairdresser whilst you get your hair cut. But he couldn't really think of anything to say.

– Been busy? he said.

– No.

Hank eased his backside on the seat and heard a twang as the rotting elastic band that held the seat covering in place snapped under his arse. The driver's yellow eyes darted up to the rear-view mirror. Hank sat still. Aware he was being watched, he pretended not to have heard anything.

– You gonna watch the Pentrecoch game this afternoon? said Hank.

– Don't watch rugby. Never liked it. Never liked it since they got that man doing the Panda act.

– No?

– No. Darts is what I does.

The *Panda act*. His sad life. The taxi travelled on through the main street. Most of the shops now had been boarded up. A For Sale sign often hung above a window. It was only the line of late-night kebab houses and pizza parlours that were doing any real business. They passed a Cash-It shop next to a closed Working Men's Institute, overlooking a launderette. The taxi stopped at the traffic lights.

Outside a bright red pizza parlour the taxi driver and Hank watched as two Asian men shouted at each other. The older man waved his arms in the air, gesticulating in surprise with a shake of his head at what the younger man seemed to be blaming him for doing. The young man was pointing his fist towards the other bloke. They were standing feet apart from each other, and from inside the taxi it seemed clear the argument wasn't going to turn into any fight. The taxi driver recognised the mature man and spoke to himself,

– Tha's Tel, used to work in the curry house I went to when I was eighteen. Always a good guy, Tel.

The light changed to green and they moved on. A mile further and into Masaki's decent street where the taxi came to a stop. Hank had reached his destination. Mission nearly accomplished. He would hand over the contract to Masaki for him to pass it on. He paid the man and struggled out.

The house was on a street where each home had a little front garden and a rusted iron gate. A stretch of front-room windows with Christmas trees inside. Hank hobbled up to Masaki's door and knocked on the white PVC with his fist. He could hear a dog barking inside and steadied himself to confront Masaki, to ask his producer the questions he needed to ask. The door was opened by Masaki's daughter, Vicki.

– May I speak to your father, please?

– He's not in.

Hank told himself he hadn't failed. To be calm. He had set out to speak to both Masaki and Tetchy. It was stalled, that was all. His task had been stalled. Not broken. He looked at his watch. He had time. He was trying to calm himself down. It was difficult.

House to House

He'd had the most fantastic dream that afternoon. It was one of his special ones. He'd been having these incredibly vivid dreams recently. Bright, vibrant visions. And he was chuffed. It involved Tom and Jerry, a chainsaw and his new Mormon friends, Ed and Betty. This one was full of the shiny colours of a Hanna Barbera cartoon. In this one the cat, Tom, swallowed the mouse, Jerry. He was meant to burp him up. But the laughing Mormons told Tom to eat the rodent. The dream wasn't meant to be a version of Itchy and Scratchy and the mouse hadn't even been able to work the mini chainsaw. Tom'd never realised how good Jerry tasted. So he swallowed him, whole. In the five hundred and eighty-nine sparkling Hanna Barbera episodes he'd seen, Tom had never managed to murder Jerry. Marshall wondered if his brain was being disrespectful.

He popped in one of his vitamin pills. His bedroom was small and Marshall felt sticky under the duvet in his T-Shirt and trousers. He checked the clock. It was 1.45 pm. He shoved his hand hopefully down into his pants and tried to push into his head the image of a girl doing things, but he couldn't banish the sight of a gleeful Tom rubbing his plump belly and the sound of a Mormon couple standing in the shadows of his dream, laughing right behind him.

– MARSHALL, WHAT'RE YOU DOING UP THERE?

His mam had shouted upstairs. She stood in the hall and slapped the wall with the palm of her hand three times.

– UP, she said. NOW. He's here already.

– Alright, alright.

Marshall got out of bed and changed. He didn't have a suit yet so had started doing the job in his decent tracksuit. Dad hadn't liked the look. Didn't think it suitable. Wasn't a good look for any house owner who answered the door. So Marshall took to wearing his old school trousers and a white shirt. Smart.

He used the toilet. Cleaned his teeth again. Watered his hair into a straight side parting. He hadn't been able to find the shampoo in days and kept on meaning to ask his mam where it was. In the mirror, the mini *Encyclopaedia of Dog training – Health and Behaviour* caught his eye, and he turned to pick it up from the top of the toilet tank. Marshall pretended he couldn't hear the sound of his mam screaming above the thin rumble of the metallic air conditioner and wandered through the pages, admiring photos of all those four-legged friends of man. After Welsh Mormonism, Marshall's other great passion was for dogs. They were farmed nearby. Crossbred beauties. Marshall thought dogs would be a good career move.

– MARSHALL, WHA' THE FUCK'RE YOU DOING UP THERE?

He flushed the toilet and stepped out into the side passage. Ready for work. He darted to the kitchen and looked around. His mam sat at the table, smoking.

– Where is he? asked Marshall.

She dragged her eyes up from the newspaper and at her son. Marshall tapped the squishy sole of his new Clarks shoes on her washed floor, making a squeaky noise. His fingers patted either side of his fat thighs in synch. She pointed at the window.

– Outside. In the car. Waiting.

– Oh.

She wiped the ash off the side of her fluffy pink dressing gown and watched Marshall put two slices of white bread into the toaster. He went to the fridge and took out the large bottle of orange juice from the door.

– What're you doing?

– Making dinner, he said.

– You know where you go today? she said.

– Doing houses down the bottom end.

– Christ, she said.

Marshall stood there slowly drinking cold orange juice from the bottle with his eyes on the toaster. His mam watched small drops of juice leak from the corner of the bottle onto his chin.

– Marshall, you're dripping tha'…

The toast jumped up. Outside his dad smashed his fist loudly on the car horn. He took the bottle away from his mouth, put it back in the fridge and grabbed the tub of Utterly Butterly Light from the second shelf, ran over to the toaster and snatched at the hot slices. His dad beeped again.

– Have you cleaned your teeth?

– Yep.

Like a cheerleader Marshall turned from the counter, showing his teeth, and twirled around waving two steaming slices of buttered toast in each hand. He kissed his mam lightly on her cheek.

– They was nice ones, those two, weren't they? he said.

– Yeah, and you bloody remember what I told you, right? Make sure you keep 'effing shtum about *them ones* in front of him. Leave it alone, said his mam. You've been fucking lucky today, boy.

– Ahhh, 'to boldly go, where no man has gone before', he said.

– Go.

Marshall shut the front door. His mam was irritated Marshall was enjoying his job. They'd given him a Community Service Order to punish him, and the little prick was loving it. She'd been furious with him all day. They were fortunate the funny old American couple didn't want to involve the police. She was getting worried about Marshall and his hobbies. He hadn't got a job since leaving school and she didn't like the idea of having to live with Marshall for the rest of her life. She didn't like the idea she'd be sharing her home in twenty-one years time with a thirty-eight-year-old virgin that was also her sad son.

Barry was outside, having a quiet fag in the car. The boy didn't drive so for the past week he'd had to pick him up. He'd offered to take over the supervision of a Probation Trust, a Community Service Order sentence scheduled for three hundred hours. He hadn't been able to get anything more physical for his fat son, litter picking or washing off graffiti. The programmes were all packed. This activity was simply door to door stuff and they'd been doing the council leafleting more or less hand in hand. Easy. Barry just had to put up with the dribble that constantly came out of Marshall's mouth. He took a sip of coffee and looked at his old house. He saw Marshall was doing something in the kitchen and beeped the horn again.

Marshall came out at speed, wobbling up the garden path, munching on a piece of toast. He opened the car door, squeezed himself in and handed Barry a piece of toast.

– Afternoon, Dad, he said.

– It's Barry.

– What is?

– I said, it's Barry. Not Daddy. Not Dad on this job. Barry. Okay?

– Yeah, right. Of course, Barry, said Marshall.

202

– Fine, said Barry.

– Yeah, cool, said Marshall.

Marshall took a large bite out of his toast and watched as crumbs bounced and rolled onto his shirt. Barry took a delicate bite out of his toast slice, without a crumb falling.

– Thanks, he said.

Barry started the engine and pulled away from the kerb.

– Had a great dream earlier, Dad, said Marshall.

– Don't want to know, said Barry.

– You'd like it.

– No, I wouldn't.

– Ever watch a Tom and Jerry? said Marshall.

– Shut the fuck up.

– Okay. Just thought you'd wanna know, tha's all.

– No.

– Alright.

– Good. Now, I got a question to ask you boy, as a policeman. You haven't been faffing around on your fucking computer again, have you? Chatting to anyone? Mormons?

– Mormons? No, course not. Why? said Marshall. You seen any?

– Just a check I need to do with you, now and again, innit? Forget I asked.

Marshall couldn't forget it. He imagined he was Barry's shotgun partner and sat in the seat with his eyes scanning the roads for his American friends. He was sure he'd spot the Americans. Didn't know how long they were going to be in the country, but he was on the look out. He hoped he'd spot the Americans. He'd taken their licence plate number. He knew if he found them again they might even take him back to America. It's what the Mormons did.

Marshall wondered whether it was going to be another cold afternoon. He could see patches of snow on the top of parked cars. Dirty heaps of the stuff, piled on the pavement. But he was in a positive state of mind. Maybe it'd get warmer.

– Not much colour around here, is there? he said.

– What?

– Colour, like. Never seems to be much colour, said Marshall.

– What're you talking about, Marshall? Don't go doing your racist act again.

– Naww, mun. I dunno, it's just like, you know, you look out the window there, and all you see is tha' shite. It's like something has been vomiting tons of concrete for miles around. And you looks over there an' it's all just stained walls and stuff. Know what I mean? Colour, like. Round here, never seems to be much of it.

Barry had been fiddling with his mobile but couldn't get a signal. He didn't know whether Marshall was playing with him or whether his son had truly fucking lost it already. He sounded like he was getting worse. Barry was doing his best to ignore him, simply staring out of the windscreen whilst scratching at the side of his nose with those sausage shaped fingers.

– I mean, it's a shame, said Marshall. When your dreams are so colourful, like, and you wakes up, and you're looking at all this shite, innit?

– Yeah, right, said Barry.

He chucked his mobile onto the backseat and turned the radio on. They were joined in the car by the voice of Frank Sinatra, his rich tones slowly telling them what it was he was dreaming of. Barry was about to automatically switch stations but stopped when he noticed Marshall had gone quiet. They weren't far from their destination and if the White Christmas song was going to be keeping Marshall zipped, Barry could bear it.

– Thaaaa's not Bing Crosby! said Marshall.

– Aaaaawwww, for fuck's sake, mun!

– But it's not, is it? That's not. It's not Bing! That's Frank Sinatra. That is Frank fucking Sinatra, mun, stealing Bing's melody! He's doing a slower paced version of Bing's favourite song there.

– SO WHAT?

– What? Tha' dirty semi-Italian rat? Singing Bing Crosby's clean white tune? Naw, naw mun, naaaw, tha's not right, is it? Doesn't fucking sound right, does it?

– Sounds fine, said Barry.

– Naw, mun. Naw. Tha's wrong.

– Well it fucking sounds alright to me.

– Naw. That's not right.

Marshall shook his head with a sombre expression on his face. They drove down to the streets at the bottom of the estate and Barry had stopped listening to the nonsense coming out of his son's round mouth. Why on earth had he offered to walk door to door with this gibbering gerbil?

Another Ride

Hank had left Masaki's place and was in the front end of a bus travelling back to the estate. He'd do it. He could. He'd at least get his trainers. And he was sure he'd be able to get back on down to Pentre for the panda routine. The fingers of his left hand picked at the dried fabric of the brown and yellow chequered bus seat, whilst he held a Greggs pasty in his right hand up to his gob and chewed. He had failed in his first task. He should not have spent money on a taxi. He had searched for Masaki and he had lost. Tetchy though, was another goal. He wanted his trainers now more than ever.

His finger stopped picking at the seat when he felt something hit his nail. Hank looked down and saw an ancient piece of chewing gum embedded flat in the fabric of the seat. The bus came onto the street and Hank let his fingers pick at the chewing gum. Tetchy would be home, the door next to his cousin's house. Hank hadn't seen Marshall for a couple of months and didn't want to stop by today. He had other, more important, things to do. Masaki had escaped him. The quest was now to regain his trainers. He would get them. The bus came to a stop and Hank stood. Holding onto the side of each seat he stepped forwards.

Outlaw Hank limped off into the street and hobbled through Tetchy's lifeless garden, avoiding the weathered plastic toys scattered across the pathway. He brought his head down and hurried, not daring to look up at his cousin's house. Tetchy's dad usually had the family goat tethered out front, but Hank couldn't see Billie. Inside, he saw the TV was on. He sucked the air in and tried to ignore the strange sensation as billions of neurons in his brain began to crackle once again. His legs felt heavy. He stood at the door with his arms on his hips, and from nowhere the theme tune to the Western TV series, *Bonanza* surged into his head:

Dum, deladum, deladum, deladum, Bo-Nann-Zaaaa!!!

Dum, deladum, deladum, deladum, dumdeladum, Dum-Dum!

The doorbell wasn't working. Hank peered through the dirty, pebbled glass, hammering at it with an agitated fist. The noise was swallowed by a narrow corridor into the house. The front door opened and a surprised Tetchy appeared. He recognised Hank and waved his forefinger in front of him.

– Wank Evans! How's it going, dude?

– I've come for my trainers, said Hank.

– You wha'?

– My fucking trainers, Tetchy.

– Wha' fucking trainers, spacca?

Both young men looked down at Tetchy's feet as he jiggled his toes in answer. Ten tiny toes. Hank blinked. The *Bonanza* theme tune once again surged in a loop inside his head. He couldn't understand it, he despised the show. Hank knew if he was to get his trainers before he went into one, he was going to have to do it fast.

He slammed his plaster-cast foot right onto Tetchy's scrawny toes and shoved him into the passage. Tetchy screamed and fell and Hank jumped onto his chest, sliding a knee to his neck.

– MY FUCKING TRAINERS, YOU CUNT.

– Wha' the fuck you on 'bout? I 'aven't gor your frigging trainers, 'ave I?

– NO? THEN WHY'D YOU WRITE THIS?

Hank managed to spread both hands against either side of

the passage and hold the wall for balance as he shifted his weight and struggled back to push the biro-signed plaster to Tetchy's face. He nudged it hard against his nose and Tetchy's eyes tried to focus on the writing.

– WHY WOULD I WRITE THA'? I WOULDN'T THIEVE A MAN'S TRAINERS AND ADMIT TO IT. TAKE A LOOK. GOAN, 'AVE A LOOK AROUND. 'AVE A LOOK.

Hank put more pressure on his hands and kicked the lying git in the side. He kicked him again with his good foot. The *Bonanza* theme tune stopped playing in his head and his foot seemed to automatically stop wanting to kick at Tetchy. Hank was waiting for the fit to happen. The new medicine wasn't going to hold one back. It had to. Hank moved away from Tetchy, rubbing at his head. He hadn't had one. Tetchy jumped up and threw his body at Hank. A large open hand was put into Hank's face. Hank's head cracked against the side of the wall.

– I never nicked your fucking trainers.

Hank didn't know whether to believe him. He knew he should look around. He moved past Tetchy and stepped into the living room. Empty lager cans on every surface. A skeletal Christmas tree was in the window, alongside the TV, showing the darts. Hank moved the plate of dried beans to one side and sat down on the sofa. He put his head in his hands and tried to stop feeling giddy.

Tetchy came in from the kitchen with a new can and sat in a chair by Hank.

– I 'aven't been over to your side in ages, mun. Cuts my own hair nowadays, don't I? Don't need Tash. Never seen no trainers. Not heard 'bout 'em. Goan. Take a look, if you don't believe us, like. Honest.

Their goat wandered into the room. Hank could feel the warmth of the goat, her breath on his neck as she smelt his sapped body. He glanced into the vacant face of the mangy looking thing. Billie's yellow eyes were waiting for him to say something. Hank didn't have anything to say to the goat. Nobody knew why Tetchy's dad kept the goat. He used to claim he was going to start a family business with Billie but it never happened. He put his hand up and brushed her away.

– I got her in this morning. Getting chilly out there. Got her in, like. Yeah.

– I can see, said Hank.

– Yeah.

– How's your brother these days?

– Dunno, disappeared.

– Oh, shame.

– Yeah, you and him used to be best mates didn't you? Always liked you.

– So you haven't seen my trainers?

– Nope. Never.

Hank rubbed his head. The fit hadn't happened. The new medication was working. Tetchy drank and raised the can to Hank.

– You want one, mate?

– Naw, said Hank.

– Heard all 'bout Cheyenne, 'en?

– Yeah. She mentioned you.

– Oh, so you visited her already? said Tetchy.

– This morning. Freelance TV journalists were up there. The arseholes are fooling her. Telling her all of this will make her famous.

– Yeah?

– No.

– Ooooh. I was thinking of going in to say hello.

Hank could hear the *Bonanza* theme tune sliding back into his skull. The one hundred billion neurons in his brain had started dancing along to the tune again and it was putting a disturbing taste into his mouth. He was aware Tetchy was talking and chuckling. Hank couldn't listen. He knew he had another matter to fix with Tetchy. It was something about Cheyenne. He couldn't think what it was. He stayed motionless, staring at the mini baubles on a Christmas tree. His eyes flicked to the TV. Where was he? Didn't he have to be at the game? It was happening. The plunge. A cluster of nerve cells were going to be firing at one hundred times a second, any second now, and Hank was not going to be able to stop them. He could see the steam train coming. Buster Keaton had a short, fat cannon pointed at him and he couldn't get out of the way. He was looking into the circular hole of the cannon, waiting for the bang.

The steam train hit his head. He disappeared into the tiny black hole at the centre of the cannon. He was out.

Tetchy stood and stepped over a juddering Hank. He snatched the stolen trainers from behind the sofa and ran into the kitchen. He opened the cupboard above the cooker and chucked them in, got another can from the fridge and went back to the living room to watch Hank wriggle.

Community Service

They stepped out of the car. Barry stretched. Marshall copied him. The blue sky was massive, the street motionless. They were days away from Christmas and most of the houses in this part of the Texas-2 estate got into a competitive mode when it came to displaying their lights. The illuminated hanging icicles or the multi-coloured lasso ropes always added an edge of glamour to a street full of knackered cars and overflowing plastic rubbish bins. A laughing Santa Claus with a Stetson hat on his head was in someone's front garden. It was lit from within and stood out amongst the concrete building-blocks which were the gateway to most of the council house semis. The colour filled Marshall's hungry eyes and took his mind away from Frank Sinatra. He was trying to imagine what the twelve-foot tall statue of Jesus might look like when it was illuminated.

– Ahhh, he said. American colours.

It was one of those moments when everything had stopped. Not a sound. Not a bit of wind. Nothing. No noise from the Cwm mountain. Marshall was already feeling his cold hands. His frozen breath in front of his nose. Barry lit a fag and pointed at the pensioner's body lying in the gutter a few feet away from the car.

– Is he dead? asked Marshall.

– I dunno, do I?

Barry looked around. There was nobody about. He took a long sip of his cold coffee and dropped the cardboard cup by his feet.

– Stuff's in the boot, he said to Marshall. Get it out.

– Right.

Marshall went to open the boot, whilst Barry went to check on the OAP lying in the gutter. The big man was breathing. The breath coming out of his scarlet lips stank heavily of whisky. The back of the man's jacket was covered in a light frost. It seemed he'd been lying there for a while. Barry poked him with the toe of his new shoe and the white-haired man grumbled in discomfort. He looked at the side of the man's face and wondered if he knew him.

Marshall was at the boot of the car looking up towards the black woods above the street. He was thinking of the dog farm. He was wondering why he couldn't hear any of the sweet barking today.

– Well, he's still alive, said Barry.

– Yeah?

– Yeah. Piss-head must have slipped.

Marshall helped Barry pick the man off the iced ground. He looked down the street. No-one was around. Barry didn't want this stinking bundle in the back of his car, and certainly didn't want to get anyone else at the station involved.

– Where do you live, sir? he asked.

The man looked up and pointed vaguely at a house a few feet away. They dragged him towards the house and up the garden path. Barry pressed the doorbell. No-one answered. They jangled him up and down to try and find his keys but the man had nothing inside his pockets. Barry rang the bell again.

– Ta boys. Ta, said the man.

– Come on. Let's just leave him, said Barry.

– Where?

– Here. Next to his front door. Some bugger'll come along and find him, won't they, boy?

– Uhh, yeah, it was us, Dad, said Marshall.

– Ta boys. Ta. Carlton, it is. Name's Carlton.

They shoved the man against the front door with a heavy thud and were about to leave when he slid down the door and into the unlit passageway. He lay there laughing at the two men who stood in the doorway.

– Ta, ta boys.

Barry and Marshall picked him up and dragged him further into the house. It was chilly in there. And it reeked. The walls in the passage were coated in a thin flowery paper that looked as if it had been put on in the sixties. Black patches of damp sweat had spread down the staircase, coating the bright carpet on each of the steps. They yanked the elderly man onto the stairs. He was mumbling.

– Ta, boys… yeah, gonna see the game today? Bet we fucking lose again, don't we. Lose.

– Hello? Anyone home? called out Barry.

– …the Pentrecoch Panda, eh? Fucking shite, boys. Shite.

Barry looked around for the light switch, but either the bulb had gone or there was no electricity. He opened the living room door and helped the man inside. This room smelled even worse. The curtains were shut but their eyes had adjusted to the darkness. They put the man down on the plastic settee next to the body of his sleeping wife. Barry was trying not to laugh, imagining the row she'd be giving him the whole week when she woke. The man opened his own eyes as Barry and Marshall were about to leave.

– Your wife's not going to be pleased is she, Carlton boy? said Barry.

– That? Uhh? Tha's not my wife! Tha's my fucking neighbour. Mrs Sparrow, mun. Looks after the nut on her other side, Boyd. Naw, you've gotten me into the wrong house, here.

The old man poked Mrs Sparrow and she slid to the side and went head first onto the orange carpet. There was an unseemly odour that caught the back of Marshall's mouth and made him want to puke. He'd seen zombie films before, and he immediately knew this one was dead.

– She's dead, said Barry.

– I know, said Marshall. What're we gonna do?

– Nothing. Come on, let's go. Get this sodden old lump back outside. We've got community service leaflets to give out. Come'n.

– We can't just leave her here, surely.

Barry and Marshall sat in the car outside Mrs Sparrow's house. They'd been arguing. The man had fallen asleep on Mrs Sparrow's settee and they'd pulled him back outside to lie against what they hoped was his own garden fence. Marshall was sure they needed to get in touch with somebody about the old woman. Barry had taken notes and tried to explain to his son that he was an experienced policeman and an old lady who'd died naturally on her sofa was not an emergency call-out. He'd deal with her later and was insisting the boy carried on with his leafleting duties. He didn't want to get entangled with a dead OAP.

– Marshall, we're not getting involved with this right now. Move it. Come on, we have to do *this*, not *that*. This. We need to do this house by house by house. It's your discipline. Community service. It's your charge.

– Yeah I know, all I'm saying is, what do you do when you finds a dead body, like? There's gotta be something. A secret phone number? The hospital, maybe? They'd know what to do, Dad.

– MARSHALL, SHE'S FUCKING DEAD. What's the hospital gonna be able to do? Racing over here with an ambulance? It'd be fucking waste.

214

– They deal with corpses there though, don't they? Hospital would want her, like.

Barry got out and went round to open the boot of the car. He was glad he hadn't hit the boy. He noticed Marshall hadn't moved and banged angrily on the roof. Marshall got out to join him. Marshall slouched to the boot. A flicker caught his eye. He stopped and was staring into the woods on the back of the Cwmgarw mountain where there was a small blip of light coming from between the dark trees. A metallic glimmer.

– Did you see tha'? he said.

– Yeah, said Barry.

– What was tha'?

– Dunno, said Barry.

– There you are, there it is again. Look.

They heard a distant *pop* and the silence of the street broke when a metallic ping exploded behind them. There was a small dent in the side of Barry's car door. They heard another distant pop and Marshall felt something whistle past him. *Ping.* The side of the car door bounced in and out. He stood there pointing his finger up at the woods.

Pop. Thud. The paper leaflets in the boot made a flutter and spread. Barry leant over and riffled through the leaflets. He pulled them apart and examined a small hole that had been blasted through several pages. *Pop. Ping.* The roof of the car rippled. Barry pulled out a splattered lead pellet from a wad of punctured paper. Someone was shooting at them.

– Get in the car.

– AAAaaaaaaaaaaaaaaahhhhh.

Marshall screamed when the top of his thumb came off. The red blood exploded into the air above his face and he quickly pulled his hand down.

– Get in the car, now, said Barry.

215

Marshall stiffened and with a childish smirk on his face showed Barry his bloodied hand.

– Now *that* is colour, he said.

Barry looked up to the woods.

– Get in.

*

They'd driven off the Bevan Estate and along the mountain road. Barry pulled up onto the bank to get a decent signal for his mobile. He was angrily talking to the supervisor at the Probation Trust office. Marshall was in the car cradling his wounded hand and watching the back of his father speak.

– No, no-one was hurt. Not much anyway. What…? Marshall… Yes, mun… He got shot, yes… No… that's not my point, is it? said Barry. I don't want to be picking pellets out of my own arse when I finish assisting my son today, do I…? We're gonna get hurt if some idiot over there is using us as target practice all afternoon.

He was stood by the side of his car, taking a piss. There was a spider between his feet and he was trying to hit it. He stood there chasing the thing with a long spray of yellow urine.

– No, no, mun. I've not taken him to the hospital… not yet. He's not that hurt is he?

Barry lifted his leg and sprayed at the dead frosty grass on the bank. He thought he'd got it and was hoping he'd taken the eight-legged devil's head off. He put his foot down and saw the bugger had jumped onto his shoe.

The supervisor was annoyed Barry and Marshall had randomly decided not to finish the job. He didn't believe Marshall could have been shot. If the boy had been shot surely his own father would have taken him to the hospital.

– Mr Evans, I'm sure I don't have to remind you that you

offered to take on this work as a professional police officer. Even though we were obviously aware of your attachment to the offender himself, we generously accepted your offer. If you are now refusing to complete the role and finish the community duties then I'm afraid we may have to take further legal action against both Marshall and yourself…

– Listen, he's been shot.

– But you are refusing to take…

The phone had gone dead. He couldn't get the signal back. He kicked the spider off his shoe and zipped up. Marshall had his hand wrapped and reckoned it wasn't hurting. He'd been in the car trying to kill a fly. It kept landing on the passenger window. Barry got in and put his aviator glasses back on. He leant over, grabbed Marshall's pale face and rammed the mound of blubbery cheek into the side of the flat window. The fly was crushed against the glass. Yellow juice ran down the one side of his son's face.

– Uhh, Dad?

– What?

– I've been thinking, said Marshall.

– Yeah, what?

– If we *were* to be going to hospital, like? Then maybe we should take Mrs Sparrow, an all.

Failed Assassination Attempt of the Pentrecoch Panda

He'd done it. It was difficult but he made it. He'd managed to do his Panda routine at the ground and was shattered. After the Tetchy incident Hank had wandered back to his own place in a haze and picked up the panda costume. He had been late getting onto the pitch because he'd had to search for scissors, but eventually found a knife under the stadium to cut through the fabric of the left panda leg. It was the only way he could push through his plastered foot. He had achieved his assignment.

Hank was now resting in a taxi a few metres down from the Bevan Community Centre and he winced every time one of the loud children ran past the car. A tingling in his left arm was beginning to match the pulse of pain in his head as he touched a sore mark. He wouldn't normally do a private job after any game but this one was different. It was Geronimo's birthday party. It was Cheyenne's family who'd booked the Panda. He had to do it. Something clicked in his head when he thought of his girlfriend. He tried to recall what it was she'd told him, but couldn't.

He felt drained after the rugby match and the Ibuprofen he'd taken hadn't reduced the swelling on the side of his head. It had appeared there after the glass bottle hit him. Their team had lost the last fifteen games and brutal fans were placing the blame on the single wobbling man hidden in the panda costume.

The darkening street filled with icy voices. People were arriving. The manager of the community centre unbolted the steel casing and opened the inner doors. Groups of young single mothers stood outside in leggings and tight tops. Chatting. Smoking. Coughing. Trembling with laughter in the cold air and peering at the crying babies in their mate's prams. Hank didn't want to move. He told himself he was being a cry-baby but it was difficult. Fuck, he'd only just come out of hospital and had had three already.

He got out of the taxi. He was spooked when he had to cover his eyes against a strong shaft of light that came down from above. The driver had parked under a new streetlight which, unlike its orange neighbours, emitted a booming white beam. The roof of his taxi glowed. Hank peered at a line of ordinary council streetlamps. Solid, lichen-stained, brown concrete poles, rooted ten feet apart, all of them with a steady orange glow coming from the top. Somebody had lost a dog and tied posters to all of the lamps except this one. He looked at this streetlamp. A special one. A new aluminium tube which emitted a harsh, blinding flicker of light like a brief warning, a blinking white eye.

Hank was disturbed. He'd lain in bed one night at the hospital imagining he could hear green aliens scuttling around the room. It could happen apparently. He'd seen a TV programme about a man in Iowa who'd gone into a coma after aliens beamed down from above had entered his home. Hank had never believed in aliens. Could aliens have crept into his own life, gently unscrewed the top of his own head, shoved in a metal tube and tugged out every atom of human energy left in his body? Surely not. Fixated by the intense white glow around his head Hank touched the roof of the taxi as it sped off. He was being silly and urged himself on.

The manager of the Bevan community centre stood on the

steps like a bouncer. Hank remembered her ashen face. He had been there before. She was smoking on the very end of a fag and chatting to a young woman with spiky green short hair. The manager tugged briefly at the lapel on her coat as Hank came up the steps.

– Sorry love, bingo's tomorrow night. Private party tonight. Guests only.

– I know, I've been invited, he said.

– You're here for the birthday party, are you? she said.

– Yes.

The manager brushed a long sliver of silver hair from the side of her face and turned to study Hank. She didn't recognise the bedraggled young man that stood in front of her.

– What's in the bag? she asked

– The costume.

– The costume?

– Yes. The panda costume?

She looked at the bag, at his plastered foot, at Hank, and wiped her grizzled hair back again.

– Wait here, she said. Let me check.

The manager flicked her fag away and went inside. Nobody had told her the panda was coming. She was upset that nobody had told her the panda was coming. If anybody had told her, she'd have brought her own bloody granddaughter along for a treat.

The young woman leaned towards Hank and studied him. He drew back his shoulders.

– The Pentrecoch Panda, right? she said.

– Yep.

– Fuck me, my boyfriend hates the Pentrecoch Panda. Fucking hates it.

– Yes, unfortunately a lot of people do, said Hank.

– How does you do the panda thing with your glasses on?

– It's a big panda head. There's space.

The manager went into her office, grabbed her mobile off the desk and texted her daughter. Her grand-daughter would love to meet a man in a panda costume. Why hadn't she been told the panda was coming? She chucked the mobile back onto the desk and shot into the main hall. She stood there and scanned the faces.

Hank had come inside and was waiting in the bright corridor next to the Events Board. The strain in his arm had turned on the swollen bleep inside his head again and he dropped the bag to lean against the radiator. He could see into the main hall. It was lit by a glitter-ball and he figured there was some Western theme going on. Most of the boys held plastic guns and wore Stetson hats and most of the girls were Red Indians. Some of the mothers were putting out crisps and tuna sandwiches on a line of light plastic tables, whilst the others took care of crying babies. The manager was arguing with one of the women in the hall.

Hank shut his eyes and let his body slide against the wall.

– Come on, this way, she yelled.

The manager walked past Hank in a huff, her pony-tail whipping at the air as she glanced back over her shoulder at him limping along.

– Come on. You can get changed in here.

They walked into the men's toilet. A short boy stood up on his tip toes, trying to pee into the steel urinal above his willy. He spun around to see who the two dark figures were.

– OUT.

The boy leapt back and squirted an arc of piss onto the floor. His toy gun fell from its holster and scattered across the tiles as he ran from the toilet in fear.

– Uhh, I'm meant to be a surprise, right? said Hank.

– You was a fucking surprise to me, love, said the manager.

– No, mun. To the children. See, the way it works is, I'm normally a surprise, aren't I?

– I dunno.

– Well, I'm not gonna be a surprise if I change in here, am I? I didn't change in here last time I was up here, did I? I was in a room at the back of the stage.

– What'd you mean, the last time?

– Last time I did performed at the centre? said Hank.

– You've never done Texas-2 Community Centre before. Think I'd know it if the panda man had ever done a party up in our centre before.

– I have.

The manager studied his face. She shook her head in disagreement. The woman the manager had been arguing with shoved her head through the toilet doorway. The bracelets on her arm jingled above the sound of the disco music coming from the hall as she pointed at Hank.

– Oi, Toni! What've you frigging got him in here for? You can't keep him in here, can you? He's meant to be a surprise, mun, in 'e? They're gonna frigging see him in here, in they?

Hank recognised her voice; this was the woman he'd spoken to on the phone. She was a friend of Cheyenne's mam who'd organised the event. The manager pushed Coleen back out of the doorway and walked past her into the corridor.

– He ain't gonna be changing in here is he, you stupid cow? said the manager. I was showing him where the bogs were, that's all, wasn't I? He's gonna be changing in the storage room, in he? Back of the stage. Come on.

The family friend held out her hand at Hank as he walked past.

– I'm Coleen, love. We spoke on the phone couple weeks ago. Pleased to meet you.

Hank followed the two arguing women across the hall packed full of tiny cowboys and Indians. They led him to the storage room behind the stage. He found a chair amongst the stacked cardboard boxes and sat. He felt bad. The tingle in his arm was pulsating in rhythm to the beat of the disco music and his mouth needed a drink. He bent forward and looked at the two woman in front of him.

– So I'm changing in here, right? said Hank.

– Right, said the manager.

Her mobile rang and she left Hank and Coleen alone. She pulled an envelope out of her purse and handed it to him.

– Fifty, right?

– Ta.

She noticed his plaster-cast foot.

– You hurt yourself recently?

– No, I'm fine, he said.

– You good to do it, with that on your foot?

– Fine. Fine.

– Okay. Get changed. Be back in a minute, love.

The shut door didn't cut out the disco beat. The sound of the adrenalin-pumped children didn't evaporate either. Hank dragged out his crushed panda suit and put it on the dusty table. He picked up the panda's head and stroked at the synthetic fabric. He hadn't washed the costume in a while and it was covered in bits of mud. His mam had always liked him to look neat for the children. His mam would never of let him put it on.

*

Hank was asleep, half-dressed in the panda costume. The door was flung open and Coleen walked in, beaming in delight, holding in her outstretched hands a three-foot long birthday cake shaped as a red sports car.

– Not bad, eh?

– Yeah, great, said Hank as he rubbed his eyes open and put his glasses on.

– Done over in Aberaman. Gloria Wyson. And she ain't frigging cheap, neither. Mind, Geronimo is only nine once, in he? And after Cheyenne's awful misfortunes, yesterday.

– Yes.

– Right 'en, so this is the plan. You is the surprise, right? Only I know you're here. And it is gonna be you tha' comes out holding tha' cake. Being dead 'effing careful, right? Gives the cake over to little Geronimo and me. And then, after kids have calmed down a bit, you does the show, right? The special stuff.

– Uhrggh, my show? said Hank.

– Yeah, you does the balloons or tricks or whatever, right?

– I don't have a show.

– You're the Pentrecoch Panda, in you?

– I don't do balloons, do I? I wave, said Hank.

– What the fuck you on about? I just hired you for fifty quid. You gotta do something more than bloody wave, surely?

– I'm the Pentrecoch Panda, Coleen. I ain't a frigging clown, am I? How am I meant to tie balloons up? Or do tricks with these big panda paws on? I couldn't scratch my own arse with these paws, could I? I'm the Pentrecoch Panda. I wave.

The manager had walked in with her arm around her grand-daughter and they laughed at the young man in the panda costume showing Coleen the big paws he had on his hands. The grand-daughter grabbed hold of the panda's head and stared at it.

– Oooohhh, nice.

– He's never been up here before, has he, sugar? said the manager.

– Yeah, lotsa times, mun, said her grand-daughter.

224

The manager looked puzzled. Coleen coughed loudly to get their attention. A sharp scowl had formed across her perma-tanned face.

– What's the matter? said the manager.

– He's standing here now, telling me he don't do no 'effing tricks or nothing. He waves.

– What you mean? He must do some tricks. The balloons or whatever they does.

The two women watched Hank slowly turn his large, fluffy panda paws in front of their faces once again.

– Then what the fuck do you do at birthday parties? said the manager.

– I dunno, I walk about for a bit. I mingle. I can sit. Yeah, you can put the kids on my knee for free. For photos, like.

– YOU AIN'T FATHER FUCKING CHRISTMAS, IS YOU? shouted Coleen. Give us my effing money back. NOW.

– Alright, calm down Coleen, said the manager.

The two womens' faces were scrunched in a look of foaming horror, and Hank was beginning to worry about the situation. The manager's grand-daughter shook her head.

– Naw, he never did much last time. Cassidy's mam was right pissed off with the miserable shite. Mind, he never had that round his foot neither.

– That's special, said Hank. The cast is a new part of my act. It's a stage prop.

Hank smiled and Coleen started to move towards him like a sumo wrestler on speed.

– Give us my effing money back. NOW, YOU BASTARD.

– No, said Hank. You just paid us.

– RIGHT.

Hank stood as Coleen tried to grab at him and whipped at the air with her arms in a violent frenzy. Hank moved to the side and Coleen tried to grab at him again.

– Alright. Alright. Calm down, ladies. Calm down, said the manager. She held a red-faced Coleen by the shoulders and let her regain her breath. Look, he's here now, isn't he? Maybe he *can* do a funny belly dance or something. Up on stage like, alright.

– Well yeah, for sure, I can dance, said Hank. You didn't say dance, did you? Sure. Course I do dancing, yeah. Snake dance, maybe.

*

Hank was standing on stage behind the rotting curtains. He had the massive cake held in his furry paws and was waiting to be announced. He didn't dance. Cheyenne always told him his dance was awful. If he couldn't dance as a fucking man, how was he going to dance dressed up as a bloody panda bear?

He listened when the noise in the hall melted into a silence. He heard the manager raise her voice, asking who they thought was standing behind the yellow curtains. Spider man was a frequent guess. A strange sounding girl hoped it was Elvis. Nobody suggested the Pentrecoch Panda. The heavy curtains were cranked back to reveal Hank and the cake. The children laughed and screamed in delight as the secret figure lurched forward. They all recognised the Pentrecoch Panda and were briefly happy with its arrival. Music came on and Hank started to dance. But his slow squiggling movements on stage to an Abba tune he didn't know didn't impress his audience.

At the back of the hall next to Coleen were the stone-faced figures of Cheyenne's mother and her seething grandmother. Coleen waved her hands at the surprise spectacle on stage whilst Geronimo's mother stood with her arms crossed and watched. Hank saw them and almost shat himself. The grandmother had recently returned from the awful rugby game and had taken great drunken enjoyment from abusing their ridiculous club mascot. Her mouth dropped open when she saw the Panda being used on stage in front of these children. It was wrong. Cheyenne had phoned her earlier to let her know who the surprise guest would be. It was why she was here. She couldn't believe it. She left the building.

Some of the red Indians had started to chant, and some of the mini cowboys fired their paper cap guns at Hank. He jumped gently from one leg to the other. The children seemed more interested in what the panda was holding. The cake. Hank had almost forgot about it. He quickly raised the heavy cake above his head and twirled around to get their attention.

He made a roaring noise and with Elvis in mind tried some tepid kind of Kung-Fu dance moves, kicking hard at the air. Hank spotted Coleen next to Cheyenne's mother, and the manager behind the children; they were all making a cut-throat gesture toward him. They didn't want him to drop the birthday cake.

The children started to jeer and hoot at a much higher level when the birthday boy waved his arms above his head and pointed towards a mean little figure standing by the main doorway. Geronimo sprinted through his crowd of friends to help this person into the birthday hall. The figure, wearing a dark balaclava, sunglasses and a lacy black cape outfit, the kids thought was part of the panda act. Their cheer grew louder when the person pushed Geronimo aside and waved a five-foot steel Highlander-Brave sword at the plodding panda.

Hank was still kicking in front of him and hadn't seen the disguised lady. He had assumed the children were cheering him on but he felt knackered and it was only when he stopped to take a bow that he saw the woman standing there with the sword. Cheyenne's grandmother croaked in her aged voice,

– I AM THE PENTRECOCH PANDA ASSASSINATOR. GET OFF OUR STAGE.

An image of JFK, somewhere in Dallas and waving his hand at a crowd, had swooped into Hank's head and he couldn't get rid of it. He felt sick. The tingle in his arm increased as it travelled toward his chest. His breathing inside the panda's head was fast. His shoulder rattled. The birthday cake fell from his hands and he caught a glimpse of Coleen screaming as he dropped to his knees on the stage. He tried to hold on to it but the cake fell and Hank fell alongside it. His head squeezing shut. His legs stiffening and vibrating. He watched as Cheyenne's mam, the manager and Coleen grabbed hold of the assassinator, herded her out of the hall, and listened to the children squeal in delight.

Find the Dogman

The place seemed dead. There was no barking as he drove up the track. The puppy farm was at a concealed spot on top of the grisly Cwm mountain, and Boyd found the unlit path which led him to the farm, a slippery drive. He pulled in between a mud-splattered Toyota Land Cruiser and an old Astra and quietly stepped out of his car with the gun.

He crept round the side of the concrete cabin and put his head into the barn. The air stank. Boyd went inside and walked up and down the lines of steel cages. Sickness spread through his body as he saw the animals lying dead in their separate cages. The Dogman must've upset someone other than himself.

The dogs had been shot at close range. They were mainly designer dogs no bigger than fifteen centimetres. He saw animals with long sharp ears, upturned noses and fangs too large for their mouths. Things he couldn't name, hybrid dogs. Dogs with bodies covered in poodle fur and heads stolen from a pit bull. Toy dogs. The dogs were cramped into their dirty cages and Boyd thought they were probably better off dead. The Dogman wasn't a dog lover. The last cage was larger than the rest and contained the body of a naked man lying face-first on the floor. Boyd found a plywood joist resting amongst some rubbish to be burnt and used it to turn the body. He didn't recognise the bloke, but knew he wasn't the Dogman.

He left the barn and went over to the living quarters. Held

his breath and opened the door. Dogman was sat tied to his chair in the middle of the floor. He had large chunks of filthy newspaper stuffed tight into his mouth with Sellotape wrapped around the back of his head. His trousers were ripped. He wasn't wearing shoes and his bare feet had been reduced to bloody, toeless stumps. It looked as if almost every one of his toes had been cut off. A plastic clothesline was tied tight against his chest pulling his arms strongly behind him to the chair. His hands had turned a dark red. Boyd didn't know whether to scream or smile.

Dogman raised his head from his chest with a sign of terror on his battered face and mumbled. Boyd went up to him, tenderly put his feet down amongst the bony pile of scattered toes and pushed Dogman's head forward to find the end of the Sellotape. He pulled at it with force, knowing it would cause the man more agony. Dogman retched out sodden, shit-smeared newspaper and yelled as Boyd stepped back with his gun raised.

– HE'S IN THE CUPBOARD.

– Who?

– BEHIND YOU.

Boyd turned in time to see the door of the farmhouse cupboard open and out step a small boy holding a Longthorne shotgun with a Scorpion air-rifle slung over his back. The mass of matted black hair on top of his head looked too heavy for his frame and made his white skin seem pallid. He was wearing a school uniform and a parka coat. He smirked at Boyd, showing a line of brown teeth.

– Alright? said Morgan.

– Yep.

– Nice gun.

– Thanks.

– SHOOT HIM. SHOOT HIM, shrieked the Dogman.

– Shut up, said Morgan.

– SHOOT, SHOOT.

– You got three seconds to shut up, or you'll be getting another one.

Morgan pointed the shotgun at a screaming Dogman Evans who instinctively went into a blubbering mass and dropped his head to his chest for cover. Boyd stood side on between them both with his gun arm outstretched, also pointing at Dogman, and his neck twisted to face the boy. Morgan was a few feet away and moved his shotgun from Dogman and back to a worried Boyd.

– So who're you 'en? Police, is it?

– It's Boyd. Who're you?

– Morgan.

– You the Dogman's son?

– Not any more. Like your pistol.

– Yeah, it's a bit heavy. Old-fashioned, like.

– You got a list? said Morgan.

– A list?

– Yeah, a wish list. You know, people you'd kill if you had a chance. Been thinking 'bout it. Figured everyone's got a list, said the boy.

– Sure, but I don't like to go public with it, said Boyd.

– Come on. Give us one of 'em.

Boyd knew his dog wasn't on the farm, and didn't want to be dealing with this. Whatever *this* was, it had happened between the boy and the Dogman. It wasn't his problem. The boy stood there, lightly hopping from one foot to the other. Waggling his heavy eyebrows in sync and flickering a brown smile at Boyd.

– Come on, give us one. One of your top ten, said Morgan. Come on.

– One of the Royals.

– Oooooh, that'd be hard.

– Yeah, but if I came across one they'd be dead before I even shook their blue-blooded hand.

– Wha'? Any-one of 'em? said Morgan.

– Yep. Cunts, the lot of 'em.

– Yeah, tasty. Like it.

– Yep, said Boyd. Even if they caught us, they couldn't kill me, could they? Locked up all my life? So wha'? I ain't gonna be dead, is I?

– Tidy.

– Wha' about you, 'en? said Boyd.

– Him.

– Yeah?

– Yeah. Been practising. So, you come up to buy one of his dogs, is it?

– No, I cocked it up. Figured this man had nicked my dog and…

– He's a dirty shite. It's possible. Bastard killed my own mam.

Morgan moved his shotgun away from Boyd to the Dogman. Boyd swiftly re-positioned his own gun and aimed it at the dangerous child. Dogman shouted fiercely with blood spurting from his open mouth, his teeth broken and loose.

– I didn't kill her! This crazy little shite killed her. Blew her fucking head off on the day of his own birthday. And her new boyfriend too. This little nut has killed off all my fucking business…

– YOU'RE LYING…

– Well, I'm sorry, said Boyd. But I'm gonna have to take the break here, guys. I ain't a counsellor. I didn't come up here to help sort out any family problems, did I? I came to get my dog back. And my dog? My dog ain't here, so…

– Your dog? asked Dogman.

– Yeah, Pinkie. My dog.

– Murdered all his own dogs, said Morgan.

– Oi, you. Put that shotgun down. On the ground, there. Lower it.

The Dogman and Morgan were both looking at Boyd. Morgan had been unaware that he'd moved his shotgun away. Boyd had him beat, and he threw his weapon onto the floor by his feet.

– Listen mate, you gotta untie us, here. Don't leave me here. I know wha' happened to your dog. Help me. I cun help you. Untie me.

– He's lying, said Morgan. He's lying.

Boyd went towards the Dogman. He knew he couldn't leave him alone with the boy. He had to untie him. The man would be bleeding to death. Boyd bent down and found the end of the clothesline wrapped around Dogman's wrists.

– What do you know about Pinkie?

– It was your girlfriend. Leanne, it was her. She come round with her sister. It was them. They took your dog. They wanted to punish you, for whatever you did. Wanted one of my swords an' all.

– You sold them one?

– I'm sorry mate, he said.

Boyd looked at him with hatred. If Leanne and her sister had taken his dog he should leave. Dogman pleaded.

– Untie me.

– Don't you fucking touch him. Don't you even think 'bout doing it, said Morgan.

Boyd saw the boy scowling at him with his shotgun raised back in his hands. He hesitated. He shook his head in apology and leaned away from the Dogman. The boy wouldn't shoot.

– What're you going to do? he asked.

– Me? said Morgan. Me? I'm leaving this place. It was good

advice a friend gave me in the park earlier today. He said, take the chance. I'll take the chance, alright.

Morgan shot at the Dogman. An enormous explosion and the force threw both Dogman and Boyd backwards against the wall. Morgan was briefly hurled under the weight of the discharge himself and went to the floor as well. He jumped and screeched with delight. Boyd shut his eyes in fear and pretended to be dead as the boy ran over to them. He snatched Boyd's gun out of his open hand and went yelling out of the cabin into the woods.

Boyd opened his eyes and looked across the carpet to see Dogman's bloody ear lying tangled amongst the broken chair and clothes line. A trickle of blood was coming from his head just above the eyebrow. Boyd put a hand to the back of his neck and winced in pain when his fingers touched splinters of wood. The Dogman was bleeding from the side of his head where his ear used to be. He groaned.

A Dead Dog

Leanne thought her sister's flat was gross. She didn't like the laughing plastic skull on the mantelpiece, the half-melted, fat black candles on the sideboard, and the dripping gold star painted on the wall. The red carpet and the white leather settee looked out of place. Donna was thinking it was lush. It was all expertly designed for her clients.

Donna was looking glamorous. She was dressed in a tight, black rubber outfit and wearing a red wig. She had dressed herself up as the Mistress X character for the unproduced dog-shoot. She squeaked with every move she made and Leanne found it difficult to hold back her laugher. Throughout the day they'd been smoking Donna's black Afghan hash to cure their hangovers and worries about their sickly cousin, Cheyenne.

– Feeling better now, said Leanne.

– Yep. Told you. Always does on this stuff. Gets rid of any nasty headaches.

The smoke from the hash lingered in the living room and erased any nerves Leanne had felt earlier. She was on the settee and laughed at her sister twirl the Samurai sword in circles around her head. Boyd's dog sat on the floor and watched her stumble and squeak. Donna stopped. She carefully flicked her thumb over the edge of the sword to feel the sharpness of the steel blade. It could cut through glass.

– I am the Mistress, she said.

– Ooooh very scary. Princess Lush this time, is it? said Leanne.

– Sod off.

Donna raised the sword above her head and pointed it at Leanne. It wasn't a heavy object and yet she felt she had to strain the muscles in her shoulders against her outfit to keep it steady. She lowered the sword toward Pinkie's neck. The dog barked.

– How hard does you reckon you'd have to, you know, hit him? To kill him, like? said Donna.

– What?

– I mean, it's pretty sharp, innit? But to get through his fat neck? I reckon it'd still have to be pretty hard, said Donna.

– Yeah. Dead hard. But don't forget, dim-wit, we ain't going to be doing that, are we?

– I know, I know. Just curious, like.

– Yeah, well come on. We got some filming to do here. It's getting late on this. Let's get going, said Leanne.

Donna pulled the sword back behind her shoulders and slashed it down jokily fast. The dog furiously barked and swiftly stood in challenge. Donna flinched in shock when the sword hit Pinkie's neck. Hard. It came out of her hands and scattered across the floor. Donna staggered on her feet, and Leanne sat there dumbfounded. The massive body of the dog lay on the carpet with a stream of blood running from its neck. His melon-shaped head lay in the far corner of the room next to the sword. His eyes had rolled back.

– Is he dead?

– You just cut its fucking head off, Donna. Yes, I think the dog's fucking dead.

– Did you film it?

Happy Is Never After the Meet

Barry had driven most of the journey keeping his eyes off the dead body in the back of his car and trying not to glance at Marshall. He couldn't believe it was taking them so long. He'd made the error of driving the mountain road to the hospital. He knew it was a faster route but it was dark now, the winter light had gone from the sky and the grim road was covered with what seemed like long stretches of black ice. Every few miles the wheels of the car were taken out of Barry's control and he had to sit there as the frozen car slid forwards and to the side on metres of ice.

Marshall was in the passenger seat with a grin on his round face they both knew shouldn't have been there. Someone had taken his thumb off. Open-fired on them. And Barry reckoned his son must've been hurting, yet he seemed to be enjoying the trip. He'd swallowed five aspirins earlier and had his eyes glued on his right hand in a state of fascination like some five-year-old kid looking at a red lollipop. He was sure someone at the hospital could fix it.

What was left of Marshall's thumb was a bony lump and although Barry hadn't said anything he didn't think there was much chance of the thumb being put back on. He knew Jean, his ex-wife, wouldn't be pleased. The car temperature read minus two and Barry had kept the heating off. Marshall's thumb sat in a styrofoam cup filled with snow in the hope it wouldn't melt. And, of course, Barry didn't like the idea of Mrs Sparrow getting too hot in the back seat. They'd wrapped the old bird up in a woollen blanket found in her airing cupboard. They'd gone back to collect her to keep his gibbering son happy and calm. Barry kept telling himself the odour hitting his nostrils was coming from the decrepit Welsh wool, rather than any rotting flesh.

There was a loud thud and Barry anchored the steering wheel in his hands when the car started to glide towards the left bank. The car was on an ice patch. He'd been looking at himself in the rear view mirror, and hadn't seen the animal. For a minute they drove at a tilted angle, jolting along in the ditch alongside the road with the car tyres grasping at a mix of snow and stone. Barry struggled and just about managed to pull the car out of the ditch and back onto the slim road.

– What was that? asked Marshall.

– Nothing.

– You'd have thought the council gritted up here, wouldn't you?

The road dipped as they went downhill and Barry was careful not to let his foot push too hard on the brake. The only way to keep control of the thing was to drive along the middle of the road with the headlight on full, hoping no teenage racer would come zooming towards them, showing his girlfriend how fast the purple GT could travel in the dark.

He'd noticed Marshall had started to make some deep nasal noises. The radio was on and he tried to ignore the boy but the constant hum Marshall made was getting louder than whatever songs came on. As they carried further on down the steep slope the noise his son produced was growing at a faster pace, and his legs bobbed along in beat. He brought his bloodied hand out.

– That is true colour.

– Marshall, come on. We'll be there soon. Keep it together, mun.

Marshall placed his hand back into the rag on his lap. His hum turned into a high-pitched, nasal whine and his legs danced in rhythm to the steady beat. Barry recognised the tune when Marshall started to whistle and chant. It was the song from the boy's favourite sci-fi series, *Star Trek*. The dancing legs next to him were causing Barry's foot to press a little harder on the accelerator.

– *These are the voyages of the star ship Enterprise…*

– Stop it, Marshall.

Marshall lurched his body towards his dad who realised he shouldn't be touching the accelerator and had to combat their speed now by using the brake in short bursts. The back of the car swung viciously from side to side.

– *…to explore new worlds, to seek out new life…*

– Marshall, come on. Behave.

Marshall let his face veer to the window and stick to the glass. He crushed his nose against the pane and his eyes drifted up over his forehead searching the black sky above. He whipped away from the window and reeled to within inches of his dad. Barry kept his eyes fixed in front of him and tightened his leather gloved hands on the wheel as he felt Marshall's breath against his face.

– *To boldly go, where no man has gone before…*

– Steady it, Marshall.

Marshall flicked away from his dad and let his body fold and flop to the tune coming from his painful whistle. He danced along in his seat like some sixties back-up singer on stage in Las Vegas, waving his hands above his head and shimmying from side to side. Barry tried to stay focussed.

*

Leanne had taken control. She was driving her sister's shabby car at speed, and with the heater on full blast. The wiped clean Samurai sword was on the seat next to her and Donna was in the back with the dog shoved into two black bin bags. She'd ordered her crying sister to clean up the bloody mess she had created and to get changed out of her stupid costume. Donna had to cut off Pinkie's legs to fit him into the bin bags. And unfortunately they hadn't been able to stuff him into the broken car boot. The massive dog was squeezed in beside Donna. Leanne was in charge. Her sister had morphed into a minging gutless slug after killing the dog.

– Only a sword, wannit? Can happen, like.

– Will you shut the fuck up, Donna? yelled Leanne.

-Sorry. I'm sorry. I didn't mean to…

– Dumb-arse.

– I'm sorry, alright?

– DONNA. I won't tell you again. Shut it.

Her sister had demolished the plan for the ransom movie, and Leanne had been frenzied. They had a dead dog on their hands without any reward. Donna had suggested taking a photo of the dog and sending it on to Boyd, but Leanne's thinking was far more pugnacious. They were going to return that sword to the dirty Dogman, and deal with Boyd. Face-to-face.

Leanne had decided. Leanne was the person in charge. Boyd was the man that had attacked *her*. Leanne was going to be the woman who would deal with him. And she would. The man had to be taught a lesson. She understood why her sister had immediately wished to hurt him. The feeling of revenge had been planted into her own numb body after learning the man had hurt their relative. True, they never really knew their second cousin, Cheyenne. And yes, they hadn't filmed the accident with the dog. But Boyd would certainly find out who had done it. She'd say it was herself.

*

They came to the bottom of the hill and Marshall'd stopped his dance routine. The *Star Trek* theme tune had finished and he was silently watching the headlights follow the white lines down the middle of the road. A blurred form leapt to life as their car's beams fell onto a lonely figure in the distance before them. Marshall excitedly prodded at his dad's arm.

– Tha's Hank. Hank, mun.

– Who?

– Hank, mun. It's Hank. Your nephew, mun. My cousin. Hank.

– What the hell's he doing all the way up here?

– Maybe he's had one.

– It's likely.

Barry slowed and stopped next to Hank, who'd been shivering by the side of the road for more than an hour now. He got into the back seat, and Barry pulled away from the side.

*

– Are you angry with me, Ed?

– Now, why the heck should I be angry with you, honey?

– Well maybe it has been a funny two days here, in this old country.

– It's been a fast two days here, sweetheart, said Ed. And as long as this dang motor lasts the journey back down the goddamned highway and over the border-bridge, two days is all we're gonna need to be spending in their country.

After what had happened with Marshall, the Mormon couple were determined not to stay any longer. It had been decided. Ed had driven them back to the motel and suggested they just pack it up and go. As far as he was concerned, the cops had finished with them. He and his wife weren't going to be spending the next two months hill-walking and sightseeing, waiting for those goofballs to find their crook.

Betty knew it was the wrong thing to do, but she wasn't going to argue with her husband. Ed had started to seem more like his past self. She was quietly pleased she'd made this dreadful vacation come to life. Whoever Marshall Evans was, he was not part of Ed's proper family. There was just the two people in Ed's real family. And he was right, it had been a fast two days. But Betty was itching. She couldn't stop thinking about the poor girl at the petrol station. If they were leaving this country, and they were, then surely they should at least check in and say their sweet good-byes.

*

Marshall turned round as Hank studied the corpse on the seat next to him. He wiped his wet hands on the corner of her rough Welsh blanket and bent his head down to wipe his face dry. The coat he was wearing had turned a heavy dark hue, soaked through by the snow. He was sniffing his hands when Barry looked at Hank in the rear view mirror.

– Thanks, he said.

– No problemo, said Barry.

– You alright? said Marshall. You had one up here?

– No, I've been shuffling along here for a fucking hour now, and nothing. Not even a frigging gritter van has gone past.

– What was you doing?

– Had one over at the community centre. Buggers hauled us into the back room to get changed and get out. I was in gaga-land. Four frigging fits in two days. Going down the street in a complete blank. I simply got into another taxi.

242

That's three in one day! Murmuring hospital, and we're on our way. I came out of it and went into fucking panic mode when I realised the tossers over at the community centre had taken all my cash and my panda outfit offa me. Suppose I shouldn't have mentioned it to him. The bastard threw us out of his cab right up here.

– Jesus.

– Yep. Never a nice one.

– Well, you got the right car now, dude, said Barry. And the nice ones in it. And the hospital is where we're heading n'all.

– Yeah. Who is she? said Hank.

– Mrs Sparrow, said Marshall. Found her earlier. Me, and Dad here, doing the door to door routines for my CS order. She was in her living room, dead. Natural. Dad thought it better to dump her at the hospital, like. Rather than get them all involved over in Texas.

– Say, Hank, is there a funny smell back there? said Barry.

– Don't think so.

– She ain't smelling too bad?

Hank leant towards Mrs Sparrow's body and smelt the air around her face. He'd seen the horror films and was expecting to jump back in fright. He knew it happened. Her mouth was slightly open and the dark gash was bound to be holding something. He steadied himself and sniffed the air again. He stared into her opaque eyes. Sniffed like a dog.

– Well yes, there is something back here, but no, no, I don't think it's really coming from her. It's this rug you got wrapped around her I think, yeah.

– Good, thanks. I thought it might be. Wouldn't want to wreck the car with decomposing flesh, eh?

They reached the main road and Barry had to stop as other cars flew past in either direction. He turned the heating on and put his foot down on the accelerator ready to pull out.

Morgan watched the cars pass beneath him. He was sat under a streetlight on the edge of the steel bridge above the dual carriageway. His hair hung down the side of his face like long liquorice strings. His legs dangled over the rail and he swayed with the wind. He had the guns, the ammo, and Dogman's cash in a large rucksack stacked against the railing, and was taking a rest on the bridge. At the far end of the road he spotted a car he recognised from yesterday. He stood up. He waved merrily and spat down towards the oncoming vehicle. He raised his thumbs high in the air above his head. He was never going to return to the farm on Cwm mountain. Morgan was crossing to live on the other side. Blackmill mountain was his future home.

*

Leanne waved back at the strange little boy. He certainly seemed to be in better spirits than when they first met. She took the swift turn into the woods and climbed the mountain road to the Dog farm. When the sisters got there and noticed Boyd's Mondeo Leanne immediately cut the headlights and drove as quietly as melting ice. She stopped by Boyd's car and looked at her sister.

– Uhrr, Leanne, love? I'm beginning to get 'effing nervous, here, she said.

– It's the right thing sis. If he's here? Then it just makes our task easier. Come on. Get Pinkie out.

Donna pulled the bin bags from the backseat and placed them on the ground. Leanne carefully closed her door and pointed with the sword at Dogman's farm. The sisters crept up to the closed door and took a glance through the dirty window. Leanne's grip tightened on the sword. Boyd stood above a sprawled sight on the floor. Next to his feet was the body of a man.

– Jesus, that's Deano, said Donna.

– I know.

The Dogman had his hands stretched out and was trying to grab at the trousers of Boyd. His blood-soaked hands jerked in pain and a whisper of "help" gargled from his mouth. Boyd turned away from him, took his car keys from his pocket, and walked to the door. He stepped into the cold dark air, and stopped when he felt the tingle of a sharp object jab him in the back.

– Get your hands up to where I can see them, Boyd.

– Leanne?

– Hello, again.

Leanne and her sister circled around to face him. He was breathing deeply in stunned shock at the sight of them both.

– What the fuck've you done to poor Dean in there, Boyd? asked Donna. You trying to become some kind of serial killer, is that it?

– Hah, he's shite at it, if that's the case. Still in the training stage, is it? said Leanne. Well, you don't go on trying to kill our family, Boyd. First me, then our cousin, Cheyenne. No.

– What? No. I didn't mean to hurt you, Leanne, I was drunk, and Cheyenne was an accident. And I came up here to look for my dog.

– Well you don't need to no more. Donna? Do the innocent man a favour here, she said.

Donna laughed and went over to her car. She struggled to pick up both of the black bin bags, and Boyd's Mondeo jumped as she slammed them down hard onto the bonnet of his car. Blood trickled out from the small tears in the thin plastic binbags, and Boyd felt sick.

– Pinkie?

– Well, we had us an accident as well, said Leanne.

– You fucking freaks!

– No. You're the fucking freak, Boyd. You! And you got yourself a little problem, here. Let's say I don't really care what you did to the Dogman in there, but you got yourself an option. You take that man to the hospital, or we'll be informing the police all about your freakish activities with dogs and with guns, said Leanne.

– You're not a snitch.

– Neither of us is, shouted Donna. But what my sister is, is a hard woman. We both is, and what she don't fucking do is take abuse from you.

– I ain't asking you Boyd, I'm ordering you, said Leanne.

Boyd lowered his head. He was sure they couldn't see his tears. He sniffed, coughed and swallowed back the acidic bile in his throat. Leanne moved towards him with the sword at his chest. She tapped his chin up with the blade and made him raise his face.

– Some people learn from their mistakes, she said. You? You were one of mine. Get the Dogman to the fucking hospital, now. We'll follow.

*

Ed and Betty pulled away from Cheyenne. She was lying still on the hospital bed.

– Can she hear us? asked Betty.

– Nobody really knows, said the nurse. Her ears aren't damaged, but chances are she's not actually using them. Same way as she's not using her eyes, or mouth. It's always one of those things being debated by doctors. Asleep or unconscious? Dreaming? Or just brain-dead. Comatose.

– How did it happen? asked Ed.

– They're looking into it, but chances are she did it herself.

The nurse told them Cheyenne'd gone into some sort of mini-coma earlier that evening. The doctor wasn't enormously worried and believed she was going to be okay, would probably wake up in a day or so. In her drugged state Cheyenne had been exhausted but excited about being on the evening news and got increasingly upset when she was informed by a nurse serving her tea that the hospital didn't have a separate television for her room. Cheyenne couldn't get internet signal on her mobile and had tried to get out of bed to watch the public television that was on display down the corridor. In a moment of childish fury she pulled out her saline drip, the morphine tube, her oxygen, and detached the four metal electrodes on her chest for the heart monitor. She got out of the bed but didn't make it to the door of the room.

Betty wiped the tears from her eyes. Ed put his hand on her shoulder. He knew it was wrong to come to the goddamned hospital. A silly idea to visit a girl they didn't even know. When they'd returned to the motel earlier Ed was ecstatic with his regained position. Ed was back in charge. He wanted out.

He couldn't quite understand how his weakened wife had talked him into coming to the hospital first, and he'd cracked. The nurse left and Ed turned to look at the young man sat in the corner. He had barely looked up at them since they first came in, his eyes fixed to his phone, snickering.

– You a relative, son? asked Ed.

– New boyfriend, said Tetchy.

– I'm sorry, said Betty.

– Who're you 'en? Americans, is it?

– Yes.

– Is you relatives, 'en?

– No, said Ed.

He turned away and the youngster continued to play with his phone. He had been taking photos of the trainers he wore and was reacting in delight to text messages sent back to him. The hoarse laughter coming from his mouth seemed either false or dumb. Ed squeezed firmly on his wife's shoulder.

– Come on, Betty, let's leave.

– Wonder what she's thinking about, said Betty.

– Girl could be thinking about anything.

*

The comatose Cheyenne was thinking she was thrilled with the size and shape of her new breasts. She'd been examining them in the toilet mirror for ten minutes now and couldn't get her top back on. They seemed to be growing every time she looked at them. She'd been checking on them at least five times a day since she'd had the operation. Her mam was happy. And Tetchy was chuffed. She'd been told by the surgeon they might be sore for a short period of time and not to let any hand squeeze or pull on them. But after ten days or so they'd be hers to do with what she wanted. They were in place. And today was meant to be her big day. It was the day she was coming out of the hospital, and the documentary crew were going to be there to film her. Cheyenne stopped chewing on her hair extension, flicked it out of her mouth, and pointed at herself in the mirror.

– Celebrity.

Sam, the director, wanted to film Cheyenne and Tetchy, her new boyfriend, leaving the hospital. They knew Hank wasn't her partner anymore, but Cheyenne didn't like the idea. She wanted some time to find herself a better candidate for the camera. Tetchy was just a fill-in. The director convinced her how it would all work to their advantage. At some point Cheyenne would dramatically tell Tetchy, on camera, he was also no longer her boyfriend and she was now going to be searching for a new man far more suitable for her figure and status. An American man, perhaps. A Mor-man. Cheyenne loved the idea. And the director thought it would be a great scene in their observational documentary. Cheyenne, the girl who'd forgiven the villain who shot her, and had become the celebrity. Her life changed. Perfect, in Cheyenne's coma.

*

Hank managed to abandon his cousin and uncle in the hospital car park. He'd thanked Barry for the lift but didn't want to get involved with the disposing of any dead bodies. Barry had nervously driven around the slush-ridden car park twice for at least ten minutes and Hank had to ask him to pull over by the main doors. They'd both seemed slightly annoyed at his departure, but Hank wanted to get into the hospital, not figure out the best spot to dump Mrs Sparrow.

He limped through the entrance into the Main Reception area with a darkened face. He'd only come out of the place yesterday and hadn't imagined having to make the journey back twice in one day. Hell, he didn't want to be thinking of Cheyenne again, he'd remembered what she had said about Tetchy and knew it was her who'd informed the frigging attack. He wouldn't be visiting the bitch again. No. Hank needed the new crutches, and the new medication wasn't working either.

Once you passed through the refurbished main hall, the Cwmgarw hospital took on a stale appearance. Hank knew the place well. The colourful plastics became pale. Hank guessed it hadn't been re-decorated since 1983. He limped through the corridor with his head held down, his eyes following his plaster-cast foot and shoe, tracing the separate tracks worn onto the chequered linoleum. He imagined these were some unlucky pathways, created over the years.

He knew the epilepsy clinic would be closed at this time but if he went into the waiting room he'd be able to get access to one of the doctors in charge of prescriptions. He'd try to get an answer about the new medication. When he got into the waiting room he started to cheer up. There was hardly anybody there. The man at the desk stretched his hand towards the line of plastic chairs two feet away. Hank ripped a waiting ticket from the wall-box, took off his empty rucksack, and sat.

*

When Tash and Belly went in for his appointment she knew they'd have to wait in the waiting room quite a while. They always did. She would always come up with Belly to the hospital for his appointments. And the crucial thing the doctor always seemed to tell her husband was that he needed to lose weight. She always knew he wouldn't always follow the advice.

They were both tidily dressed. Tash in her floral trousers and pink blouse and Belly in his beige trousers and lined shirt. Neatly ironed. Tash had been wandering around the reception area, exploring and examining the fancy new cafe, reading notices on the wall, whilst Belly sat in the line of seats with his head down. Tash came over with some excitement and compassionately said to him,

– You can 'ave one, if you want.
– 'Ave wha'?
– Coffee. A Cappuccino, if you like.

– I don't want one, he said.

– It's free, mun. You're entitled to one, she said.

– I don't want nothing, mun. Just had dinner, wannit?

– Cos you're a patient, see? Free, for you. Whatever you'd like: coffee, cappuccino, tea, water...

– I don't want it, do I? I don't like coffee, mun. You 'ave one.

Tash hurriedly stood. She went to the nearby water cooler, filled a plastic glass and came back with it to Belly.

– What's tha? he said.

– Water.

– What for?

– For you. If you wants. Or I can go get you a coffee, love. Says so on the wall over there.

– On the wall?

– On the notice. On the wall. Patient entitlement. Look, I'll go get you one.

Tash stood again and went up to the counter inside the cafe area. She came back with one steaming china cup and saucer, together with a little biscuit. She handed the cup over to Belly, who took a sip. He pulled a face and gave it back to her.

– You don't like tha', do you, love? Too strong? Mind, 'ave to pay now, if you wants another one.

– I don't, he said.

Tash handed Belly the small biscuit, and drank her lovely Cappuccino. She'd noticed Hank had come into the room. Either he hadn't seen her or he was ignoring her. She couldn't tell. He'd sat down in the first row of chairs, directly in front of the main desk.

– Found your trainers 'en, love?

He jumped when he heard her speak. He hadn't seen them.

– Oh, hi. No.

– Shame, they was nice ones 'em, weren't they?

– Yep.

251

– Still. Things like tha' always happens.

– Spose.

– One of 'em things, innit? You gotta accept it, like.

– Spose, said Hank.

– Yep. It's life, mun.

*

Boyd wondered whether he was wasting his time taking Dogman to the hospital. He shouldn't even be helping the cruel bastard. Pinkie was dead right now. And this shite had helped those sisters. The sickening thought of it bounced uncontrollably around his head. He shouldn't be assisting the fucking demon.

– You dying back there yet? he said.

– Don't think so, said the Dogman.

– Naw? Why not?

– Must be the Lord. Man must like us both.

Boyd looked at the Dogman on the back seat, his face crunched in pain with his arms stretched around his raised bloody legs in a fixed grip. He couldn't walk because of what the evil boy had been doing to his feet. And he couldn't hear much because the boy had taken off his ear. It was a bad shot. He'd missed his head, it was the ear and the skin on one side that'd been removed but only because of the passing fiery blast. Boyd had had to drag him, crying with pain, to his car, his bloody stumps wrapped in dirty towels. It had been a struggle, whilst those two witches simply watched and chuckled. He'd wanted to call for an ambulance but Leanne had insisted. He was to be taken to the hospital immediately by him.

– We there yet? Speed up, fuck's sake.

– Don't dare make things worse for yourself.

Donna's car banged along down the road, the aerial flapping against the wind as they followed Boyd to the hospital. Donna was behind the wheel now, and they'd both agreed to keep the heaters on high.

– We ain't gonna be staying up here too long, is we? said Donna.

– You and me will be staying for as long as we have to.

They weren't far from the hospital. Boyd was trying to overcome the loss. Pinkie had gone. He drove on. And as he did he had to idly struggle to push the entertaining thought of murdering the Dogman to one side. The boy had stolen his gun. He would have to search in the boot to find a suitable weapon. Something heavy? A crow bar, perhaps. A car jack. He didn't know if he had a car jack. He'd never used one before. He didn't know whether you had to buy a car jack, or whether the car jack actually came with a car. Boyd couldn't stop grinning when he realised he kept a knife in the side door. Could he at least hurt the man on his back seat? Or would it be a waste of time? It'd be a waste of time. He knew it. After all, there were also those two behind him. Following. He'd have to deal with the sisters as well.

*

– Goddamn women, mumbled Ed.

– Yep. Always the same, said Belly.

Ed had had to pause in the waiting room whilst his wife bought coffee to take away. He'd started to explode when he watched her begin to chat to another woman browsing around. And he had to rest his weary frame when he noticed Betty had actually begun to cry in front of this nosy lady.

– Sorry fella, it was probably mine that set her off, said Belly. Tash. She probably heard the accent. Always going off to America is Tash. Looking. Searching. Digging up info 'bout her past relatives. Claims they was Mormons or something. You ain't Mormons, is you?

Ed looked at the fat man next to him and sternly shook his head.

– Yeah, bit of an obsession, innit? It's her maiden name, see. Yendell. Tash Yendell. Always trying to find herself another frigging Yendell, in she? Yendell match. Tell her, Tash *Evans* is her married name. Stick to it. Naw, *Yendell*. Always sounds better, she reckons.

Both of the women were sobbing. Hugging each other. They were sobbing and smiling. Staring in surprise and admiration at each other.

*

Leanne watched the car in front of her, whilst concentrating on the stream of words coming out of her sister's gob. Donna had started to speak. Words flowing rapidly as soon as she saw the sign for the hospital whip past the car in front of them.

– What the fuck's he doing? said Donna.

– I dunno, said Leanne. Slow down.

– We can't mun. He's going on. He's going…

– Slow it, Donna. Maybe he's missed the sign. Flash your lights. Slow the car.

– Leanne, the fucker's getting away from us.

– Take the chance, said Leanne. Flash the headlights, now. He's just missed the turning, that's all. Stop the sodding car, Donna. NOW.

Donna cried out in panic and frustration as she put her foot on the brake and their car skidded to a stop. The lights flashing and the horn beeping before the actual turning to the hospital.

*

Boyd threw his left arm over the seat, twisting his body around. He had missed the turn to the hospital. Through the back screen window he could see the road was clear. Donna was flashing her headlights and beeping angrily at him. He shoved the Mondeo into reverse and hurtled backwards non-stop at sixty miles per hour for about six hundred feet.

– WHA' THE FUCK'S HE DOING? yelled Donna.

– Take the chance, Donna. Keep it calm. Just take the sodding chance. Don't reverse. Don't move. Wait.

– LEANNE, HE'S GONNA FUCKING RAM US.

– Stay put, Donna. Keep it cool. STAY.

– LEANNE, I'M NOT A FUCKING DOG. YOU GONE BLIND, WOMAN? HE'S GONNA FUCKING HIT US.

– STAY, DONNA. STAY PUT.

Boyd raced back at speed. And with their eyes wide open and unable to blink Donna and Leanne let out a synchronised shriek of terror when in a few seconds Boyd rammed his Mondeo to a stop, only inches in front of their bumper. He beeped lightly in apology and waved his hand out through the window to make the turn. Donna and Leanne loosened themselves to regain their composure. They followed him into the hospital car park.

– Donna? I'm sorry, Donna. I'm sorry all this has happened. Donna didn't answer her sister.

– I know I shouldn't have got you involved in all this.

– Naw, Leanne. You did. And I'm glad, you did. You needed to do it. So did I. I'm sorry. I met someone yesterday.

He said you should call him. He said we should call him whenever you or me need to. Leanne? I think we should call him. Now.

Donna took Barry's card out of her pocket and lovingly slipped it over to Leanne's open hand.

*

Hank had left the waiting room before Tash and Belly had even received their appointment. It had been a short trip. The night nurse had refused to change his medication. She had given him the new crutches and a large stash of Valium to calm himself. He had to get a drink of water and was surprised when Masaki stepped out of the elevator in front of him.

– Hank?

His head looked raw. His face looked concerned. Hank could see new black hair shooting up through the coarse bandages wrapped around his skull. There was a solemn glint in Masaki's red eyes as he held his hand up into a fist and flourished it with intent.

– My friend, he said.

Hank looked down at the hospital linoleum. He moved his plastered foot forward and scraped it back alongside a dirty mark. He wondered where his damned trainers were. He gave Masaki a sheepish grin.

– Hank? My friend?

– We were, I suppose. This? No. No longer. This was your proposal, Masaki. We've taken the money. We changed. I don't know where these people came from and where you found these financiers. But you did. And it's gone.

– You have not signed? No, Hank, it is not my project. Not this. This is not for us. We are different to these people. We have the moral rights, Hank. It is not our film that they wish to create. Do not sign. You cannot sign. Hank? Please, tell me you have not signed. Hank?

He looked at the garbling Masaki. He felt low. The Valium hadn't yet clicked into his bloodstream and he felt the plunge was imminent. Dark electric waters swirled beneath him, pulling his body down to drown. He rested one of his crutches against the wall and clumsily took the contract out of his back pocket. He handed it over to Masaki who opened it and scratched at the side of his face.

– I thought it was what you wanted, said Hank.

Masaki looked ashamed. He tore the contract in two and watched it float to their feet.

– Why have you done that? said Hank.

– Because it is worthless. There is nothing to apologise for, my friend. There is no deal with these filthy people.

Hank was unsteady on his single crutch, and Masaki put a hand out onto his shoulder to stabilise him.

– There is no contract without the *two* signatures, my friend. And they? No. They would only have had the one. I will not sign. I have not signed.

Masaki pulled Hank towards him. Hank hugged him as they shook hands in sturdy agreement.

*

Ed and Betty were resting in the hire car. She was concerned he was not fit to drive, and they knew it was a long journey back to the airport. He barely had the energy to sit straight behind the wheel and she suggested they stay put another night. Ed wasn't listening to his wife, he was looking at the hospital parking lot. It was full, apart from the two spaces on either side of their own car. Rows upon rows of mangled,

257

metal vehicles he was sure'd be deemed un-roadworthy in the US of A. He wondered how ill the patients were if their goddamned automobiles were this bad. Ed managed to pull his weary body forward and denied his tired condition. He pointed at the steering wheel and looked at his wife.

– I'm the man here, sugar-pie, and I'm the one who's gonna be driving us out of this nasty little country. So, let's hope this thing doesn't clatter all the way back.

– I'm sorry for bringing us here, honey.

– I know, he said. I can forgive you sweetheart.

They watched as an ambulance hurried into the hospital grounds with its lights flashing. It made its way over to the emergency doors and two paramedics came out the back of the van bringing with them a man lying on the trolley. He was wearing the bottom half of what looked like a panda costume with an oxygen bag covering his face. They wheeled the man inside and the van pulled off.

Betty could see Ed wasn't going to listen to her, something had caught his attention. Ed had noticed the car that had been creeping around the parking lot a few times had come to a stop next to the exit sign. He watched it turn the wrong way and drive into the lane marked No Entry. The car went across a series of red stripes and parked in the disabled zone. Two men stepped out of the Honda Accord; the tall one lit a cigarette and looked around him then nodded at the other one. They opened the back door of their car and dragged out a stiff woman wrapped up in a piece of carpet.

– Hey, isn't that Marshall?

– Yes, said Ed. It's him, alright. We've met the other one too.

– What're they doing, Ed?

They watched as Barry and Marshall held the woman under each arm, Marshall with a pained expression on his face, Barry with a fag in his mouth as they struggled to half carry, half drop-and-drag Mrs Sparrow through a bank of snow over to the hospital Exit doors. They dropped the corpse in the 'no smoking' zone and Marshall sat slumped on the pavement next to the body as Barry took out his mobile to answer a phone call. He frequently started to speak and pay the caller serious intention, whilst furtively scanning the surrounding car park. Ed sighed and Betty looked in shock at her husband.

– Jesus, Ed, these people do need saving.

An ugly car pulled up on the left hand side of Ed's car. Ed could see there was a man who may have been dead and was flat out on the back seat. The driver of the car had his mouth open, his head tilted back, and was making barking noises, snatching at the air in front of his face, his hands holding a knife. Ed and Betty turned their heads to the right as another car pulled up alongside them. The young woman behind the steering wheel looked like she'd taken something. She was trying to ignore the jubilant woman in the passenger seat who was talking hurriedly into her mobile phone and angrily punching in happiness at the air to the side of her own head.

Betty put a hand to her mouth and pulled away from the window, a weary confused expression on her face. She slipped a hand into her pocket and felt in comfort for the piece of paper Tash had given her. They had met. She couldn't believe it. It was an address and a name. Her name: Yendell. She smiled. It was there. Ed without thinking reached out for her.

– Come on, honey, let's go. There's nobody to save in my old country.

He turned the engine on and gently eased the car out of its space, leaving a cold gap between the two parked cars on either side.

*

Hank waited alone at the hospital bus stop with a strange wonderment rattling through his body. His head bobbed along, floating above the plunge. He watched the hospital activity with a wild joy. These were indeed his characters. The quick and the dead. The lost and the found. His people. His black sheep. He sighed. He closed his eyes tight. He knew now he would never leave the place. He would breathe the Valley air forever. He swallowed, and opened his eyes.

Parthian
Fiction

Hummingbird
Tristan Hughes
ISBN 978-1-91-090190-8
£8.99 ● Paperback

Winner of Edward Standford Award

**Winner of Wales Book of the Year
People's Choice Award**

Pigeon
Alys Conran
ISBN 978-1-91-090123-6
£8.99 ● Paperback

Winner of Wales Book of the Year

Winner of Rhys Davies Award

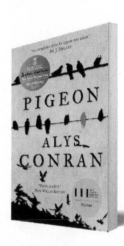

Ironopolis
Glen James Brown
ISBN 978-1-91-268109-9
£8.99 ● Paperback

'A triumph'
– *The Guardian*

'The most accomplished working-class novel of the last few years
– *Morning Star*

Women Who Blow on Knots
Ece Temelkuran
ISBN 978-1-910901-69-4
£9.99 ● Paperback

Winner of Edinburgh Book Festival
First Book Award

PEN England Translates Award

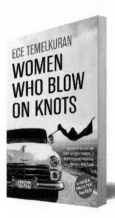

The Golden Orphans
Gary Raymond
ISBN 978-1-91-210913-5
£8.99 ● Paperback

'Intense, unnerving and brilliant.'
– *The Spectator*

Bad Ideas \ Chemicals
Lloyd Markham
ISBN 978-1-912109-68-5
£7.99 ● Paperback

A Betty Trask Award Winner

PARTHIAN